KINGPIN

AN ITALIAN MAFIA ROMANCE

WS GREER

Kingpin
Copyright © 2016 by WS Greer

Cover design by:
Robin Harper, Wicked by Design

Interior Design and Formatting by:
Christine Borgford, Perfectly Publishable

Never water-down what you love just to fit in. Take pride in being outside the norm. Be yourself. Be different . . . on purpose.

This one's for me.

~WS~

PART ONE

2001

ONE

Alannah Sullivan

"ALRIGHT, SO ARE YOU READY?"

I look out the window at all the kids streaming into Barry Elementary School, and it makes me nervous. My face feels hot and my hands are sweaty.

"I hate the first day of school," I reply, still staring out the window.

"Well, technically it's not the *first* day of school. You've been in fifth grade half a year already," Dad answers. I can tell he's smiling without even looking at him. When I turn around to frown, sure enough, there's that big goofy grin.

"Dad," I start, cutting my eyes at him. "You know what I mean. It's the first day at this school for me, but not for them. I think that makes it worse, actually. I'm going to be the only new kid."

Dad takes his hand off the steering wheel and turns his body towards me. He's completely clean shaven because he's in uniform and on his way to work after he drops me off. As corny as he is sometimes, his smile still makes me feel better.

"I know, sweetie," he begins. "I know this is hard, and I'm sorry we had to move in the middle of the school year, but we know that's how the military works sometimes. All you have to do is be the strong princess that you are, and you're going to be just fine. You'll make friends in no time, and before you know it, you'll be running this place. Everybody is going to want to be Alannah Sullivan's friend. You just have to get past this first day. Okay?"

I twist my mouth into a frustrated frown as I exhale and reach for the door handle.

"Okay. Thanks, Dad."

"You're welcome, sweetie. Now, go have a great day. I love you."

"I love you, too." I pop open the door as Dad leans over to kiss me on the cheek, then I'm out and headed towards the school.

I was born in San Antonio, Texas, on Lackland Air Force Base, eleven years ago. My current home, Scott Air Force Base in Belleville, Illinois, is my dad's third and newest assignment. We only got here a week or so ago, but my parents are already forcing me to go to school. Ugh. I'm not ready to get back to it yet, but they say I have to.

So, here I am, walking on the sidewalk with my red and black backpack slung behind me. I'm surrounded by a bunch of other kids I don't know, who all look comfortable because they've been here forever. They've gotten to know each other and have grown to become friends, but not with me. I'm the new kid who's stepping into class for the first time after half the school year has already gone by. My mom, Dana, has been telling me since before we left our last home in California that the first day is always the hardest. She kept saying it as we walked through the school a couple of days ago to get familiar with the building, and she said it this morning, too, as she drove in to her new job at Belleville Hospital for the first time. So, I've been trying to remind myself of what she said.

The first day is always the hardest.

I know where my new class is, so I walk straight there without looking anywhere but forward. I know my new teacher's name is Mr. Bishop, but I haven't met him yet. Other than his name, I don't know anything or anybody here. So, as I walk into class for the first time, my heart feels like it might pop any second now. Especially when I stand in the doorway because I don't know where I'm supposed to sit, and other kids are in their assigned seats staring at me like I'm crazy. It takes Mr. Bishop at least five minutes before he sees me standing here.

"Oh, hello," he says, finally. He has a higher voice than I expected for a man his size. He's really tall and has thick black hair that looks like it's been slicked back with grease, and his face has a lot of wrinkles in it. "You must be Ms. Alannah Sullivan. Is that right?" he asks, walking towards me.

"Yes, sir," I answer. I'm so nervous now, my words almost didn't come out.

"Well, it's nice to meet you, Alannah. My name's Mr. Bishop." He makes me shake his hand like I'm a grownup. "You can go ahead and have a seat while I get you some text books. Okay?"

I look around the room again as the teacher walks away, but there's no place for me to sit. All the desks are taken, so I have to stand there with the whole class staring at me while I wait for Mr. Bishop to grab books out of the closet. It feels like it takes forever, and I'm sure there are girls in the far corner of the room who are laughing at me now. I ignore them until the teacher finally comes back.

"Umm, excuse me, Mr. Bishop. There's no desks," I say as quietly as I can.

He looks around and sees I'm right.

"Oh, I'm sorry. Give me a second while I go grab one from Mrs. Webb's class across the hall." He walks over to me and hands me the four text books to hold while he leaves the room. Now, I'm standing at the back of the class holding books that are so heavy I'm turning red as my arms start to shake. I know for a fact those girls in the front are laughing now, and so are two boys sitting right in front of me. How could this possibly start off so bad? Mr. Bishop must be taking his sweet time to find that desk, because I'm starting to sweat and my grip on the books is slipping.

"Oh my god, look how red she's turning," someone says, but I can't see their face.

I try to hold on, but my fingers slip and the books fall to the floor. The entire class starts laughing at me like I'm a standup comedian, and I'm instantly embarrassed. Mr. Bishop walks in holding a desk, and he frowns at the class when he sees they're all laughing at me and I have tears in my eyes.

"Hey, you all stop that, now," he barks, and the class quiets. "Sorry about that, Alannah. I didn't realize the books were that heavy. I guess I should've just put them on my desk, huh? That's my mistake. You don't have to cry, sweetie. I know being new is difficult, but once you get past this first day, you'll be good to go. You'll make friends, I promise."

The first day is always the hardest.

Mr. Bishop sets the desk down and picks up the books for me. He puts them on the desk and gives me his warmest smile.

"Here you go, sweetie. Have a seat right here," he says. My desk is in the very back of the class, and I'm the only one in my row. Embarrassing.

Everyone finally turns around once Mr. Bishop walks to the front of the class and starts talking. My life in Belleville, Illinois has officially begun.

THE FIRST HALF OF THE day goes by pretty fast. We had two lessons—one on math, and the other on science. Mr. Bishop talks like he's in a hurry and has a lot of energy, but he's really nice so far. I didn't have to interact with anyone besides him, so my nerves calmed down after the horrible book incident. However, it's lunch time and I'm walking in line towards the cafeteria. The walls in the hall are painted blue, white, and yellow—the school's colors—and all six of the classes in this hall are going to lunch at the same time. Everyone's talking, and the boys are being the loudest while the girls are being quiet because they're sneakily whispering to each other. No one has talked to me, so I haven't tried to talk to anyone else.

When we get into the cafeteria, which is really the school gym filled with tables for us to sit at, I'm surrounded by kids. Somehow, I still feel alone, though. As I look around and see things and people I don't recognize, I feel homesick. The only place I can remember living is California, so everything here is new to me. Even as I take my seat with a tray full of things I won't eat, I'm too shy and nervous to speak. Everyone else is so caught up in their own conversations and craziness, it's like I don't even exist. I'm all alone in a crowd.

Once we're allowed to go outside for recess, I watch all the other kids in groups playing with each other. There's a big basketball court full of boys playing everything from dodgeball to four square. There are girls with hula-hoops, and some drawing pictures on the concrete with chalk. The playground in front of me is a big field with swings and big metal jungle gyms for us to climb all over, but I'm just not feeling up to it. All I really want is for this day to be over. I just want to go home to my parents. At least I recognize them. At least the furniture is familiar. My mom and dad will talk to me.

I walk over to the swings and sit down. I let out a sigh and watch the other kids run around like they've been waiting to do it all day and now they're finally free. It's loud and annoying, but I'm pretty sure we only have a few minutes of recess left, so I'm just going to sit here and wait. The swings are right in front of the door we're going to have to go back into, so I'll be first in line.

As I wait to hear the bell, out of the corner of my eye, I see a boy running from girl to girl. Every girl he's around lets out a scream, and then he runs to the next girl. He's a chubby kid with red hair, wearing blue jeans and a green military jacket like the ones my dad used to wear before they switched them.

I scrunch my forehead as I watch this kid run over to another girl and smack her on the butt. The girl screams, and the chubby boys runs to another girl and pulls her hair. He's just going around tormenting every girl he sees, and I don't see any teachers around to stop him.

Eventually, the chubby kid sees me. I suddenly feel anxious as he runs in my direction, but my dad taught me to never let a boy touch me in any way I didn't like. So, when the kid reaches me, I have no plans of letting him get away with smacking me on the butt. I press myself into the seat of the swing so he doesn't even have a chance.

I don't recognize this kid from my class, but I probably wouldn't even if he was my classmate. He stands there for a moment, looking at me with a strange grin, then he walks behind me and tries to smack my back, but I jump up before he can. He tries to run around me again, but I turn around and make sure we stay face to face.

"Stop it," I say to him, which seems to irritate him.

"Don't tell me what to do," he responds, before he steps closer to me and tries to pull my hair.

I reach up and smack him on the arm, knocking his hand away. From the sound of the impact and the look on his face, I know it hurt. I may have done it a little harder than I meant to, but I can tell he doesn't care. He looks angry now.

"That hurt!" he yells, just before he reaches for my hair again.

I turn around and try to walk away from him, but the next thing I know, I'm shoved in the back. I fall forward and land face down in the sand under the swing. When I try to get up, I feel something on my back, then I feel his hands on the back of my head. The chubby boy is sitting on me and pushing my face into the sand.

"Stop it!" I scream, as tears sting my eyes. The pain of my cheek grinding into the sand is too much to take. "Please stop!"

"Shut up," he responds.

I try to lift my head, but he pushes it back down and now my nose is in the sand and I can't breathe. I try to scream, but I can't even open my mouth. I try to breathe, but I snort sand instead. I feel panicked, and I'm terrified, but only for a second.

Suddenly, the weight on my head and back is lifted off me. I hear the *thud* of a person hitting the ground, followed by a yelp of pain. When I raise my head, I see the chubby boy on the ground looking up at someone standing over him. He has his back to me, but I can tell he's bigger than the chubby boy. He's wearing black pants and a black, long-sleeved shirt, and he has short black hair. The chubby kid looks up at him like he's scared to death, and he doesn't say a word as the kid turns around to face me.

When he looks down at me, he has a scowl on his face that frightens me. He has blue eyes and lips that look too big for his face. Something about him reminds me of an evil villain I'd see in a movie—he's the guy beating the crap out of the hero.

"Are you okay?" he says. His voice is deeper than every other boy's voice I've ever heard.

"Umm," I begin, but the chubby kid steals my attention when he gets up and walks towards me.

"She hit me first, so I'm allowed to hit her back. So, move, Ugly Dominic," the chubby kid says with a chuckle.

It all happens so fast after that.

The big kid snaps around and punches the chubby one in the face. Chubby stumbles backwards, but the big one grabs him by his shirt and throws him on the ground right in front of me. Sand goes flying everywhere as the big kid jumps on top of the chubby one and punches him in the face again, just before grabbing him by the hair and yanking his head over so that he's looking at me.

"Apologize," the big kid says, calmly. "Look at her and tell you're sorry. Now."

The chubby kid looks up at me as blood streams from his nose and tears fall from his eyes.

"I'm sorry. I'm so sorry," he says, just before he loses it and starts bawling like a baby as he cover his nose with both hands.

I don't even know what to say. I look at him for a second, then I look up at the other kid. At first, I was terrified of him, but now I'm not sure what to be.

The big kid lets the chubby one go, then helps me up off the ground. As I stand, he reaches down and starts knocking sand off my clothes while I struggle to get it off my face and out of my hair. The two of us walk away from the crowd of kids who are gathering to look down at the boy on the ground bleeding and crying.

"He won't mess with you, anymore," the kid says. He looks at me with an expressionless face, and my heart pounds with anxiety.

"Thank you," I reply, nervously.

"You're new here, right?"

"Uh-huh."

"My name's Dominic," he greets, but he doesn't smile so it's not very comforting.

"I'm Alannah," I reply, just as the door behind me swings open and three teachers come out. The two women go tend to the crying boy who's still on the ground, but Mr. Bishop comes trotting up to us.

"Dominic, can I talk to you for a minute?" he says. He doesn't look happy. "I was told you beat up Billy Hannigan. Punched him in the face and threw him on the ground. Is that true?"

"Yeah," is all Dominic says in response.

"Why'd you do that, Dominic?"

"He was trying to bully Alannah." He says it like he's not even concerned with getting in trouble.

"He bullied Alannah, so you bullied him? Is that right?"

"Yeah, that's right. That's what he gets for putting his hands on the girls."

"Well, that's not how we do things, Mr. Collazo. Violence is not how you solve your problems. I'm going to need you to come with me to the principal's office."

Dominic shrugs like he doesn't have a care in the world as he starts to follow Mr. Bishop towards the school. Before he steps inside, he turns around.

"Bye, Alannah" he says, then he smiles for the first time. Why would he smile when he knows he's about to be in trouble with the principal?

I feel tingly all over as I smile back at him, but before I can say bye, he's already inside.

For the rest of the day, I don't speak to anyone except Mr. Bishop.

The only kid I speak to my entire first day of school is Dominic Collazo.

TWO

Dominic Collazo

"I GOT SUSPENDED YESTERDAY."

My father, Donnie, puts his Cadillac in park and stares straight ahead. He lets out a sigh of frustration before he turns to me. He's completely clean shaven with blue eyes that are enhanced by his thick glasses. His black hair is slick and the scars on his left cheek remind me of how hard a life he's had. I'm proud he made it through it all. He's one hundred percent Italian, thirty-five years old, and doesn't take any crap from anybody. He's my idol.

"What'd you do?" he asks, glancing towards the windshield at the packed parking lot in front of us.

"I punched Billy in the face. He was being a jerk."

"A jerk, huh? What was he doing?"

"He was running around putting his hands on all the girls. Smacking them on the butt and stuff. He even tried to shove this new girl's face in the sand. He wouldn't let her up so I took care of it."

I see a smile stretch across my dad's face.

"Good. He deserved it, right?" he says, grinning.

"Yeah, he did."

"And you did what you felt you had to do, right? You handled it?"

"I did."

"Good boy. It's unfortunate, but that's what you have to do sometimes. I know you're only eleven, but sometimes kids your age are assholes and need to be dealt with. I'm proud of you. I bet your mother was pissed, wasn't she?"

I chuckle to myself, remembering how mad my mother, Gloria, got when the principal called her and told her to come get me. She doesn't like having to leave work to come deal with the school, and she was extra mad because this isn't the first time she's had to do it.

"Yeah, she was *really* mad," I reply.

"I bet she blamed it on me, didn't she?"

"Kind of. She said some stuff about how I'm growing up to be like you, and it makes her sad. I told her I loved both of you, and that I was sorry about getting suspended. She calmed down after that."

Dad laughs a little, but stays focused on the parking lot.

"Hey, you did the right thing, Dominic. Okay? No matter what your mother says about it, you did the right thing. A man isn't supposed to hurt a woman. That's the rules. If a man hurts a woman, that's breaking the rules, and breaking the rules is cause for punishment. So, I'm proud of you, son."

I feel the tingling sensation of pride spread through my body. "Thanks, Dad."

"Fuhgeddaboutit," he says, smiling at me.

I know the words are *forget about it*, but the way Dad says them makes me laugh. That's his Italian roots making their presence known. I don't know why, but I love it when he says it.

My dad's eyes snap forward when there's movement in the parking lot. He leans forward and squints, trying to see who the man is getting out of the black Mercedes that just parked. When he recognizes him, he looks at me, his jaw tight.

"Stay here. I'll be right back."

He doesn't give me time to respond. He gets out and walks across the street like he's on a mission, his black leather jacket flapping at his sides, and smoke billowing out of his mouth from the cold. The man he approaches is also wearing a black leather jacket, but he has a thick beard that matches it. That's all I can make out from here.

All I can see now is the two of them talking. My dad is gesturing as he talks, and I know that's a sign he's not happy about something. The other guy looks afraid, but he's standing his ground. He hands my dad an envelope, which my father calmly takes.

Then, everything changes.

Suddenly, my dad punches the guy in the face. He stumbles backwards, clutching his mouth while Dad pulls a gun out of the back of his pants. My heart quickens as I watch my dad point the gun at the man's face. The guy puts his hands up like he's being arrested, then Dad hits him the face with the gun and he falls to the ground. Dad leans over the man's crumbled body and aims the gun at him again as he yells at the guy. Then, he reaches back and slams the gun into the man's face two more times, before finally walking away. My dad walks quickly towards the car as the guy behind him lies lifelessly on the ground, and he stuffs the thick envelope into the inner pocket of his jacket.

I'm not sure what I feel as my dad approaches. Part of me is scared. Part of me is proud of him. My nerves are on high alert and I feel excited with fear. I'm not surprised by what just happened because it's not the first time I've seen my dad involved in something like this. Like I said before, my dad doesn't take crap from anybody, and I like that.

When he gets in, he's breathing heavily as he reaches into the glove compartment and grabs a white towel and a plastic bag. He hands the towel and the gun to me before he starts the car.

"Clean this off and put it in the glove compartment," he says as he looks out the window at the guy who's still on the ground.

I use the towel to wipe the blood off the gun. I scrub it as hard as I can and make sure it's completely clean before I toss the gun into the glove compartment and close it. I drop the blood-soaked towel into the plastic bag and shove it into my pocket as the two of us drive away. When we find a dumpster far away from here, I'll be sure to get rid of the bloody towel.

This is how my weekend with my father begins, and I smile the whole ride back to his house.

THREE

Alannah

IT'S BEEN THREE DAYS SINCE I started school in Belleville, and I haven't seen Dominic since he beat up Billy on my first day. I've made a couple of friends, however, so I'm not completely alone when we walk to lunch now. Lisa and Maggie are with me, even though I'm pretty sure they're the two girls who laughed at me my first day in class. Both of these girls are blonde and they love to gossip about everybody they see. Honestly, they're the complete opposite of me. My hair is brown, and I don't like talking bad about other people, so when they do it, I just tune them out.

"Look, there's Kevin. He's so cute," Lisa whispers to Maggie, even though we're supposed to be walking quietly to the cafeteria.

Maggie whispers, "I know, right?" then looks at me to see if I agree. I pinch my lips together and slowly nod. I'm not a fan of boys who have hair almost as long as a girl's, but I guess the guy they're talking about is okay.

Once we're through the door of the cafeteria, kids are ignoring the monitors and talking super-loud. I've learned that the six classes in my hall are the upper classes of the small school. There's two fourth grade classes, two fifth grade, and two sixth grade. The other fifth grade teacher is Mrs. Webb, who I haven't met yet, but she's old and looks like she hates kids. She has lots of wrinkles, gray hair, and everything she says sounds mean, even when she says hello. Her class comes in after ours, and none of them are talking, probably because they don't want to get yelled at.

"There's the wicked witch," Maggie jokes, giggling at herself.

"Oh look, there's Ugly Dominic walking in right behind her," Lisa says, laughing.

Dominic walks in behind his teacher as she leads the class to the back of the line. While Lisa and Maggie are laughing their heads off, I watch Dominic. He's standing there keeping completely to himself, wearing a St. Louis Blues sweater. His classmates behind him are chatting up a storm, but not with him. He's standing with his back against the wall and his head down, staring at his feet. From looking at him, you'd think it was his first day of school. Even after he gets his tray and sits a few tables down from me, no one talks to him. I don't know why that is. Do they *all* call him Ugly Dominic? People are so mean.

Dominic is too big for his age, his lips look huge on his face, and he's got some acne, but he doesn't deserve to be called ugly. He's obviously different from everybody else, but he also saved me the other day. He's a nice person. Nobody else tried to get Billy Hannigan off of me, yet he's the one they're making fun of and avoiding like he's got a flesh-eating disease. I watch him the whole time I'm eating, and it really makes me sad. Not one person speaks to Dominic, and after he dumps his tray, he walks outside to the playground all alone.

When Maggie, Lisa, and I get outside, I immediately start looking for Dominic. It's hard to make anyone out with so many people running and screaming, but I eventually find him sitting on a bench next to the wall where we go to check out sports equipment. He's got a basketball and he's dribbling it behind his legs as he sits. There's a group of kids playing basketball and he's watching them like he really wants to play, but he can't bring himself to ask if he can join. He doesn't look sad about it, it's more like he's used to watching them instead of actually playing.

"There's Ugly Dominic being a stalker again," Maggie says as she taps me on the arm.

"Why won't they let him play?" I ask.

"Because he's weird, that's why. Look at him," Maggie goes on.

"What's so weird about him?"

"Umm, his face," Lisa chimes in. "The fact that he's, like, The Hunchback of Belleville, Illinois."

Maggie bursts into laughter and Lisa joins her. While they laugh, I look at Dominic again. He sees them laughing, but he ignores it and goes back to watching the others play. I can't stand the fact that he's sitting there by himself. He helped me before anybody else would, and they're laughing at him. I don't like it, so I walk away and leave them standing there.

"What are you doing?" Maggie asks when she notices, but I don't even respond. I ignore her and go sit next to Dominic on the bench.

He looks over at me and studies my face for a minute. He squints and wrinkles his forehead, before moving his attention back to the basketball court.

"Hi," I say, softly.

He looks back at me like he's surprised. "Hi."

"Haven't seen you in a few days. They suspend you?"

He smiles a little. "Yeah, they did. Just three days, though. No biggie."

"No biggie? My parents would be really mad if I got suspended. Especially my dad."

"Yeah, my parents are different. Especially *my* dad."

"Must be," I reply. "So, I wanted to thank you again for saving me from that kid last week. My neck is still a little sore, but it would've been worse if it weren't for you."

"Fuhgeddaboutit," he says, his eyes still on the game in

front of us.

"What?"

"I said fuhgeddaboutit."

"Forget about it? What do you mean?"

He finally looks at me and smiles, holding back a laugh.

"I just mean, don't worry about it. You're welcome. He deserved it."

Now I smile. "I usually wouldn't say something like this, but I guess I have to agree with you. He did deserve it. I still can't believe your parents weren't mad about you getting suspended though."

"Well, my mom was mad, but my dad wasn't. My dad laughed, actually," he says, grinning with pride.

"He laughed? Wow. My dad definitely wouldn't have thought that was funny. My dad's in the military. He's strict with stuff like that."

"Oh, your dad's in the military? So, you just moved here?"

"Yeah. My dad got stationed at Scott. We moved here from California." I look up and see Lisa and Maggie glaring at us, but I ignore it.

"You like it here so far?" Dominic asks, his eyes back on the game.

"It's okay, I guess. I mean, I did get pushed down and have my face shoved in the sand on my first day of school."

Dominic looks at me and smiles. Even though his face looks a little weird because of how big and pink his lips are, he still has a nice smile. But he must not like it because he doesn't show it often.

"Well, that makes sense," he replies behind a chuckle. "I don't know why some guys don't understand that you can't treat girls that way. My father taught me that hurting a girl was against the rules."

"That's good. I wish everyone would teach their kids to be nice to everyone. At least your dad is teaching you right."

"My dad's awesome. He teaches me a lot. I want to be just like him when I grow up," Dominic says. I can tell he really means it.

"What does your dad do?" I ask. Dominic grins a little, but then pulls it back.

"My dad . . . he does a lot of stuff. He gets money from a lot of different places. He's a business man."

"Interesting," I reply, but only because I can tell he's lying.

"Yeah. He lives out in St. Louis."

"Wow. He brings you to this school all the way from St. Louis. That's like forty minutes away."

"No, my mom brings me to school. My dad lives in St. Louis. My parents aren't married. I stay with my mom mostly, but I hang with my dad on a lot of weekends. Joint custody agreement, or something like that, I ain't really sure."

"Oh, I get it now. My dad's a doctor for the Air Force and my mom's a nurse, *not* for the Air Force."

He nods, then goes back to the game again. At that moment, the bell rings and lunch is over. All the kids run to put their equipment away and line up to wait for the teachers.

"Well, I guess I'll see you tomorrow," I say to Dominic as we both stand. Dominic puts the basketball away before turning to me with a confused look on his face.

"What'd you say?"

"I said I'll see you tomorrow."

"You're gonna talk to me tomorrow?"

I frown. "Sure. Why wouldn't I?"

"I don't know if you've noticed, but nobody really talks to me here. They're either afraid of me or they're secretly making fun of me. So, I just kind of stay to myself."

It doesn't seem to bother him, but just hearing him say that makes me feel bad for him. It's not fair that people ignore him like that. He doesn't do anything to anybody, but they still treat him like crap. It's not fair. He defended me.

"Well, I don't know what's wrong with everybody," I say, walking to the back of my class's line. "I don't care what other people think. You saved me on my very first day of school, and made that guy apologize for hurting me. So, *I'm* gonna talk to you."

He smiles at me again as he reaches the back of Mrs. Webb's line, just as the doors swing open and the teachers usher us in.

Once we're inside, Dominic looks over at me again, still smiling.

"Okay, well I guess I'll talk to you tomorrow then," he says.

"Okay. Talk to you tomorrow."

We walk into our respective classes and I ignore Maggie and Lisa as I take my seat. I feel their eyes burning into me.

"Why were you talking to him so long, Alannah?" Maggie inquires.

"Because I wanted to," I say, instantly feeling frustrated.

"Nobody really talks to him, though. He's so big and weird-looking," Maggie says.

Lisa jumps in. "And he's mean. He's beaten up, like, four people already this year. I'm surprised he didn't try to eat you."

"No, he didn't try to eat me, Lisa, and he didn't beat me up, either," I snap. "If he's mean to you guys, it's probably because you call him Ugly Dominic and ignore him all the time. He's nice to me, and that's all that matters. So, I don't care what you guys say."

And that's the last of it. Maggie and Lisa glare at me for a second longer, but they don't say anything else. Mr. Bishop steps to the front of the class and starts talking about something that happened a long time ago, and I smile to myself because I feel like I actually made a new friend today.

FOUR

Dominic

"THERE YOU GO, SWEETIE,"

"Thanks, Ma," I reply, immediately taking a sip from the Coke my mother just put in front of me. "I'm starving. This is gonna be so good."

My mom, Gloria, takes her seat on the other side of the table and smiles. Her puffy cheeks have big dimples that always make me feel calm. She's dressed up for dinner like it's a special occasion, even though it's not, with a black dress and a pretty silver necklace my father bought for her when they were still together. Dad doesn't hang out here much because Mom doesn't like what he does, which is why they never got married, but I can tell they still like each other. I like seeing them together, but I really like hanging out with my dad on the weekends, too.

"So, how was school, Dom?" she asks, looking up at me while she chews. I absolutely hate when she shortens my name to Dom, but it's Ma, and when you're dealing with Gloria Giaculo, fuhgeddaboutit.

"It was fine. Normal."

"Normal? So, no trouble today?"

"No, Ma. No trouble today." I know she's really asking if I got into a fight today. It's been a tough year in school for me, and that affects her too.

"That's good," she says, nodding. "Anything interesting happen?"

"Not really. Well, I may have made a friend. I don't know, Ma."

"A friend?" she chirps. "What kind of friend?"

"I know where this is going, Ma. Yes, it's a girl. No, she's not my girlfriend, and no, I'm not in love."

"What? I didn't even say anything."

"Yeah, but I know you were about to."

"No way. Of course not. I wouldn't do anything to make you feel uncomfortable." She takes a second to finish chewing, then she continues with what I knew was coming. "So, what's her name? Is she pretty?"

"Ma!"

"What? I'm just curious if the girl's pretty. What's the big deal?"

"Ugh. What happened to not making me feel uncomfortable?"

"I love you, Dominic."

"Oh, whatever. Her name's Alannah."

"And?" she says, grinning like The Joker.

"Yeah, she's pretty."

"Is she Italian?"

"I don't know, Ma. I doubt it. Her father's in the Air Force."

Mom frowns. I know she'd prefer I thought an Italian girl was pretty, but we live in Belleville, Illinois. Italian girls are hard to come by.

"Well, does she at least look Italian?" she continues, not letting it go.

"I don't know, Ma. Who *looks* Italian? She has dark brown hair and brown eyes. I didn't know we had to look a certain way to be true Italians."

She puts her hands up like she's showing me they're empty. "I'm sorry. I don't mean to pry. I just think it's nice, that's all. I hope you two can be really good friends. Dominic and Alannah. That sounds nice."

"Oh my god, Ma."

"I'm sorry, I'm sorry. Let's talk about something else," she says, but that sneaky smile is still lingering. "I forgot to ask you earlier since you got home so late; how was your weekend with your father?"

An image flashes in my memory . . .

"Clean this off and put it in the glove compartment," he says as he looks out the window at the guy who's still on the ground.

I use the towel to wipe the blood off the gun.

"It was good. Fun," I reply, smiling as I chew. I make sure to keep my eyes on my plate.

"Yeah? He take you anywhere?" she asks, suddenly serious.

The smile melts off my face, but I keep looking down. I know she's staring at me.

"Umm, nowhere special. We just hung out," I reply.

I'm not stupid. I know why my parents aren't together, and my father has told me plenty of times that there's things I can't say in front of my mother. My father hasn't changed at all. The things he does when we're together are the exact things my mother hates about him. It's weird, because I know she still loves him, there's just certain things she hates about him. Grownups are strange.

"Don't lie to me, Dominic Giovanni Collazo," she snips. Ugh, my full name. Now I have to look up at her, and she's glaring at me with an expressionless face.

"I'm not, Ma," I lie.

I look back down at my plate even though my lasagna is almost gone. I hear her take a deep breath, which is the signal that she's about to give a speech.

"Listen to me, Dom," she begins. I know how this goes, so I put my fork down and prepare to listen for a while. "I love your father, I really do, but I also know the truth about him.

And I know you're getting to that age now that you're learn-ing the truth about him, too. I know what your father does, and who he hangs out with, and I know it's dangerous. He loves you, though, and I'm not gonna try to deny him his right to being your father. I'd never even think of doing that, but I need you to know something. Your father's life might seem glamorous. He's got a lot of money, and he knows a lot of people who fear and respect him. But what your father does isn't glamorous, Dominic, it's dangerous. Maybe you haven't seen that much of it yet, but I know Donnie, so I'm sure you will. You have to be smarter than that. Make some friends the right way, and do something good with your life. I don't want you to be like your father."

"Why would you say that?" I snap. "My father is respected by everyone in St. Louis. They all know his name. Me? People treat me like crap at school, and I just let them get away with it. They laugh at me, they call me Ugly Dominic. Nobody likes me, Ma, and you want me to *not* be like Dad. I wish I was like him. He gets respect, but not me. I'd rather be like him than be like me."

"Don't say that, Dominic," Mom answers, softening her tone now. "I know how rough school can be, and I know some kids are little shits, but you have to be above them, just like you have been. You're better than those kids who are calling you names. Don't bring yourself down to their level. Don't let them bother you with their words."

"Their words hurt, Ma!" I yell. I didn't mean to, it just came out that way.

Both of us are silent for a moment, my words hanging in the air like a cloud above our heads. The tension in my moth-er's face eases as she gets up from her seat and kneels in front of me. She takes my hand and looks me right in the eye, and I can see she has tears in hers.

"I'm sorry you have to go through that. Kids are brats, and

their parents should teach them better. I can't control that, but I can teach you better. Don't let the hatred of others bring you down. You're above all those kids who are mean to you. You don't have to fight all the time. You win by being smarter than all of them. You're gonna be the one, out of all those little A-holes in that school, to be somebody big. They might not respect you now, but I guarantee they're gonna respect you later. You'll see, Dom. I just want what's best for you, that's all. I want you to have a better, safer life than what your father has, Do you understand?"

A better life than my father has? A better life than the nice cars, and the money, and the women, and the respect of every man in the city? How does it get better than that?

I hear her words, but it does nothing for me. It'd be impossible to convince me that my father's life is somehow bad. He has everything. I want everything he has, and I'm so tired of trying to be the nice kid my mom wishes I was. The things that I think aren't nice. The things I want to do to those kids who call me Ugly Dominic aren't nice. I'm not who my mother thinks I am, but I don't want to break her heart by telling her that I'm more like my father than she knows. So, I hear her words, but I let them go in one ear and out the other. Just like my father would do.

"Yeah, Ma. I understand."

FIVE

Dominic

FRIDAY. EVERYBODY LOVES FRIDAY, EVEN me, but what I'm even more excited about is that I'm about to see Alannah again. She's really been going out of her way to talk to me all week long. I don't know why she does it, but I like it. In fact, I think I like her, but I'm not going to say anything about it. She gets enough crap from people just for hanging out with me, so the last thing I want to do is make her feel uncomfortable by telling her how much I like her. So, when she sits down next to me during lunch—for the fourth day in a row—I just smile at her and keep eating.

Okay, she's here. Just stay cool, Dominic, I think to myself.

"Hi, Dominic," she says as she sits. She's wearing a pink shirt with a picture of NSYNC on it, and I instantly have a new hatred for Justin Timberlake. Her brown hair is so pretty, and it hangs over her shoulder like it was always meant to be there. She smells good, too, like flower scented perfume made just for her.

"Hi, Alannah. What's up?" I reply, making sure I don't let my inner thoughts slip out.

"Not much. Nothing but wishing I would've packed a lunch today instead of eating this," she says, gesturing towards her tray. "Seriously, what the crap is this?"

"I think it's meatloaf," I answer, smiling. "Or, wait, maybe it's lasagna. No, it's a cheeseburger."

She laughs, and now I smile because she's smiling and I like it.

"You're funny, and I think you're right. It's a combination of, like, ten different things. So gross."

"Almost as gross as the picture on your shirt." She looks down at stupid Justin's face and gasps.

"Leave them alone," she jokes as she hits me in the arm. I notice we're getting some stares from people, but I ignore them. "You wish you had curly, Ramen Noodle hair like JT." Both of us laugh, and I do my best to think about what my mom was telling me earlier this week. I'm trying to be nice, but the girls a few tables down from us are starting to get on my nerves with their gawking.

Alannah and I finish our food and get up together. We dump our trays and ignore the whole world as we walk outside. Our hands are so close together as we walk they're almost touching. I really have to concentrate because the closer our hands get, the faster my heart beats. I don't think she even knows how close we are.

The two of us walk to the center of the playground to a big, dome-shaped jungle gym and climb to the top. It's not really that high, but it feels cool to be off the ground with the wind blowing around us. We watch the other kids coming out of the cafeteria, some of them grabbing basketballs and soccer balls to play with, others running over to the swings in front of us. Then, out strut the cool kids.

Lisa and Maggie stride in step, surrounded by a few other girls who are looking to get or stay on their good side. As they walk, they look at everyone else like they're beneath them, like they don't deserve to be on the same playground as the two of them. It's annoying. I hate the looks on their faces and the closer they get to us, the more I wish I could make them cry for how rude they are to other people. Some people don't deserve nice.

"You really hate them, don't you?" I hear Alannah say. I look over and see she's staring at me with a smile that looks more nervous than anything else.

"Umm, I don't hate them," I start. "They just aren't very nice to people. Especially me. I've seen the way they've been treating you, too, since you started talking to me. It's just not right, that's all."

I look at her, hoping my words have made her less nervous about the way I was glaring at the two of them. She smiles and turns her eyes towards the girls as they walk at a glacial pace across the grass like two predators stalking prey.

"Yeah, they haven't been very nice, but I'm not worried about them," she says. "I don't care if they don't like me."

"Are you always nice when people are mean to you?" I ask.

"I try to be," she begins, but she stops herself. "Sshh, they're coming over here."

I turn to find Lisa and Maggie glaring at us from below like we did something wrong by just existing. I take a deep breath and wait for them as they come closer and stop right in front of us. We're looking down on them, which I find ironic. It's something my mom would say. They're literally beneath us.

"Are you two in love or something?" Lisa asks, giggling in a way that instantly annoys me.

"You obviously are," Maggie answers for us. "I just don't understand how you could like him so much, Alannah. He's so ugly. Something must be wrong with you."

Alannah sighs. "Nothing's wrong with me," she says. "I just don't let people like you decide who I'm allowed to be nice to."

"Shut up," Maggie snaps. "You're just too stupid to know that hanging out with Ugly Dominic makes you just as ugly as he is. So, now you're dumb and ugly."

"Yeah, you're actually worse than Ugly Dominic," says Lisa. "We're gonna call you Dugly. Dumb and ugly."

The two of them burst into laughter and lean over at the same time like two ignorant twins. I glance at Alannah, and I can tell she's upset, especially when another kid comes over and they tell him their new nickname for her. He starts laughing too, then he tells one of his friends, and from this view above them all, I can see it spreading already. Before we know it, every fifth grader will be calling Alannah Dugly. I can't let that happen. She doesn't deserve this.

As I watch the tears make their way out of her eyes, I feel a new sense of anger in my belly. I've been mad before, but this feels different. I might be madder than I've ever been, but I don't lash out, I control it as I lower myself from the jungle gym and drop to the ground. As I stand up, the two girls stop laughing. They look at me like they're worried now, even taking little steps back as I approach them. They're scared, and it makes me feel good. I like that they're afraid. They *should* be afraid.

"You better not touch me, Ugly Dominic," Maggie says, spitting her words at me. "I'll go right to Mr. Bishop and have you suspended *again*."

I lean in close so that my head is between both of theirs, and I can basically feel them holding their breaths.

"You think I'm dumb enough to touch you out here in front of everybody?" I begin, turning my head and making eye contact with them both. I make sure I whisper the rest, as I look into Maggie's eyes. "You think I'd let people see it? Nah, I'll wait until you're walking down Thornton Street on your way home, like you do every single day after school. And when you walk past that alley, you know the one that looks dark even in the daytime, you'll know you're not alone. When you're lying on your face in that alley with no one around to help you, you'll know it's because you started calling Alannah that stupid name. It'll be your own fault, and nobody will see anything happen. So, how would you be able to tell Mr.

Bishop then? How will you be able to tell anybody if I make it to where you can't fucking talk anymore?"

The two of them look like their stuck in a block of ice together. They're both frozen in time—barely blinking, barely breathing, unmoving.

I turn to the guy who was laughing earlier, because I'm sure he could hear what I was saying.

"What? You don't think I'm funny? Or, do you only laugh when you know it's hurting a defenseless person's feelings?"

He doesn't say anything, but I see him swallow hard. I don't even know who he is, but I chuckle at him as I climb back up the jungle gym and take my place next to Alannah. She isn't crying now, and that makes me feel better. The two of us watch Maggie and Lisa slowly step away from the jungle gym, and they keep walking until they're on the other side of the playground, like they're trying to get as far away from me as possible.

"Are you okay?" I ask Alannah.

She smiles. "I'm fine. What'd you say to them?"

"Just not to mess with you like that," I reply. "I told them I'm not gonna put up with that crap anymore. You don't deserve it."

"Thank you, Dominic," she says behind her beautiful smile. "You didn't have to do that, though."

"Yeah, I did," I interrupt. "Look, I don't like many people in this stupid school, but you're the only one who has been nice to me. And you don't do it because you're scared, you do it because you want to. You're a nice person, Alannah, and you don't deserve to have people talking crap to you like that. Nobody's gonna mess with you now—not while I'm around. Okay?"

She seems to take a second to think about it, then she smiles from ear to ear, and my heart does the same.

"Okay, Dominic."

TWO YEARS LATER

SIX

Dominic

"DO ME A FAVOR, REMIND me again, because maybe I have a bad fucking memory. Maybe I'm old and I have fucking amnesia or something. Remind me again; what's today's date?"

He knows what the date is. He didn't forget, but I've been here enough times now to know how this is about to go down.

Lorenzo Solento, owner of Solento Deli, seems to have forgotten that he has to pay tax to my father. He didn't have to be in this positon, he put himself here. It's simple; the first of every month you pay the ten percent you owe just like everybody else, and as long as you do that, nothing bad will ever happen to you. Nobody can touch you, or they'll have to explain to Donnie Collazo why they took money out of his pocket. Nobody wants to do that, so all you have to do is pay the tax. If Lorenzo would've paid his tax when he was supposed to, my father and I wouldn't be here right now. But he didn't, so it is what it is.

"Today's the third," I reply, but my father's not really listening anyway. He's just staring at Lorenzo.

"I gave you two extra fucking days to pay, and you want to stand there and expect me to accept your pitiful fucking apology," my father snarls. "How long you known me, Lorenzo?"

"A long time, Donnie. Me and yous go way back," Lorenzo pleads. I can see beads of sweat on his forehead, and he's fidgeting with nerves. "You've always been real good to me, too. I'm really sorry about the inconvenience. Really, I am."

"Shut your fucking mouth," my father interrupts. He knows he can't let Lorenzo get away with this. I know he can't. I know he won't. "You make me have to come down here on the weekend with my thirteen year old son to collect from you. I'd rather be at my fucking house getting my dick sucked in the bedroom while my son plays PS2, but instead we're both here, and you're apologizing. I'm *not* getting my dick sucked, my son's *not* playing fucking PS2, and you're apologizing." My father glances at me. "Dominic, lock the fucking door."

I do as I'm told, and before I can flip the sign from Open to Closed, I hear the sound of my father's fist bashing into Lorenzo's face. I whip around to see Lorenzo on the floor curling himself into a ball while my father kicks him in the back of the head. His body jerks with every stomp and there's blood on the floor that's smearing onto Lorenzo's white jacket.

"You stupid fuck!" my father yells as he keeps on stomping Lorenzo's face and head. "You trying to make a fool out of me? You think I'm gonna let some dumb fuck like you hold out on me? You pay just like everybody else does, you cock sucker!"

I watch my dad kick Lorenzo about twenty times before I start to feel bad for the guy. I mean, he really should've known better than to hold out on my dad, but sometimes people make mistakes and have to be taught a lesson. My dad has to make an example of Lorenzo so people know they can't get away with not paying on time, but I'm starting to feel like he's had enough already. My dad's still kicking, but the guy isn't really doing much to cover up anymore. He might be unconscious already. I take a deep breath and decide to step in.

I jump in front of my father and slowly push him backwards. "Okay, Dad, he's done. I think you knocked the fucking guy out already." My father reluctantly backs away.

"Alright, alright," he says, looking around me at the bloody mess on the floor. "Get the money off the counter."

I turn around and walk to the counter where Lorenzo dropped the envelope full of cash when we walked in. As I reach for the envelope, I see a figure come running out of the back. It's a boy—maybe a few years older than me—and he's screaming as he runs towards me with a meat cleaver over his head. He's ready to bash my head in, and my dad's too far away to help, so I have to act fast.

He's wild and out of control, so I let him swing the cleaver. He misses by a mile, and the momentum makes him tumble forward. As he tries to regain his balance and turn around, I reach back and punch him in the face. I hear a loud cracking sound and blood explodes from his nose, splattering all over the place. He drops the cleaver and falls to his knees.

"Stupid fucker tried to hit me with a meat cleaver," I turn and say to my father. He looks at me with amusement, but doesn't say anything.

I feel furious. I know this guy is probably related to Lorenzo—maybe his son or nephew—and he was just looking to protect him, but I was the one trying to keep my father from killing Lorenzo. I got him off of him, and this is how I'm repaid for being nice. This is what I get for showing remorse? This is why my father has always told me not to show remorse. He has always told me to bury my feelings deep down so I don't even know they're there, so when a situation arises, I can act without letting feelings get in the way. I should've listened.

I bend down and pick up the meat cleaver off the floor.

"I went out of my way to protect Lorenzo, and here you come with this fucking thing trying to kill me for it. Do I look like some kind of easy target to you? I'm Donnie Collazo's son, you stupid fuck! You hear me? You better remember it forever. I'm Dominic Collazo."

He tries to shield his face with his hands, but it does nothing to stop the impact of the meat cleaver on the side of his face. When he falls, there's more blood on the floor, and his cheek looks like a fleshy mess. It looks like his jaw is out of place, too, but I don't feel bad. I drop the cleaver and grab the envelope as my father and I walk out together. I make sure to leave the sign flipped to Closed.

When we get in the car, I can feel my father staring at me as I close my door.

"What?" I snip.

"You did good, Dominic," he replies with a wide grin. "You did real good. There's three things I need you to take from this, though. One: don't ever fucking jump in my way ever again. If I'm kicking the shit out of some *stronzo* for being late on his taxes, I don't care if he's been dead for twenty fucking minutes, you don't get in my way. Ever. You understand?"

"Yeah," I reply, afraid to look up at him now. "Sorry, Dad."

"Number two; when you hit that guy, you splattered blood everywhere and got some on your shoes. Now, I'm gonna have to explain to your mother why you got blood on your fucking shoes. So, get a rag out of the glove compartment and wipe that shit off before it stains permanently. If you're gonna keep coming with me, you're gonna have to learn to protect yourself from shit like this. Always clean up your messes."

I reach into the glove compartment and pull out the rag while he keeps talking.

"And three; what you did in there was a thing of beauty," I stop wiping the blood from my shoes and look at him. He's smiling from ear to ear. "That guy could've hurt you real bad with that meat cleaver, but you did what you had to do. That's it, Dominic, you have to act. You didn't let your thoughts get in the way of what you needed to do. And the way you told him your name . . . fucking genius. I wish I would've thought of that. That asshole is gonna remember that for the rest of his life, and that's exactly how it should be. I'm proud of you, Dominic. You made your old man proud in there."

Now it's my turn to smile. I know it seems odd for my

father to tell me he's proud I hit a guy in the face with a meat cleaver, but my dad isn't like other dads. My dad's a gangster. He knows I know it, too, and he doesn't care because he knows it doesn't bother me. No matter how many people I've seen him beat up over the years, he's still my dad, and he's the only hero I've ever had. My dad's a gangster, and I'm proud of him. I'm proud to be his son.

"Thanks, Dad," I reply, still grinning as I lean forward and get back to work on my shoes.

My father opens the envelope and counts the cash right there in the parking lot. I hear him let out a sigh of frustration.

"Fucking peanuts," he snips, grinding his teeth together as he counts the money. "Look at this shit. How am I supposed to earn on little shit like this? How am I supposed to get upped like this? I've gotta show that I'm an earner, and this ain't gonna cut it!" He stuffs the money back in the envelope and shoves it into the glove compartment. "I've gotta get with the guys and work on a bigger score, because I'm just not doing it big enough with these little shops and delis. I'll never be a capo this way."

After all the time I've spent with my father over the years, I know what it is he's trying to achieve. He wants to be promoted to a more powerful position in the family he's a part of. It means more to him than anything, and I know the only way he's going to be promoted is if he makes a lot of money and proves to the bosses he's a good earner.

"Sorry, Dad," I say to him. "I know how bad you wanna get upped, and I know you've been working on it a long time. It'd be different if you could make the casinos downtown pay a tax. Ten percent on them would be way more than ten percent from Lorenzo."

My dad slowly turns his head and looks at me with eyes bigger than saucers.

"What did you just say?" he asks, and I'm instantly scared

to answer.

"What? Nothing, I was just talking."

"Casinos. Tax the casinos."

He doesn't say anything else for another thirty seconds, but I'm too scared to break the silence, so I wait for him to do it.

"You're a fucking genius," he says, but he still has the big eyes. "All those expensive casinos and hotels in downtown St. Louis. That'd be the biggest racket the Giordano Family has ever seen, especially if we can reel in two or three of them. That'd take a big fucking crew, and we'd have to be extremely organized, but if we pulled that off, it'd be huge. Holy shit, Dominic, you're on a fucking roll tonight!"

My father finally starts the car and drives away. Luckily Lorenzo is unconscious or the cops would've been here already.

As we leave the parking lot my father turns to me again.

"I've got an idea of my own," he says before turning his eyes back to the road. "We're gonna make a little trip, okay?"

"Okay. Where are we going now? It's not another collection, is it? Because I just got my shoes clean."

"Nah, it's not another collection. I'm gonna introduce you to some people. Some friends of mine. That okay with you?"

I nod my head. "Sure. Of course."

As we drive on the highway back towards St. Louis, I can feel it. Everything I thought I knew is about to change.

SEVEN

Alannah

"ALANNAH, WAIT UP."

I hear Dominic yelling for me as I walk down the hall towards the exit. School just let out, and now I have the luxury of waiting for my dad to drive from his job to come get me. Yay me. Luckily, Dominic has to wait too, so we get to spend some time together before we go home. His mom usually shows up before my dad does, though.

I turn around and watch as Dominic strides across the tile floor towards me. He smiles when we make eye contact, and everybody else in the hall disappears. He's different now, in a lot of ways. Something has definitely changed about him over the couple of years we've known each other. For one, he's much more confident lately. He carries himself with a certain pride that's really obvious. He's always looked like he has no fear, but now it's different. It's like he knows there isn't a thing in the world that can touch him. He's not arrogant, but he carries himself like he knows something the rest of us don't. He doesn't have a fear in the world.

Dominic's also growing into his body. His shoulders have filled out and his lips don't look too big for his face anymore. Nobody's calling him Ugly Dominic now that we're in junior high. His jaw is chiseled, his lips are full, and he has way more muscle than anybody else his age. He isn't ugly. I'm not sure what I'd call him, but it definitely isn't ugly. Those days are over.

"Hey, how was your last class?" I ask, as he catches up to me and we start towards the doors.

"Ugh, fucking stupid. Mrs. Shelton should *not* be allowed near kids," he replies with a grin—the grin I'm starting to find myself liking in a way I didn't used to. We're both thirteen now, and Dominic is starting to talk and act like he's twenty already. He's definitely the most mature guy I've ever met, cuss words and all.

"Mine was dumb, too," I reply. "Having Mr. Harrison for my last class just sets me up to be depressed for the rest of the day. He's so annoying and monotone."

"Oh yeah, I have him for first period. I blame him for my days being shitty."

The two of us walk on the green grass and sit down at a bench in front of the parking lot. It's a beautiful day outside with the bright sun shining in our faces making us squint. While Dominic settles himself on the seat and looks out at the road to see if his mom's coming, I take a second to just look at him. His posture is big and bold, his clothes don't have a bunch of brand names on them, but they're really nice—a little too old-looking for his age, but it's fitting, given Dominic's demeanor and maturity. He carries himself like a guy who has already graduated from high school and now he's just visiting, feeling above it all. I'd be lying if I said it didn't look good on him.

"Mom running a little late today?" I ask, drawing his attention.

"Nah. Ma's not picking me up today," he says, still looking out at the road.

"No? Your dad?"

He smiles, but he doesn't look at me. He's smiling to himself. "Yeah."

"Spending more time with him, huh? Usually it's just the weekends."

"Yeah, well, the arrangement between him and my ma has changed a bit. He wants to come get me and spend more time with me now."

"What changed all of a sudden?"

He looks at me like he's thinking about something I'm not supposed to know. I can see it in his face—that look you get when you're wrestling with what you want to say next.

"You don't have to tell me if you don't want to," I jump in before he can say anything.

"I know, but I kinda want to."

"Okay."

Dominic turns his body towards me and leans in like the conversation just became our little secret, so I lean in too.

"You're my best friend, Alannah, you know that?" he says quietly.

"Yeah, I know. You're my best friend, too, Dominic," I reply, a little thrown off by the start of the conversation.

"Good. We've known each other a while, and we're best friends, so if I tell you something, you'll keep it a secret, right?"

"Of course I will. You're honestly freaking me out a little."

"It's nothing to get freaked out about. I told you a little bit about my dad, right?"

"What do you mean? Like, what he does?"

"Yeah."

"Yeah, you told me he's a business man or something."

"Well, he is, kind of. My dad's a part of a family in St. Louis that conducts business together. I'm still kind of learning about it all, really, but the reason my dad's gonna be coming to get me more is because I kind of started working with him. Well, for him, I guess."

"You work for your dad?" I ask, frowning. "How is that? You're only thirteen."

"I know, but it's not like it's flipping burgers at McDonald's or something. I'm just doing little stuff for him and The

Family, and I get money from the stuff I do."

My frown is still holding on strong. "So, what kind of stuff do you have to do?"

Now it's Dominic's turn to frown. "I can't really say, mainly because I'm not really sure yet, but the stuff I have to do . . . isn't always good."

"What? What do you mean it's not good? Like, illegal?"

"Sometimes . . . I guess."

"So, your dad does illegal stuff, and now you're doing illegal stuff with him?"

"Look, the only reason I'm telling you is because you're my best friend in the whole world, and I like that I can tell you stuff about me. Stuff that nobody else knows. So, I don't want you to judge me. I don't need that. I just want us to be able to tell each other everything. That's what best friends do. Right?"

I pause for a minute to let all of his words sink in, then I answer. "Yeah, that's what best friends do. I'm not gonna judge you, Dominic. I told you when we were in fifth grade, I only care about how you treat me. And I promise not to tell anyone. Ever."

He smiles at me and I feel butterflies in my stomach, although I'm not sure why.

"Good," he says, just as a dark red Cadillac turns into the parking lot, and he grabs his backpack as he stands.

"Is that your dad?" I ask, marveling at the nice car with the tinted windows so dark I can't see inside.

"Yeah. I gotta go. I'll see you tomorrow, Alannah," he says as he starts walking towards the car.

"Okay, see you tomorrow."

As Dominic walks to the car, the passenger window slides down and I can see his dad's smiling face. He's got slick black hair and the same strong jaw as Dominic, but there's something about him that makes me feel nervous. Even as he smiles at Dominic, he looks like a person who you want to be your friend, not your enemy. I guess that's probably the same way people see Dominic.

I don't know exactly what Dominic was talking about when he was saying all that stuff about his dad. I don't know how he could be working for him when he's only thirteen, and I don't know what illegal stuff he was talking about either, but it doesn't matter. Dominic really is my best friend, and there's no way I'd say anything to anybody about what he told me, and nothing he said changes the way I feel about him or the way he treats me. We'll always be close. No matter what.

EIGHT

Dominic

"I'M GETTING READY TO GO."

"You're getting ready to go where? Like, out?"

"Yeah, Ma has to work tonight, so my dad's coming to get me here in a few."

Alannah pauses for a moment like she's surprised. I can basically see her scrunching her forehead and pinching her lips together like she does when she's confused. I've always liked when she does that.

"So, your mom has to go to work, and your dad is about to come pick you up and take you into St. Louis? It's, like, nine o'clock at night. I'm actually getting ready to go to bed," she replies.

"Yeah, it's weird, I know. I finished my homework for history just before my mom told me to get ready."

I hear Alannah's father come into the room and tell her it's time to get off the phone.

"Well, have a good time, I guess. I have to go. Bedtime, well, at least for some of us it is," Alannah says behind a giggle.

"Okay. I'll talk to you later," I reply.

We hang up as I hear the doorbell ring. My father's here. Time to go.

IT'S REALLY DARK OUT HERE. I feel the gravel under my shoes, but I can't see it. I even lift my hand to see if I can make out the outline of my fingers. I can't. It's too dark. The lights from the city are way down the road, so they're doing nothing to brighten this area. It's dead quiet, too. So quiet, in fact, I'm almost scared by it. Almost. I know what's going on, and I know what I have to do, so I'm not afraid, I'm nervous.

I've never done anything like this before, and I don't want to mess it up. I have to do it exactly right, or I could ruin things, so there's no time for screw ups. I take a deep breath, because I think I hear a truck coming. I look down the road and see headlights coming towards me and the dust kicking up behind the big truck.

Here we go.

As the truck approaches, I kneel down in the road and put my hand in the air. I wave at the truck like I need help, and sure enough, it pulls over. It's a Best Buy truck, probably on its way to drop off a bunch of electronics or something. I bet it's loaded with stuff.

The truck stops just a few feet from me, but I don't get up. I wait. I hear the door click open and the driver starts to get out, and that's when it starts. Without warning, my father and his crew climb out of the shadows of the ditch and rush the driver with their guns drawn. The guy is completely caught off guard as they run up to him and my father immediately punches him in the face. The guy falls down right in front of me. We make eye contact and I see his face turn to complete terror when I smile at him and climb to my feet. I dust my knees off and make my way over to the back of the truck where my dad's friend, Frankie Leonetti, is cutting the lock with a big pair of bolt cutters.

Frankie's a big guy, and he honestly looks like he could be my father's brother with the same slicked back hair. I don't know much about him yet, except that he and my father are on the same level as soldiers for the Giordano Family. He chuckled when my father named me as an associate in his crew, and even said my dad was crazy for it, but in the end he was accepting and called me Boy Wonder, although I'm not sure why. Frankie gets the lock off and pushes the big door open.

"Would ya' fucking look at that," he says, his voice thin and high pitched. "Look at all this shit."

Frankie shines a light into the back of the truck and illuminates all the DVD players, TV's, and laptops anyone could ask for. The truck is full of Best Buy merchandise, and the guys are ecstatic.

"Holy shit, Donnie, come look at this," Frankie says, still staring into the truck.

"Don't you fucking move, asshole," I hear my father yell at the driver who's still on the ground with a gun to his head. "You act up and you won't make it off this road alive. Stephano, watch him."

Some guy named Stephano walks up and takes my dad's place watching the driver, while Dad comes to look into the truck with the rest of us.

"What a beautiful fucking sight," he says with a bright smile on his face. "We hit a big one, boys."

"Fucking right!" Frankie chirps.

The whole crew starts to laugh and pat each other on the back. I laugh, too, but out of the corner of my eye, there's movement.

I look over and see Stephano laughing with the rest of us, but the driver he's supposed to be watching is reaching into his pocket. I don't think, I run over to the driver and kick him in the face, then I stomp his head three times for good measure before my father can pull me off of him.

"Hey, what the fuck is wrong with you?" he asks.

"He was reaching for his pocket," I explain. My father looks baffled, then he looks down at the driver who's covering his face in pain. Dad pulls his gun from his waist band and kneels down next to him.

"What did I tell you? Are you trying to die out here on this road? Huh? You want me to fucking kill you out here? How about I give you a closed fucking casket so your mother never sees you again, you fucking cock sucker!" Dad hits the driver in the face with the pistol and I see a couple of his teeth fall out. Then my father stands up and directs his attention to Stephano. "And you, you fucking moron. I told you watch him, and you take your eyes off him so long my thirteen year old son has to come save your ass. You stupid son of a bitch!"

"I'm sorry, Donnie," Stephano says.

"Hey, we don't have time for this shit," Frankie interrupts. "We made the score, now it's time to go. Wrap it up."

Right on cue, everybody starts moving. Frankie shuts the door in the back, Stephano climbs into the driver seat of the truck, and the rest of us run towards the cars that are hidden in the darkness up the road. My father hits the driver in the back of the head with the gun, knocking him out, and we leave him there in the darkness.

Once we're back in the car and driving away, my father can no longer hold in his excitement about how things just went down.

"Holy shit, this is huge!" he exclaims. "Did you see how much shit was in the back of that truck?"

"Fucking beautiful," Frankie agrees. "You know what else was beautiful? Fucking Boy Wonder back there. Did you see him kick the shit out of that guy?"

"Oh my fucking god, I know! What did I tell you?" Dad yells.

"He's a fucking natural, Donnie," Frankie says, turning back in his seat to look at me. I smile, because I don't know what else to do.

"You did real good back there, Dominic," my father says, looking at me in the rearview mirror as he drives. "Real fucking good. I'm proud of you. You hear me?"

"I hear you," I answer, still smiling. "Thanks, Dad."

"Fucking Boy Wonder," Frankie says again, still looking at me and shaking his head like he can't believe it. "Congratulations on your first score, kid."

NINE

Alannah

I GET TO THE BENCH before Dominic does today. It's not as beautiful outside as it normally is. Maybe that's my subconscious making it seem worse than it actually is, I don't know. I feel nervous. Anxious, even. On one hand I'm excited, on the other hand, I feel terrified and I don't even know why. I have no reason to fear Dominic. Other people might, but not me. Yet, as I place my back pack on the ground in front of me, I feel like he's about to be upset with me, and these days, nobody wants Dominic Collazo to be upset with them.

I hear the door to the school slam behind me, and I know it's him. My heart quickens and I have to make myself breathe or I might not do it right. I hear his footsteps because he's big and he walks heavy. Even his walk is intimidating. He sits down across from me and smiles, so I smile back to keep it light.

"Hey," he says.

"Hi."

"Why you looking so nervous?" he asks, so I know I already messed up the smiling part.

"I don't know. I'm not nervous." That's a lie.

He chuckles a little. "Okay. So, you said you wanted to talk to me, and now I come out here and you look like you're about to get the electric chair. You're making *me* nervous. What's up, Alannah?"

"Nothing's up, really. How was your day?" I ask, stalling.

"My day was fine, but you ask me about my day all the time and you never look this nervous. Your note said you needed to talk to me, so just get to it, crazy."

He's being playful and smiling, so maybe this will go better than I thought.

"Okay, so I need to tell you something," I begin. Dominic puts his big arms on the table and leans forward to listen. "Do you know Bobby Pistone?"

He twists his mouth and looks down, thinking.

"Bobby Pistone. Oh yeah, Bobby Pistone. Tall eighth grader on the basketball team, really skinny, blonde hair."

"Yeah."

"I don't really associate myself with guys on the basketball team, so I don't really know the guy, but I know who he is. What about him? Did he do something to you? He say some shit to you?"

"No, no, it's nothing like that," I reply, making sure I clarify. I don't want Dominic to get the wrong impression or it could be a problem for Bobby.

"Okay, so what about him, then?"

"Well, I have, like, five classes with Bobby, so we see each other all the time." He nods, and now that I've started, my heart is going crazy. "He's always looking at me and stuff, and kind of flirting, and I guess I was kind of flirting back a little. He's always making jokes. He's really funny. I bet you'd like him if you guys got to know each other. Umm, anyway, so me and Bobby were talking in third period today, and he told me he really liked me. I was super nervous, but I told him I kind of liked him, too. And umm, he kind of asked me out this morning. I mean, I was beyond nervous because nobody has ever asked me out before. I've never had a boyfriend or anything like that. So, anyway, I said I'd go out with him. I told him yes. So, I guess Bobby is kind of, like, my boyfriend now. Or something."

Dominic doesn't respond, and his eyes drop down to the table between us. He's completely silent and it's making me feel bad, so I have to keep talking.

"I wanted you to be the first person to know," I continue, but he doesn't look up. "You're my closest friend, and we tell each other everything, so I wanted you to know this." He still doesn't look up at me. "Dominic?"

He takes a minute and it looks like he's trying to gather his thoughts. He stays silent, and the only sound is our breathing and the rush of the wind around us. Of course, today would be the day our parents are slow to arrive.

After two minutes of silence, Dominic finally moves. He reaches down and grabs his back pack off the ground and places it on the table. He starts reaching inside of it like he's looking for something, until he finally pulls out a little white box and places it on the table in front of me. He slides the box over until it hits me in the chest, and then he stands up.

"I got this for you a couple of days ago," he says, looking at the box instead of me. "I meant to give it to you and talk to you about some stuff, but I couldn't quite bring myself to do it. Guess it's too late."

I look down at the box. "What's this?"

"It's an iPod. I got it from Best Buy a couple of days ago."

"You got me an iPod? Wow, aren't these expensive?"

"Yeah, I guess so. Just take it, it's yours. I'll talk to you later." Dominic hoists his back pack over his shoulder and walks away, never making eye contact with me.

"Dominic, what are you doing? You have to wait for your ride," I plead, but as soon as I finish, I see his mother's car driving towards the parking lot.

Dominic walks to the road and waves her down. He climbs into the passenger seat, and they drive away without him ever looking back at me.

As I watch them go, I feel like I just messed something

up—like an opportunity has been missed. Something about it feels wrong, but Dominic and I are strong, so no matter how wrong it feels, I know we're strong enough to survive it.

TWO YEARS LATER

TEN

Alannah

YOU EVER GET THE FEELING something bad is about to happen? It's like a little warning inside of your heart that tells you to watch out, because everything is about to go wrong and you need to be prepared. Well, that's how I feel waking up this morning. It's in my stomach like a cancer waiting to be discovered—it hasn't been officially diagnosed yet, but you can feel it eating away at you from the inside.

There are rumors about Dominic now. Over the past couple of years, the kids in school have been drawing their own conclusions about what he and his father do to make all the money they obviously have. Donnie Collazo has had a different car every year, and Dominic is one of the best dressed kids in school now. Not to mention the fact that he seems to have every electronic device known to man. Last year, he gave me a new iPod before that version was even available for purchase. Kids are nosy, so when a guy goes from being normal to being picked up and dropped off at school by Italian guys that look like they'd have no problem slitting someone's throat, people talk, and since Dominic and I are best friends, they talk to me.

I spend a lot of my time trying to convince people that Dominic's father is simply a casino business man. I say that because that's what Dominic tells me to say. Apparently, a year or so ago, Donnie Collazo became part owner of River City Casino & Hotel and started making big bucks. Around the same time, all these news reports and newspaper articles started popping up about potential organized crime going on in downtown St. Louis, and the FBI started looking into it, but they didn't have anything solid yet. Even my father started complaining about Italians coming in downtown and running big businesses. The next thing I knew, there were rumors and stories about people going missing and being beaten up inside the casino by people who looked like they worked there. There was even one story about a young Italian kid helping to cut off some guy's pinkie finger for trying to pocket chips at River City. Once that story started spreading, everyone thought it was Dominic. His level of respect went through the roof. Anyone who was brave enough—or dumb enough—to disrespect him when we were younger, wouldn't dream of doing it now. *Teachers* respect Dominic Collazo. The principal talks to Dominic like he's the president. Everyone believes that he's somehow connected to this wave of Italians downtown, but they don't know for sure.

I do.

The best thing about my relationship with Dominic is that we tell each other everything. It's been four years since we met, and we get closer every single year. Even through the few boyfriends I've had—all of whom Dominic has despised—and the few girls he's been interested in, he and I are still close. That closeness brings honesty.

And trust.

And secrets.

We're best friends, so when Dominic told me he got the new iPod from Best Buy, I knew he didn't mean he bought it. He didn't come right out and say it, but I understood what he meant, and he knew I knew it. When he took me out to dinner after we graduated eighth grade and paid for it with a wad of cash that was nearly too thick to fit into his pocket, I didn't think twice about it. When I asked him about the pinkie story and he grinned like The Grinch without saying a word,

I knew it was true. When he bought me a watch for my fifteenth birthday that was nicer than anything my mother has ever owned, I just smiled and accepted it—and hid it from my parents, of course. Dominic has never said the words mafia or mob to me, but it's been implied enough times for me to know, and I don't care.

Our relationship is complicated. The truth is, the things I know about Dominic only make me like him more. I love that I know things about him that other people wish they knew. From the very beginning, Dominic has done nothing but make me feel safe and special. He's the reason I'm the only popular girl in school who doesn't have rumors being spread about her. Nobody talks about me behind my back, and guys wouldn't dare disrespect me like they do other girls in the school. Like I've always said, nobody wants to be on Dominic Collazo's bad side. Dominic goes out of his way to make sure I'm taken care of, and he's been doing it since the day we met, so I would never break the bond we have. I'd never betray his trust, and he'd never break my heart.

A few guys have come and gone, but Dominic has always been there. Even though I think I've always known the way he feels about me, he's always supported me when it has come to dating. He'd do his best to convince me he wasn't upset about anything, but when I got a new boyfriend, I could always tell it was killing him inside. I just never thought of Dominic in that way.

Until this year.

The Dominic Collazo I met in fifth grade is not the same Dominic Collazo I know now. Dominic is five-nine, about a hundred-sixty pounds, and he doesn't have an ounce of fat on his body. He has the most beautiful lips I've ever seen, and his incoming facial hair makes him the most gorgeous thing roaming the halls of East Belleville High School. Girls fall over each other trying to catch a glimpse of Dominic, and the rumors of his mafia ties make him the bad boy they all wish they had. But Dominic doesn't pay any of them any mind. His way of thinking isn't anything like other guys in high school. It's like he's already an adult. I mean, he basically is. He's working with his dad, he's making money, and from what he tells me, he even helps his mom with some of her bills—although their relationship has soured over the past couple of years. When he walks into the school, the other guys become little boys. He's bigger, more confident, and more mature than all of them. To these high school girls, Dominic is like the big, sexy guy who graduated and went on to college, except he didn't. He's a freshman just like me, but it's like he's from another planet, and it takes everything in me to ignore how I feel about him now. We've always been friends, and even though I've always known how he feels about me, I'm worried that my feelings towards him will somehow ruin what we have, and I couldn't handle it if that happened. I need Dominic in my life, and I can't risk what we have by crossing that line. So, as I walk down the stairs for breakfast, I ignore thoughts about what it'd be like to go to homecoming with Dominic instead of the guy I'm actually going with.

"Good morning, sweetie," my father says when I reach the kitchen. To my surprise, my mother is sitting at the table. Usually, she's gone by now, but she's wearing her scrubs, so I know she'll be leaving soon.

I grab a box of cereal out of one cabinet and go to reach for a bowl in another.

"Good morning," I reply. "Surprised you're still here, Mom."

"Yeah, I'm getting ready to go in a bit," she replies. "I told them I'd be late this morning. There's something me and your father need to talk to you about before I go, though."

The look on her face worries me. She's scrunching her forehead and glancing back and forth between my father and me.

"Okay, what's up?" I ask as I pour my Froot Loops into the bowl.

"Umm, well I have some news," my dad chimes in. "It's about my job." When I don't reply, he's just spits it out. "I got orders last night."

I set the box of cereal on the counter and turn around so I can face them.

"You got orders?"

"Yeah."

"So, we're moving?" I ask, even though I already know. That's what getting orders means in the Air Force. The military is making us move to another base.

"Yes," my dad answers, looking at the floor. My parents know how much I love living here.

"When is this supposed to happen? And to where?" I press, feeling hot all over.

"We have a couple of months left," Dad answers. "And it's to Joint Base Elmendorf-Richardson. In Anchorage."

"Alaska?" I snap, making my mother jump. "We're moving to Alaska? Are you freaking kidding me? A couple of months? That's insane!" I feel tears already starting to sting my eyes.

"I know, sweetie. It's a little short notice, but you'll still be able to go to homecoming, at least," my mother says, trying to show me the silver lining.

"So what!" I snip. "I've been here since the fifth grade. All my friends are here. Dominic is here!"

My parents glance at each other with that look they have when I mention Dominic. They've never liked him because of who his father is and the rumors that go around about them.

"I know, sweetheart, but you know this is how the military works," my father reminds me. "We don't stay in one place for too long. The good news is, we'll be able to stay in Alaska long enough for you to graduate high school. You'll be there your sophomore, junior, and senior year. So, you'll have made plenty of friends by then. Graduation will still be awesome."

"Stop it, Dad!" I yell. "It's not about that. My whole life is here, and I don't want to move to fucking Alaska!"

"Hey! You watch your mouth, young lady! Where do you get off talking like that?" my dad barks, but I don't care. The tears are flowing and I'm too upset. I get up and stomp back up the stairs, leaving my parents and my bowl of cereal behind.

Somewhere in the back of my mind, I knew this day would come. Now that it's here, it feels worse than I ever imagined it would, and my head is filled with questions I don't have answers to.

How can I just leave Belleville after all this time? And move to Alaska, of all places! Why now? Why does it have to be so soon? How am I supposed to prepare myself for this? How do I tell my friends?

How do I tell Dominic?

It's official. The cancer has been diagnosed, and everything's about to change.

ELEVEN

Dominic

"WE'VE GOT A PROBLEM."

My father looks at Frankie Leonetti like he's definitely not in the mood to hear bad news, but Frankie presses on anyway.

"Sammy and his brother, Alfonse, are here," Frankie says in my father's ear. Dad looks over at the security monitors and sees the Cestone brothers standing outside his office with their arms folded, already defensive. This won't be good.

"Fucking kids don't learn, do they?" Dad replies as he pulls a cigar from his desk and lights it. "Let them in."

We're about to have drama, and that's a shame because things have been going so well for us. My father finally got the promotion he was looking for, and he's now a captain in the Giordano Family. He isn't the guy he was before. He's calmer now, more controlled. It probably has a lot to do with the fact that he's in charge of a crew who takes care of most things for him, and now he can sit back and collect money from the casino.

My dad took my idea about taxing casinos and ran with it. It didn't take long for him to pull strings and move in on the owner of River City. It started out just as a tax, but when the owner kept falling behind on his payments, my dad forced him out and became owner of the casino as a whole, so the money's just pouring in. Most business is conducted from his office in River City, so the casino is almost like headquarters now, and Dad started making money at the perfect time. It came down to a decision between my dad and Frankie for who was going to be a captain, and the boss, Leo Capizzi, chose my father because he was the better earner. The casino money put him over the top. Now, Frankie works for my dad, and business couldn't be better.

Everything has been running smooth for a long time now. The Giordano Family is making money all over St. Louis, and I'm developing a little reputation myself as an earner working for my dad. I'm fifteen years old and they're still calling me Boy Wonder—which I fucking hate—but it's not the name that matters, it's the fact that I have a reputation already. Dad fronted me some money and taught me a thing or two about taxing and loan sharking, and even though I have to hide everything from my mother, it's worth it. This is exactly the person I want to be. I love being a part of this family, and I love making this money. I wouldn't trade it for the world. The small bit of attention we've gotten from the nosy ass FBI is nothing, because they don't have shit on us. So, fuck the FBI, as my father would say.

The only source of annoyance we have is from the two cock suckers walking into the room right now, Sammy and Alfonse Cestone. These two pricks are older than me, but younger than Frankie and my dad. They're immature, and they want street cred, and since my dad and his crew are focused on bigger things with the casino now, Sammy and Alfonse have started really stepping up their street activity in our absence. They're pulling a lot of robberies and taking a lot of trucks, which is fine as long as they don't hit the one's we already own, and they don't touch the trucks that are on routes that belong to my father. They've abided by the rules for a couple of years, which is why Frankie and Dad have let them do it, but they're getting greedy now, and that's going to be a problem. Rumor has it they have serious ties to one of the Five Families in New York, which isn't anything new because we all do, technically, but they seem to think they're connections gives them a power the rest of us don't have. They don't know how wrong they are.

"How you doing, Donnie?" Sammy says as he saunters in with his hands in his pockets. He has sharp facial features—a long jaw and a pointy nose and chin—and his brother looks just like him, except he's a little plumper in the belly. They walk to the front of Dad's desk and wait to be addressed. Still following the rules, for now. Sammy and Alfonse aren't made guys, they're simply a crew trying to gain credibility on their own, so rules must be followed.

Dad blows smoke into the air and eyeballs the two goons. He knows why they're here, and he doesn't like it. Frankie takes a seat in the corner behind the Cestone brothers and folds his arms. Everyone is tense, even me as I sit next to dad and glance out the big window overlooking the casino floor.

"What the fuck is this, Sammy?" Dad begins. "You coming over here unannounced? I don't like it."

"I apologize for that," Sammy says, remaining calm. "We don't mean no disrespect, Donnie, we know you're a capo now. We just had some business we'd like to discuss with you."

Dad exhales in annoyance, but he relents and tells them to sit down. They do, and Sammy gets started while Alfonse remains silent, looking past my father like he's not even listening.

"We had an idea. This casino thing is looking pretty lucrative. I mean, I don't know how you pulled it off, but becoming owner of this place was fucking genius, Donnie, I gotta tell you."

"I appreciate that, Sammy, but what's the fucking point?" Dad snips.

"Well, I'm glad you asked. You know who my Uncle Carlo is, don't' you?" Sammy asks. He leans back in his chair and makes himself comfortable.

"Why would I know who your uncle is?" Dad asks.

"Because he's the don of the Lucchese Family now." Sammy throws one leg over the other and smiles. He's trying to play the "my uncle's a boss in New York" card, and you don't do that without having an agenda. You don't try to trump a capo with a guy who's not even in the same state, even if they are related to you, and even if your relative is a boss of one of the Original Five Families of New York.

"Okay, your uncle's a boss in New York," my dad says with venom in his voice. "What the fuck do I care? What's that got to do with me?"

Sammy exhales and somehow manages to sit back even further. Considering the tone of the conversation, he's entirely too relaxed. He's an arrogant asshole and it's rubbing my father and Frankie the wrong way. He's even managing to get on my fucking nerves.

"The reason it's important to you, Donnie, is because I know you don't wanna piss off a head of one of The Five. You don't need that kind of drama in your life. So, to avoid any unnecessary suffering to your thriving crew, I think it'd be a good idea if you and I went into business together. You know, kind of as a favor to New York."

Dad doesn't say a word. Frankie sits up and taps his jacket like he's looking for a pack of cigarettes, but he's really making sure his gun is where he expects it to be.

"You understand what I'm saying, Donnie?" Sammy asks, narrowing his eyes. "I don't even need to be seen, hell I don't want to be seen. I'll just be behind the scenes. My brother and I were thinking you kick us seven percent every week and everything will be good to go. Everybody's happy. Especially New York."

The air in the room is thin, and the tension is thick. Dad glances at me, then his eyes bounce to Frankie before he finally stands up and straightens out his suit. He puffs on his cigar and blows the smoke right into Sammy's face. Sammy doesn't flinch.

"You got alotta balls, kid. Coming in here and thinking you can tax me on my casino is the ballsiest thing I've ever seen, and I admire that. It's also the dumbest thing I've ever seen. The only fucking person I kick up to, is *my* boss, Leo Capizzi. Anybody else thinking I owe them something is a fucking moron, and that includes you and your ugly fucking brother. I don't even know your fucking uncle, but if he has a problem with that, he can fly his ass down here and take it up with Leo. You fucking kids have no respect. This isn't how we do business in Our Thing. Now, you two fucking idiots are gonna get up and get out of my casino, and on your way, you're gonna thank the Virgin Mary that your uncle is a boss in New York, because that's the only reason I'm not having both of your bodies thrown in the fucking Mississippi River tonight. Now, get the fuck up, and don't ever let me catch you on this street again. Consider this a restraining order. If anyone in your crew comes within five hundred yards of River City Casino Boulevard, we're gonna have problems."

Sammy's jaw is tight and Alfonse just stares at my dad like he wants to kill him right here, but neither of them make a move. The last thing they want to do is have a problem in this casino, so they both stand.

"Okay, Donnie. I apologize. I didn't mean no disrespect." Like twins, the two of them turn around and walk towards the door together. Frankie gets up and opens the door for them, but just as they exit, I see Sammy glance at me. We make eye contact only for a second, then he steps out and Frankie closes the door behind them.

"Can you believe those little motherfuckers?" Frankie snaps. "If you want me to handle this, Donnie, just give me the fucking word. Those arrogant cock suckers need to learn a lesson." Frankie is livid and pacing around the room. I know he'd love to get his hands on those two. Frankie would have no problem clipping them both.

"It's okay, Frankie," Dad replies as he sits down. He turns around in his seat and watches the Cestone brothers walk through the casino towards the exit. "They're just young and ambitious. But it's gonna get them killed if they don't keep it in check. I'm in a good mood. We'll give them a pass today."

"UGH, YOUR MOTHER IS GONNA fucking kill me," Dad says as he looks down at his watch. "I didn't even realize what time it is. Here Dominic, take the keys and go start up the car. I'm gonna wrap shit up here and I'll meet you down there."

I take the keys to the Cadillac and make sure I have everything before walking out.

"Later, Frankie," I say as I open the door.

"Take it easy, Boy Wonder," Frankie replies.

I make my way through the casino floor and the lobby and take the elevator down to the garage. It's eleven at night on a Wednesday, so it's pretty quiet down here. I can hear the echo of my steps as I walk through the concrete structure, and as I approach Dad's car I pull the keys from my pocket, but I accidentally drop them.

"Shit."

I reach down to pick them up, and as I'm reaching, I hear footsteps echoing, getting louder and louder as someone runs towards me. I go to look up, but before I can see anything, I feel the pain of a kick to my stomach.

I can't breathe. I fall to the ground in the fetal position trying my best to get some air into my lungs, but it's barely working. My eyes, however, are working fine, and I can see Alfonse Cestone standing over me. He has a small knife in his hand and the look on his face says he's ready to use it. He *wants* to use it, and there's no way he would've touched the son of a made guy if he didn't plan to.

"Dominic Collazo," he says, glaring down at me as I gasp for air. "Didn't expect you to be down here alone like this. Was waiting for Frankie to come out so we could give him a little message, but since you're here, it's even better. I think Donnie will really get the point if it's you."

Alfonse lifts his foot and sends it crashing downward, stomping me in the head. My skull bounces off the concrete and my vision immediately goes blurry. The pain is intense and I feel like I'm about to pass out. My hearing is muffled and I'm pretty sure I've lost all control of my body. I see Alfonse, but there's three of him and they're all dancing around and through each other. I think he's talking, too, but I can't make out the words. It's like his voice is playing on a recorder in slow motion, deep and slow.

I'm too confused to be afraid, but I see Alfonse drop to his knees and bring the knife to my face. The tip of it is near my cheek, then I can sense it's near my neck. I want to move, but I can't. He leans over me and I feel the prick of the blade on my throat, but then I hear a loud pop that makes me jump.

Just one pop, and Alfonse is gone.

I'm staring at the blurry ceiling of the garage with my back on the cold concrete. I hear muffled voices and words I can barely understand—something about sending a hand some-where, and dumping something else in the river.

"Dominic," I hear a voice say. I think it's my dad. "Dominic, are you okay? Come on, get up. We gotta go."

I feel my father lift me up off the floor, but I'm still groggy. Everything is still blurry, but as my father helps me walk to the Cadillac, I look back and see a body on the floor, and there's blood.

I know it's Alfonse.

Even through blurred vision, I know I just saw a dead body for the first time. More importantly, I just saw my father kill a man.v

TWELVE

Alannah

"MY GOODNESS. YOU LOOK BEAUTIFUL, honey."

My mother snaps another picture of me in my off-white homecoming dress as I stand next to Marcus Smart, my date for the dance. Marcus is wearing a dark gray suit and he really looks great in it. He's sixteen and just under six-foot tall, with skinny arms and short brown hair. Apparently I have a thing for basketball players, because every boyfriend I've ever had has played for the school's team, and Marcus is no exception. We haven't been going out for long, but he's a nice guy. He's sweet and is always going out of his way to spoil me, which can get a little annoying at times, but it's better than dating an asshole. He's definitely not a bad boy, though, and I'm not sure if that's a good or bad thing.

Tonight's the homecoming dance, and it's been a week and a half since I've seen Dominic. I don't know what's going on with him but he hasn't been at school at all, and I haven't even gotten an answer when I've tried calling him, which is unusual. I'm worried about him, but one thing I know for sure is that Dominic Collazo can take care of himself, so I try not to let it bother me too much. I've just been wanting to see him since my parents told me we're moving to Alaska soon. I've tried to use the time to figure out a way to tell him, but I haven't come up with anything.

Marcus and I spend another half an hour posing for pictures before my parents finally let us leave. Marcus, a sophomore, is driving his mother's red Honda with one hand like he's been doing it his whole life, and he puts his other hand on my knee. I smile when he places it there and he smiles back, then looks straight ahead.

When we get to the dance, there are people and decorations everywhere. The school colors are purple and white, and it's like those two colors have taken over the world the second we step out of the car. There's purple and white flashing lights bouncing off the walls outside, and even more of them dancing around the room when Marcus and I step inside. Purple streamers lay spread across the floor and music blares from gigantic speakers in every corner of the basketball court that's been turned into a dance floor for the night.

"Wow, they went all out," Marcus says, raising his voice so I can hear him.

"Sure did," I reply. "You wanna dance?"

"Not yet, let's mingle a bit. I wanna see if any of my people are hear yet." Marcus speaks to me without looking at me as he scans the room for his friends. He starts to walk away and I contemplate following him, but I see something out of the corner of my eye that makes me stop.

I notice people looking in the same direction, watching as a figure struts into the room. It's pretty hard to tell with the purple and white lights, but I'm pretty sure he's wearing a black suit with light gray pinstripes. Everything about him is attractive: styled black hair, strong jaw, wide shoulders, and even his intimidating scowl. Every girl in the vicinity is looking over at Dominic as he walks in like he owns the building.

There's something different about him. I don't know what it is, but it's there. The way he holds himself is bigger, prouder, like something has changed him. He's surer of himself, straddling the line between confidence and arrogance with absolute perfection, and it looks just as good on him as the suit he's wearing.

I watch him walk and I'm almost in awe of him. When he sees me, his demeanor changes. His scowl turns into a smile that's only meant for me, and my heart seems to skip a beat. Dominic is gorgeous, and it's like I'm seeing him for the first time right now.

"Hey," is all he says as he approaches, hands in his pockets.

"Hi," I reply with a feeling of nervousness I've never had around him before. "Umm, where's your date?"

He shrugs. "Don't have one. Just wanted to come see what this was all about. You look beautiful, Alannah."

Another skipped heartbeat.

"Thank you. You look . . . really handsome. That suit is awesome."

"Thank you." Dominic glances around before settling his eyes on mine. "Where's *your* date?"

Now it's my turn to look around. Marcus is nowhere to be found.

"Oh, umm, I guess he walked off. I think he's looking for his friends or something. I don't know."

"Hmm." Dominic pinches his lips together, just as Mariah Carey's *We Belong Together* starts up on the big speakers. "So, you wanna dance?"

I smile to myself, but then I take a second to look around for Marcus, but Dominic stops me.

"He's more concerned with finding his friends. I'm interested in you. So, how about it?"

I twist my mouth to try to keep from smiling, but I lose the battle.

"I'd love to."

Dominic smiles slyly, then he takes my hand and leads me to the dance floor. We don't have to push our way through the couples that are already dancing, because they seem to move out of the way for us. Dominic couldn't seem to care less, but I notice their eyes. They're glued to us from every direction like we're covered in pig's blood, and Dominic walks us right into the middle of the pack. He faces me and puts his hands on my waist, still oblivious to the stares.

"They're really staring a lot," I inform him, but he shrugs it off.

"Fuck them. It's just us in here. We're the only ones on this dance floor."

I lose the fight to another smile as I wrap my arms around his neck and we start to dance to the music. It only takes a second for me to forget about the people glaring, and eventually they go back to minding their own business, so I give my full attention to Dominic.

"So," I begin. "Where have you been the past couple of weeks?"

"I was in the hospital," Dominic replies without hesitation. "I had a concussion."

"Oh my gosh. What happened?"

He looks me in the eye, seemingly thinking about his response, but eventually gives it in the form of a whisper.

"Some guys tried to move in on my dad's casino. Dad wouldn't budge, of course, so they tried to come after me. Roughed me up a little. No big deal."

"Are you serious?"

"Ain't I always?"

I feel my heart start to race like something bad is happening right in front of me.

"That's crazy, Dominic," I say, suddenly feeling overwhelmed. "Well, are you okay, at least?"

"Fuhgeddaboutit," he says with a smile.

"What do you mean, forget about it? I can't just forget about it. What did they do to you that gave you a concussion?"

I hear Dominic sigh and he looks at me sideways.

"Alannah, the last thing I want you doin' is concerning yourself about me. Sometimes things like this happen, but I survived and I'm here now. I'm here with you, so everything's good."

"We've been close for four years, Dominic, you can't expect me not to worry."

"I didn't know you cared so much all of a sudden."

"Well, I do," I snip, my emotions starting to get the best of me. "And it's not *all of a sudden*. I do care about you, maybe more than you realize."

Just as the words escape me, the music stops and it's silent. All these people surrounding us and it couldn't seem quieter than it does right now, with all this air and tension between the two of us.

Dominic and I look each other in the eye like it's a staring contest, like we're trying to see who'll turn away first, but neither of us budge until we're interrupted by a voice.

"Alannah," he says quietly, almost like it's a question. It's Marcus, and he looks scared and angry at the same time—angry because I'm dancing with someone else, scared because that someone is Dominic.

Both of us look over at Marcus just as the music starts up again—this song's more upbeat and happy, the opposite of my mood—and I clear my throat to try to make it seem less awkward. It doesn't work.

"Umm, hey, Marcus. I was looking for you. Where'd you go?" I ask, barely able to look him in the eye.

"I was talking to Julia and Janelle, but when that last song came on I was hoping we could dance together, but I couldn't find you," he says. He makes sure to only look at me, and Dominic makes sure to only look at him.

"Umm, yeah, sorry about that," I begin. "I needed to talk to Dominic, but umm, we can dance together now if you want."

Marcus smiles at first, but it fades as he tries to figure out how to get between Dominic and me, because Dominic hasn't budged. It's awkward again.

"Dominic," I say, stealing his attention.

"There's something I need to talk to you about," he replies, finally ending his death stare at Marcus. "Something I need to tell you, and it's important. I'm gonna go for now, but maybe after this thing is over we can meet up."

I clear my throat again. This has to be making Marcus feel uncomfortable.

"Umm, actually, there's something I need to tell *you*. It's really important, too. So, that's a good idea. We'll talk later."

"Okay." Dominic steals another glance at Marcus before walking away.

The next couple of hours is spent switching between dancing with Marcus and dancing with my girlfriends, but always thinking about Dominic. Seeing him for the first time tonight in almost two weeks seems to have put a spell on me, and it takes a lot of effort just to not talk about him throughout the night.

When it's all over, Marcus insists on going to an after-party, but I insist on going home. I can see it pisses him off, but I really couldn't care less. He drops me off in the driveway of my house and I never look back as he drives away. I quietly make my way inside, where my parents are already asleep, and I call Dominic.

TO MY SURPRISE, DOMINIC SHOWS up to my house driving a black Mercedes with dark tinted windows. I couldn't even see it was him inside as he pulled into the driveway. He smiles at me through the windshield as I walk to the passenger side and climb in. He's not wearing a suit anymore, just a black t-shirt and black sweatpants, but he's still gorgeous, sweats and all.

"When'd you get your license?" I ask, my brow furrowed.

Dominic smiles.

"What license?"

He places the car in drive and we're off, rolling away from my housing area and headed for the highway. It's a quiet trip. Dominic doesn't say much, and I'm all in my head with thoughts of the conversation I had with my parents a while back, and how I'm going to tell Dominic about it. I'm wondering about what happened to him, too. How did he end up with a concussion, and what the hell is really going on in his life that puts him in situations where someone can give him a concussion? There's a lot of questions, and as we stop in an abandoned parking lot behind an apartment complex in Belleville, I'm ready to start getting answers. But it's Dominic who starts talking first.

"So, there's something I been meaning to tell you," he begins, his Italian accent seemingly getting stronger by the minute. "I've thought a lot about it, and all the shit that went down at River City made me *really* think about it. About you. About us. I've learned that life can be extremely short. One minute you're lounging in an expensive casino office, and the next minute you're on your back with a knife to your throat."

I feel my heart drop into the floor of the car.

"This isn't easy, Alannah, so just bear with me here, alright," he keeps going. "Umm, I know we're getting older all the time. I mean, we're fifteen now, and we've known each other for four years already. But the truth is, since the day I met you when we were in the fifth grade . . . what I'm trying to say is . . . what I *need* to say is . . . I think I'm in love with you, Alannah. I think I been in love with you since the day I pulled that asshole off of you your first day of school. I think I been in love with you since the first moment I ever saw you. You're the best thing in my life, and not having you be a part of me is the only thing in this world I'm afraid of."

I let out a sigh as my body heats up, and I get a million

goosebumps that all have legs to crawl across my sensitive skin. I look down at the air conditioner to see if it's been switched to heat, but it hasn't. I clear my throat, trying to buy time to think of a response, but Dominic keeps going.

"I know that's probably a lot to take, and I don't mean to overwhelm you. I know I'm different from the other guys in school. My father and I aren't a normal father and son, and I know my life's the complete opposite of yours. I've seen the guys you've been dating, wishing with all my heart it was me, and when it would end, a part of me would be happy, because they were never good enough for you anyway. That guy you went to homecoming with tonight was an asshole, and he didn't deserve to be in the same room as you, let alone be your date for the night.

"All things considered, including our differences, nobody will love you as much as I do, Alannah. I'd give everything to protect you, and I'd be as loyal to you as I am my own family. I mean that. I want you to be mine, and I want to be yours. So I don't wanna hide how I feel anymore. Life's too short for that. I want you to know how I feel about you, and to be honest, I think you feel the same about me. If I'm wrong, just tell me, but I don't think I am. Am I wrong? Is it just me who feels this way?"

I feel tears climbing up, stinging my eyes as they reach the summit. I'm overcome with emotions, and I know I was supposed to tell him something important just now, but I can't remember what it was. All I can think of is how good it feels to hear him say he loves me.

He loves me.

"You're not wrong," I reply as the first tear achieves its goal of reaching my cheek. "I didn't know how I felt for a long time, but I know with absolute certainty now. I love you too, Dominic. I do. I love you."

My brain tries to remind itself of what I'm supposed to tell

Dominic, but my body is no longer willing to wait until my brain figures it out. It goes rogue, and my hand reaches up and pulls Dominic's mouth to mine like it has a mind of its own.

It's the first time we've ever kissed, and now that it's happening, I wonder how I ever went so long without doing it every single day. It's like I've discovered the air my body's been craving, and now that I'm breathing, I can never hold my breath again. Our tongues collide and dance together, and I swear I can hear the Mariah Carey song playing again, because the words are so true. *We Belong Together.*

We kiss like we're trying to make up for all the years that we didn't, and I feel things I've never felt before. This is a new feeling of heat, a new level of passion, a new degree of desire and yearning, and it's uncontrollable.

Our hands roam freely over each other's bodies, and although I've done my share of kissing in my fifteen years, everything in this moment is a first. The things I want right now, I've never wanted before.

Dominic leans in and kisses me on the neck, and I lift my head to make it easier for him. My father would be so pissed if he knew what I was doing, but the concoction of emotions flooding my body drown out any thoughts of this being wrong. I only think of Dominic.

I use both of my hands to pull Dominic over to me, and even as he struggles to get over the shifter and my seat clumsily falls back into a lying position when I pull the handle, I don't care, because I want him on top of me. I want to do things with him I wouldn't dare think of doing with anyone else. I don't think to stop when he starts to pull my dress up to my waist, or when his fingers start to touch me over the top of my panties. No, I don't think to stop, I only surge forward, my skin on fire with sensitivity I never knew.

I push his pants down, he slides my panties off, but I never want to stop.

Who would I rather lose my virginity to? Marcus Smart? Bobby Pistone? Of course not. There isn't a person in the world I'd rather lose my virginity to than Dominic Collazo. So, when he slides himself inside me, I ignore the burning sensation and the pain of it all, because he makes it worth it. He takes his time with me, going just as slow as I need him to, and even though neither of us really knows what we're doing, something about it feels right. It feels like love, like this is what we're supposed to do.

We Belong Together.

It's a beautiful pain, and although it barely becomes pleasurable physically, I love it because it's with him, and it feels right in my mind. We're each other's first. We're going through it together like we were always meant to, and I love that.

I love him.

WE MANAGE TO FIT OURSELVES together in the passenger seat of the Mercedes, our bodies intertwining with one of his arms under me, and the other across my chest. The windows were fogged, so we let them down so the breeze could sweep over us as we look out at the stars.

I lay on Dominic's shoulder thinking about why it took so long for us to admit our feelings to each other, and how excited I am now that we have. I think about what it's going to be like for us now that we're finally a couple. The thought of us walking through the halls in school with everybody staring at us doesn't make me uncomfortable, it makes me smile. We'll be like Bonnie and Clyde. That's probably what they'll call us behind our backs, but nobody would dare say it to our faces. We'll be a power couple forever, still going strong all the way up to graduation.

That's when it hits me.

Now that the passion-induced haze has been lifted, my brain finally starts to do its job again, and I remember what I was supposed to tell Dominic. The words hit me like a ton of bricks to the chest, especially after what we just did and how much it meant. It's unbearable to think about it and the tears make a comeback. The first one slides down my right cheek, but the second goes down the left and lands on Dominic's arm, drawing his attention.

"Hey, what's the matter?" he asks, probably confused by the sudden tears.

"There's something I forgot," I begin. "I got distracted by everything that was going on, and I forgot the whole reason I needed to talk to you tonight. There's something I need to tell you, Dominic."

He sits up and angles his body to look me in the eye, which just makes it that much harder.

"Dominic, I'm moving," I blurt out, as I lose all control and the tears roll out in bunches. I can't believe I'm saying it, and I still can't accept that it's actually going to happen.

Dominic still looks confused.

"What? What are you talking about?"

"I'm *moving*. My dad got orders to Alaska and we have to move."

"Are you serious right now?"

"Do I look like I'm kidding? I wouldn't joke about this, especially after what just happened. I've been meaning to tell you, but you haven't been at school, and you weren't calling me back because you were in the hospital."

Dominic looks like his world just collapsed on top of him and he can no longer breathe.

"What the fuck, Alannah?" he snaps. "When is this supposed to happen?"

I somehow manage to cry harder when I start to say the answer.

"The military needed to fill a vacant position in Anchorage, so they gave him short notice orders, and we found out a few weeks ago. We're only a couple of weeks away now. That's all. Just a couple of weeks."

"Goddammit!" Dominic barks as he jumps up and opens the door. He nearly falls out of the car and starts pacing around outside, pulling the drawstring on his sweats to keep his pants up. "Who's this saying you have to go? Who said you have to go, because I'm not gonna let this happen, Alannah. You have to stay here. You tell me who it was, and I'll tell my dad. You won't go anywhere."

"It doesn't work like that, Dominic," I bellow as I exit the car myself. "This is the military we're talking about. The United States Air Force. They say we have to go, we have to go. Nobody's stopping it."

"Then I'll talk to your dad. I'll tell him you gotta stay here. Let's go, I'll go talk to your dad right fucking now."

Dominic starts to walk to the driver's side like he's really going to do it, and I have to run over to him to stop him.

"Dominic, please stop," I beg. "There's nothing we can do about this. I always knew this could happen, and I guess I just hoped it wouldn't. I'm sorry I didn't warn you, and nothing hurts me more than knowing I have to leave Belleville, but I don't want to do anything to make things worse. I don't want to feel any worse than I do right now, so please don't confront my dad. It's his job, and I'm his daughter. There's no way he can stay here, and there's no way he'd let me stay. You know that."

Dominic stops moving and just looks at me. It takes a second, but for the first time since I met him, Dominic's eyes fill with tears. He tries to push them away, and when he can't, he turns his face so I can't see him, but I know it's happening. All I can do is wrap my arms around him and cry with him.

"I'm so sorry, Dominic," I whisper as we lean against the

car and sob together.

The truth eventually sets in. After all this time, we're finally together, but we know it won't last, and it's the hardest thing either of us has ever had to accept.

THIRTEEN

Dominic

"WHY AIN'T YOU BEEN RETURNING my calls?"

I close the door to the Cadillac as I sit, but I don't buckle my seat belt. The way I've been feeling the past few days, I wouldn't care if we crashed into a brick wall and I flew through the windshield.

"You hear me talking to you?" my father snaps. He sounds pissed, and that's all I have to go on because I haven't looked at him yet. "I said, why ain't you been returning my calls, Dominic? You missed out on two scores last week. That's the kind of thing you need to be around for. What's the matter with you?"

"I was with Alannah," I reply, finally glancing at him for a second before staring out the window again. Dad steps on the gas and aims for the highway, back to River City.

"You were with Alannah? That's all you have to say for yourself right now?"

"She's moving soon, Dad. To Alaska, okay? It fucking sucks, and I've been trying to spend as much time with her as I can before she leaves. Cut me some slack here."

"Cut you some slack?" he snaps, repeating me again. "So, you're all depressed over some girl? You think you've got it bad right now, do ya'? Your personal life becoming too much for you to handle? Well, let me fill you in on what's been going on this past week with The Family while you were sulking in your fucking bedroom. The FBI has been all over us. They claim they have store clerks and truck drivers coming forward, say-ing we're extorting them. How about that? We got guys out there ready to rat. That make you feel better?"

"What? Of course not," I reply with a furrowed brow.

"Nah? Well, how about this? The cops found Alfonse Cestone's body in the river two days ago."

"What?"

"That's right. That fucking guy who tried to slit your throat in the garage at River City, fucking guy floated back to the top, and some family saw him and called the cops. Feds are trying to pin that on us too, claiming they know it was a mob hit. Feel better yet?"

"Why would that make me feel better?"

"You think you've got it so bad, Dom, and you have no fucking idea. How about this? Frankie got arrested yesterday. He's in jail as we speak. The Feds say they got him on credit card fraud and money laundering, and if they got him, then that means I'm next."

I don't even have a response to that one. I can't imagine what it'd be like if my dad got put away. I couldn't manage. I had no clue any of this was going on because I haven't been around. I've been trying to spend all my time with Alannah before she leaves, and The Family's been taking a hit, and Frankie's in jail. This is too much on one kid's plate.

"The point I'm trying to make, Dominic, is that if you're gonna be a part of Our Thing, you're gonna have to get your priorities straight. If there ever comes a time that you get to be a made guy, you're gonna have to take an oath, and pledge to put this family above everything else. Above *everybody* else. The Giordano Family isn't one of these huge families in New York. We're small out here in St. Louis, so we need loyal guys who know and follow the rules put in place by Anthony Giordano way back in the day. We have to keep the tradition going, and if Leo ends up making you the way he made me, you're gonna carry the burden of keeping this family alive. Nothing comes before La Cosa Nostra. Nothing. We're too small of a family to be getting heat from the Feds that can put guys away like this. The Commission is gonna open the books one day, and when they do, I want you there, Dominic. But you gotta earn it, and you're not gonna do that if you're stressing out over some girl. You understand?"

I pause so I can really think about my answer. Do I really understand? Do I understand that I'm going to have to put La Cosa Nostra before important people in my life? Do I accept that The Family has to come first? Am I willing to put The Family before Alannah? I'm not really sure, but I need to re-assure my dad. Me being a part of This Thing of Ours is re-ally important to him, which means it's important to me. So, even though I'm figuring out how I feel about certain things, there's no question about how I feel about my father. I'm loyal to him, no matter what.

"Yeah, Dad, I understand. I'm sorry," I reply. "I'll do better."

Dad takes his eyes off the road to make eye contact with me, his jaw tight and his eyes narrow. "Good."

It's been a fucking struggle. Everything going on with Alannah has taken the wind out of my sails. She's all I think about. Well, the fact that she's leaving is all I think about. After all we've been through, right from the moment we met on the playground at Barry Elementary, after all of the feelings, after all the friendship, after giving our virginity to one another, it's going to come to an end. The truth is, I'm struggling. Between what I need to be doing with my father and what I want to do with Alannah, I feel stuck between a rock and a hard place. I want to be just like my dad, but I want to be with Alannah, too. Regardless of what I want, though, Alannah's leaving, so I guess the decision is being made for me. I just hate the fucking decision.

Dad drives slow, like always. He's never in a rush to get

anywhere. Business at River City isn't going anywhere, and now that Frankie has been arrested, The Family is going to be losing money. Frankie was a good earner and sure to be getting upped soon, so his being arrested will definitely have an impact on us, and just like Dad said, the last thing we need is for the FBI to start coming after Dad, too. Looks like a change is coming.

We turn onto River City Casino Boulevard and approach the last stoplight on the road leading to the casino. As we drive, Dad looks to me.

"Listen, we're only gonna stay here a couple of minutes, alright," he says. "I'm gonna go make sure everything is good to go, then we're out. With all this heat getting started, I don't wanna push my luck by being seen in too many places where our business is being conducted. How about when we're done here, I take you to go get some ice cream? Sound good?"

I roll my eyes, but I smile too.

"Dad, I'm fifteen, not five," I snip in jest. "But I'm not gonna turn down ice cream."

"Ah, that's what I thought," he replies behind a laugh. "Wise guy or not, everybody loves ice cream."

"Fuhgeddaboutit." Both of laugh just as the light ahead of us turns red and Dad stops the car.

While we laugh, a white Honda pulls up to the light next to us. There's two men inside, staring straight ahead, but I'm not an idiot. Something about them seems off, like they're trying *too* hard to look straight ahead. I feel my brow furrow all on its own as I look past my dad at the two guys next to us. I don't recognize the driver at all, but the passenger looks familiar.

It takes a second, but eventually my mind finishes flipping through the images of faces I've seen recently, and recognizes the guy. Those facial features are what catch my attention: sharp chin, pointy nose, strong jaw clenched tight. It's the guy who had the balls to try to tax my father a few weeks ago. It's

Sammy Cestone.

As my memory grasps the name, the stoplight turns green. Dad sees the change in lighting and directs his attention to the road, pressing his foot on the gas just as Sammy's arm comes out the window holding a black nine millimeter pistol.

"Fuck! Dad watch . . ."

Before I can finish the sentence, the nine millimeter explodes into a flurry of gunfire. I immediately duck down and cover my head with my hands as the bullets come flying through the car. There's glass shattering and I can hear the distinct sound of bullets piercing the metal of the car. The sound is so loud I can't hear myself think. Panic sets in and tears fill my eyes as I try to dig myself lower and lower into my seat. I can't seem to get low enough though, and suddenly, a hot stinging sensation rips across the back of my neck, and I feel warm liquid rolling down the back of my shirt. It hurts like hell, but I know better than to move. The shots seem like they last forever, but eventually they stop, and tires squeal as the Honda rushes away.

Now, there's silence. Nothing but the terrifying scream of silence and the ringing of my ears. I know I heard the car drive away, but I'm scared to move.

I open my eyes first. There's broken glass on the floor beneath me, and a white smoke is hovering through the car as it floats off the bullets and shell casings. I see drops of blood next to my feet just as I rub the back of my neck and wince at the pain. Sure enough, there's blood all over my fingers when I inspect them. It's not a hole, so I assume a bullet grazed me as I ducked. It hurts, but I think I'll be okay. Now, I need to get up.

"Dad, you good? I saw who it was," I hear myself say, but my voice sounds muffled and my ears ring louder when I speak. "Dad, I saw them. Dad?" I force myself to sit up and look over at my father, but the second I do, I wish I wouldn't have.

My father's slumped down in his seat, his neck bent down and to the right so much that his head is resting on his own shoulder like a pillow. His entire torso is covered in blood.

"Oh fuck! Dad!" I scream as I lean over and try to lift his head up, but when I grab his face, my fingers sink into a hole on the left side of his head. I scream when I feel it and let go of him, and his head falls back down to the position it was in. "Oh my god. Oh my fucking god! Dad!"

I muster up the courage to lean over and look at the other side of his face, because I have to see it. I have to know. When I do, I crumble. There's two, maybe even three holes—there's too much blood to tell for sure—in the left side of my dad's face, and I know there's no chance he could possibly have survived what I'm seeing.

I let out an uncontrollable scream that burns the back of my throat. My tears have a mind of their own and come rushing out of my eyes faster than I ever thought possible, as I stare at my hands covered in my father's blood. I hear police sirens approaching, and there's bystanders on the sidewalks staring into the car. None of them are doing anything to help, they're just staring at us. At me. At my dead father. I don't even bother asking for help, either. They're obviously too stupid to recognize I need it. Fuck them. *Fuck them!*

I look at my father again as I sob uncontrollably. My stomach heaves up and down from the crying, and my heart hurts from the sight of him slumped over, unmoving, breathless, lifeless. I can't think, I can't see straight, I can't move, I can't live. My thoughts collide and jumble together to form an incoherent mess of words and emotions that multiply over and over again, and produce a hatred and anger I can't understand. I don't know if I'm in shock or if I'm just scared and mad. I don't know anything.

The sirens get closer and I still can't move. Soon, the cops will be here and they'll ask me questions about what happened, and if I saw anything. The same fucking cops who arrested Frankie yesterday, and the same ones who would've been coming after my father tomorrow.

I won't tell them anything. I won't tell them about Our Thing, or River City, or my father, or Alfonse Cestone's death, and I won't tell them about Sammy Cestone either.

I won't tell them it was Sammy.

It was Sammy.

Sammy . . .

My world closes in around me. Alannah's leaving. My father's dead. There's nothing left, and I have no reason to think of anything positive. Everything positive is gone.

As the cops arrive with their sirens blaring, I look at my father one last time. I think about how his heart is no longer beating, and I realize mine isn't either. It has gone too cold. Or, maybe it just left my body altogether. I don't know. I don't care. Either way, I'll never be the same. I don't even want to be.

Everything good in me has died with my father.

FOURTEEN

Alannah

Dear Dominic,

Another eight days has gone by, and I haven't seen or heard from you, so I'm writing you now because I don't have any other options at this point.

I've called you a bunch of times, but your mom doesn't answer the phone much, and when she does, I can tell she's barely even listening to me, and I know she won't give you the message. I understand why, though.

Everybody heard about what happened to your dad. I can't begin to tell you how sorry I am, Dominic. I know how much you loved him and how close you were, and I won't pretend to know what you're going through right now. I just wish you would've talked to me so I could help. But like I said, I understand why you'd want to be alone. My love for you is making me a little selfish, though.

I miss you, Dominic. I miss the way we talked and how much we made each other laugh over the years. Nothing puts a bigger smile on my face than the night of homecoming. It was the most amazing, special night of my life, and I'll never forget it. Not ever.

"HURRY UP, ALANNAH. WE HAVE to go. You know I don't like to rush," my father yells back into the house. He and my mother are outside talking to the housing inspector, who's making sure we didn't leave the house in some terrible condition before we go.

Today's the day we leave for Anchorage. I sit in my empty

room remembering everything that happened while I lived here. All the good things, all the bad things. The best memories are the ones that involve Dominic. All the nights I spent in here on the phone, talking to him when I knew I wasn't supposed to because it was late, but my parents were asleep so I did it anyway. I remember how I laid on my bed and thought about him after my first day of school, when he saved me from Billy Hannigan. I remember the day my parents told me we were moving to Alaska, and I came to this room and cried as I realized I was in love with him. Four years of incredible memories that put a smile on my face even as it all comes to an end.

"Alannah!" my dad barks again, pissed I haven't answered him.

"I'm coming, Dad," I shout back. "I'm just finishing it up."

I push away the memories with plans to revisit them later, and put my pen back on the paper.

I want you to know that the past four years have meant everything to me, Dominic. I don't take the time we've spent together for granted. I'll never forget the laughs we've shared and the stories we've told, and the lives we've lived together. I hope you don't forget them either, but I'm worried you will.

As I get ready to fly to stupid Alaska, I'm worried you'll forget about everything good we've experienced. I'm worried that when I leave, you'll change, and I'm scared to death of what might happen when I'm gone.

I need you to hang on to the parts of you that I love. I know there's things about you that I choose to ignore, but please know that I love EVERYTHING about you. I love your smile, and your sense of humor, and your willingness to open up and be honest. I love your loyalty and your protectiveness. I love your passion. I love YOU, Dominic. Please don't ever forget that. Don't forget that I love you, and don't forget the things I love about you.

Please don't forget.

Who knows, maybe one day we'll be together again.

I love you, Dominic. Forever always.
Love, Alannah.

I write the last few words on the page and put my pen down, just as my emotions take over and I have no choice but to sob. Not just little baby tears that cloud my vision, but real, heavy tears that are strong and powerful. They overtake my face and make my eyes red and puffy.

It's more emotion than I thought possible. Even though I knew this day would come, there was never enough time to prepare for the emotions. There wouldn't have been enough time in a million years. The fact that I haven't seen Dominic in over a week makes it even worse, and the fact that his dad died and I haven't been there to help him through it makes it unbearable.

I cry as I fold the letter, and I cry as I tuck into the envelope. I cry on my way down the stairs, stopping only to tell my parents I'm okay so they won't worry, and then I start up again as we drive away, leaving all of my memories of my bedroom behind forever.

My parents, though, were nice enough to promise to take me to Gloria Giaculo's house to drop off the letter. I've only been over once or twice, but seeing it now makes me feel like it was a second home.

I knock on the door, but Dominic's mother doesn't answer. I clutch the envelope tighter, willing the door to open so I can make sure this letter gets to Dominic, but after five minutes of standing there and my parents telling me we have to go, I finally give up. It's like everything connected to Dominic has evaporated, and I'm left all alone. I tuck my chin into my chest and meander back to the car, sulking the whole way.

Just before getting in, I notice the mailbox at the end of the driveway. So, I decide to take a shot in the dark and hope for the best. I place the letter in the mailbox and say every prayer I can think of, hoping with everything in me that Dominic gets it.

I don't say a word as we drive to the airport. My parents ramble on about how everything will be okay, and how I'll make new friends in Alaska, but they don't understand that it's not about making new friends, it's about keeping the only one I really want. It's about my love for him, and since they can't understand that I love him, I don't listen when they tell me I don't know what love is because I'm only fifteen. They won't attempt to understand, so I won't attempt to make them.

I'm silent when we check in at the counter. I'm silent when we board the plane, and I'm silent when we take off. I want to be silent forever, because everything I've grown to love is being left behind.

As we reach our peek altitude, I say another prayer for Dominic, hoping that since we're so high and closer to heaven, God will actually listen. I pray the whole flight, but I'll never know if my prayers are answered.

PART TWO

TEN YEARS LATER

FIFTEEN

Alannah

"THREE, TWO, ONE. HAPPY NEW Year!"

The glasses tink together and there's plenty of hugs as a big 2016 flashes on the screen over and over again. There's confetti and kisses, and my parents' house never looked so full of joy. It's January first, 2016, and I feel more anxious than ever about the future.

"Alright, alright, everybody gather around," my mother says, interrupting the happiness. Everyone quiets down and gives her their attention. "Okay, so now that we've brought in the New Year, it's time for the second reason we're here tonight."

The twenty-or-so people in the room all seem to turn to me at the same time. They know what she's talking about, and I feel a wave of heat rush over me.

"As you all know," my mom continues, her purple dress flowing around her ankles. "Our beloved Alannah is moving away to start her own life in the mid-west, and we wanted to take this opportunity to get together one last time to show her how much we love her, and how much we're going to miss her when she's gone. I'm going to be worried to death every single day, but I know she has her mind made up, and she's going to do big things with her life. So, if you all could raise your glasses one more time for my baby girl, Miss Alannah Sullivan. Cheers."

The group of friends I've made over the past ten years raise their glasses towards me and say "Cheers" in unison, followed by a loud applause I wasn't expecting.

"Speech!" someone shouts from the back, then a few more people repeat it, egging me on.

"Come on, Alannah. Give us a speech," my mother says, adding to the peer pressure. Her mascara starts to mix with her tears and streak down her face, but she wipes it away. Ugh, peer pressure is a bitch.

I nod to the group as I step over next to my mom. The room goes silent as I realize I have no idea how to begin.

"Umm. I don't really know what to say," I start.

"Well, that's a first," Derrick Coleman says from the back, making everyone laugh. I give him a look that says *shut up*. Derrick thinks he knows me because we dated a few years back. He doesn't, which is one of the many reasons we're not together anymore.

"Umm," I begin again. "Well, I don't know. I, uhh, I feel lucky to have lived here in Anchorage all this time. The past ten years of my life have been amazing. I've made awesome friends and awesome memories that I'll never forget. I appreciate all of you being here and being supportive of me moving out to St. Louis all on my own. I know it's a big change, and it's scary, but I look forward to it. I think it'll be good for me to build my own life. I'm going to miss all of you, especially my old college friends, and my girls from the hospital. It's going to be hard nursing it up in St. Louis without you ladies, and without my mom, but like I said, I look forward to the adventure. Mercy Hospital seems really nice, and they're anxious for me to get there, so it should be fun.

"I'm going to be in touch with all of you, I swear. I'll never forget where I came from or the impact all of you have had on my life. I love you all, and I'll be here to visit all the time, so you better be ready to have a blast when I'm in town."

"We love you, Alannah!"

"I love you, too, Jessica! Alright, now that's enough of a speech. I don't want to start crying. Thank you, guys."

They all applaud again and pat me on the back as I go hug my mother. She squeezes me like she's afraid she'll never see me again once I get on the plane in a few days, and I can tell she's fighting back her tears. I am too.

It's been a long road getting to this point. All the relationships—good ones and bad ones—all the school, all the family stuff—good and bad. It's been an adventure, and Anchorage has become a great home for me and my family. It's been so good that my dad decided to retire from the Air Force and live here for good, which is why he can't understand why I want to leave. He's still supportive, but me moving away is still a sore subject between the two of us.

My father, always the skeptic, believes that I'm only moving back to St. Louis for one reason. Even though I've told him he's wrong, my father is hard-headed, so he just gives me that look and we change the subject.

My mother's thinking is in line with my dad's, but she doesn't give me as much grief about it. I think it's because she just wants to be supportive of her daughter, just like she always has been. When I told her I wanted to become a nurse like her, she had my back, and gladly paid my way through college so I could get my BSN in nursing and work at Providence Alaska Medical Center with her the past couple of years. Mom has been in my corner the whole time, so the emotion she's showing tonight isn't a surprise.

"So, there's nothing I can do to make you change your mind?" Mom says as she follows me into the kitchen. I put my wine glass in the sink and face her with a smile.

"Not likely," I reply. "But I'm glad you care so much."

"Well, I do," she replies as my dad walks in and stands behind her. He has a stern expression on his face and folds his arms with an attitude. "So, can I ask you a question? And I want you to be honest with me, Alannah. Okay?"

I feel a pang of nervousness hit me. Where is this about to go?

"Kind of freaking me out with the sudden seriousness."

"Well, me and your dad are just curious about this whole thing. I mean, how do you even know he's still there?"

My face grows a mind of its own and twists into a confused frown.

"What are you talking about? Who?"

"Don't play, Alannah," my father finally chimes in, breaking his night-long silence. I'm still not used to seeing him with a beard, but he's growing it out since he retired. "Let's not pretend you're moving back to St. Louis because you love it there. Let's just be honest, alright? We know who this is about."

"Oh my gosh, Dad. I get so tired of having this same conversation," I snip, folding my arms and mirroring his demeanor. "I'm moving to St. Louis because Mercy Hospital hired me, and I did always like it there, whether you believe it or not. I loved St. Louis, and I didn't want to leave. So, I'm twenty-five years old now, and I'm moving to a place I know I love. That's all there is to it."

The two of them glance at each other like they figured I was going to say that and they're amused I actually did.

"I don't want to argue about it, especially since you're leaving in a couple of days," my father says. "We just want to make sure you're doing this for the right reasons, and I don't want to see you get hurt because you're hoping to rekindle something you had when you were fifteen. I just don't want you to get your hopes up because I don't want you to be disappointed."

"Ugh. Well, thanks for caring, but it's not about that. I mean, come on, it's been ten years. I'd be crazy to still be thinking about Dominic after all this time. I was a teenager. It's just time for me to venture out on my own, and I want to do it in the place I loved the most as a kid, so that's what I'm doing."

I know they don't believe me. It's written all over both of their faces and sewn into their body language, but they don't say it. They decide to drop the subject for now, and the three of us go back into the living room with the guests, where we spend the rest of the night reminiscing and ignoring the tension between us.

Dominic doesn't get mentioned again for the rest of the night, but after the party's over and I'm in the taxi headed back to my place, the truth about Dominic is all I can think about.

Of course I've been thinking about Dominic this whole time. It doesn't matter that it's been ten years. The way I felt about Dominic when I was fifteen is still the way I feel about him now. It's not like we ended with some horrible breakup that made us hate each other. It ended against both of our wills. Neither of us wanted it to be over, and it just so happened, something horrible took place with his father right before we moved away. It's not Dominic's fault his dad died, and I don't blame him for disappearing like he did. I probably would've done the same thing, and I can only imagine how terrible it must've been for him to lose his father and then lose me too. He had it rough, and I understand.

Over the years, I was always looking for him. I'd watch the news to see if there was anything big happening in St. Louis, hoping maybe I'd see his face on TV in the background, or I'd see his name pop up. Then again, I was hoping I *wouldn't* see his name pop up, too. I was never naïve about Dominic's life. Now that I'm twenty-five and I've learned a lot, I know Donnie Collazo was in the mafia, and I know Dominic was a part of that as well. It never changed the way I felt about him, though. If anything, knowing it just made me more interested in him. Strange, I guess, but I suppose that's how love works. It never mattered what Dominic did, he always treated me with so much love and respect, and that's all that's ever mattered to me. I've known guys who were as nice as can be out in public, but they treated me like absolute shit behind closed doors. Dominic never did that.

There was a period where I was worried to death about Dominic, even though we hadn't spoken in years. I was checking in on St. Louis like I always did—especially in the beginning—and some members of the FBI and St. Louis Police were really going after the Giordano family. According to the police, everything picked up when they found a guy named Alfonse Cestone in the Mississippi River. He had his hands and feet cut off. They even had pictures of the body on the internet. It was gruesome, and it was all the St. Louis PD needed to open up a case against the Giordano family.

After that, all hell broke loose. Donnie Collazo was next to go, in apparent retaliation for the Cestone death, then Sammy Cestone went missing. It was just hit after hit after that, in some war between the Giordano's and the Cestone crew. The FBI got involved and got a couple of informants to snitch on some of the Giordano guys, and a lot of people either went to jail or died. After it all, St. Louis PD was basically shouting from the rooftops that they "Decimated the St. Louis mob." They were proud of the mob's collapse in their city, claiming all the important members of the mob were now either dead or in jail. But I never saw Dominic's name. Not even once.

I scrolled and scrolled through headlines and articles, but I never saw his name. I even went as far as reading obituaries in the city, and I was relieved that I never saw him. I always knew that just because I didn't see his name didn't mean he'd made it out of all that drama unscathed. The mafia has a way of getting rid of people without them ever being found—just like Sammy Cestone—but something told me that didn't happen to Dominic. He's too strong for that, so I know he's alive. I know he's okay, and it fuels me.

A whole decade has passed, and Dominic Collazo is still on

my mind. I'm not ashamed of it, and I don't care what my parents have to say on the subject. So, I'll board the plane in a few days, and I'll fly back to the place where I left my heart, hoping the whole way that Dominic did survive the St. Louis mob's collapse, and praying that he took my letter to heart. I don't know anything for sure. Hell, I don't even know if I'll ever see him when I get back. But a girl can hope, right?

Well, I'm hoping.

SIXTEEN

Dominic

THEY STOPPED USING SOCIAL CLUBS back in the nine-ties because the Feds kept bugging them and fucking guys with their own words. So, the guys back in the day adjusted accordingly.

The Lodge is what those old social clubs used to be. Leo Capizzi's the first boss to go back to social clubs to discuss family business, but he did it smart. He kept The Lodge completely off the books and disconnected from his name. The building is in the name of a guy Leo extorted over a decade ago, someone unrelated and unknown, so the Feds have no clue. Leo made sure The Family would have a safe place to meet up. We come in through the back and Leo has the place swept for bugs every single day—a welcome inconvenience—and the lights are bright so everything and everybody can be seen. There's guys standing in every corner of the room for the sole purpose of watching all movement. No cell phones are allowed inside, and you don't want to be the idiot who forgets to check his at the door. Leo Capizzi is not the guy you want to piss off, and it doesn't matter how old he is.

I'm the first one in. I take a seat in the red leather chair and cross one leg over the other, my pant leg raises and exposes the red sock that matches the pinstripes on my suit. The large table in front of me is made entirely of glass, even the legs. It looks great, but it also keeps things from being hidden under the table, and it can't be drilled into, which means no recording devices can be planted inside of it. Leo covers all his bases. The guys in the corners of the room eyeball me, but not out of disrespect, they're just watching. It's their job. They're not dumb enough to disrespect any of the men who are about to enter this room. Not many people are that stupid.

The boss called on every captain in The Family, which makes me wonder what this meeting is going to be about. It's not often we get together in a group like this, it's bad for business. More than likely, something big is about to go down.

Our family has undergone a change over the years. This isn't my father's family anymore. We've had to keep everything completely quiet over the years because the Feds have a hard-on for us, and anything that even looks a little like organized crime makes the fucking pigs blow their load all over the streets of St. Louis, which is how we ended up with so many young guys becoming made members. Back in the day, you could be a made guy in your twenties, but you'd probably be in your thirties or forties before you were upped to capo, and probably would never become boss unless a lot of people died and the position basically fell to you. That was then.

Now, after all the shit that has gone down over the past decade, capos in this family range from twenty-five to thirty-five. Well, there's only one capo who's actually twenty-five years old.

Me.

I wasn't handed this position, contrary to what some of the old heads might think. I wasn't upped because I'm Donnie Collazo's son. After the FBI started using RICO cases against our acting bosses while Leo was in hiding, and our other capos got killed in the Cestone war a few years back, I was upped because of what I bring to the table. For one, I'm the best earner. My casino, River City, is the best money maker The Family has, not to mention the other rackets I've had going since my father showed me the ropes when I was a kid. I own River

City one hundred percent, the business is ninety percent legit and legal, so it's damn-near untouchable, and I'm part-owner of two more casinos, and working on another. It was me who planted the seed in my father's head about taxing casinos in the city, so I know this business better than the rest, and because I know how to keep my casinos clean, St. Louis PD can't fuck with me. I'm a legit business man, so the feds can suck my dick. Nothing earns stripes in Our Thing like being an earner, and that's part of the reason I am where I am. The amount of money I kick up to Leo trumps everyone else in The Family, but I earn it through smarts as well as hustle.

Being an earner is only part of it, though. The other part is almost just as important. I've been a part of La Cosa Nostra since I was in elementary school. I live it. I breathe it. I take it seriously because it's my life. My father died in this game, and he was my biggest role model, so I proudly follow in his footsteps. Everything I do is to make him proud, and I don't give a fuck who tries to get in my way. I have absolutely no remorse for anybody who makes a mistake when it comes to me and my business, and it all started the day I watched my father die right next to me. That day changed everything, and when Sammy Cestone *went to Australia*, I knew I was in this for life. Everything I do is La Cosa Nostra. It's all I know, and it's all I care about. The rules will be followed, and if they aren't, there are consequences that I have no problem carrying out. To be frank, I don't fucking care if somebody has to die. No one cared when my father died. I learned that the hard way, and if someone else has to learn it the same way I did, so fucking be it.

You better remember it forever. I'm Dominic Collazo.

My train of thought is interrupted by the sound of the door being opened by one of the guards. I watch as another one of our capos, Big Sal Bagano, comes waddling into the room, his belly poking out like he's in his second trimester. Big

Sal has been around for a while. He's in his late thirties, but he just isn't a good enough earner to ever make it past capo, but he's a good guy who I respect. He knew my father, and when I meet guys who were connected to him, I hold them in higher regard.

Sal's followed by our newest capo, John Salvatore, who's got a bad habit of flaunting his wealth with expensive shit: cars, jackets, and jewelry. John's thirty, and he's got a big mouth, and is developing a reputation for saying inappropriate things to the wrong people. I don't like him, but he's a made guy, so it's something I just have to put up with. There's just something about his face that pisses me off.

"Dominic!" Big Sal says when he sees me. He approaches with open arms, and I stand to embrace him. We hug lightly, patting each other on the back, as is tradition.

"How you doin' Sal?" I ask with a smile.

"Good, good. Just wondering why we're meeting up like this, is all. I don't like us being in the same place. You get one bomb in here and that's it for all of us."

"Jesus, Sal, relax," John interrupts. "So paranoid. You're gonna scare Dominic." He says it with a playful smile, but I'd love nothing more than to slap that smile right off his face. "Haven't seen you in a while, Boy Wonder," he says to me jokingly.

My heart rate picks up, but I don't let him know he just hit a nerve with that name. I'm not a teenager anymore, and I damn sure ain't a boy, so I don't like people calling me that. However, this is a friendly meeting. I exhale and let it slide. This time.

"Yeah, it's been a while," I reply through clenched teeth. "How you been?"

"I won't complain," he answers as we hug. "How are the casinos? Still rolling in the dough?"

"Something like that," I reply. I don't like putting my

business in the streets, and he should know better than asking about it, doesn't matter if we're in The Lounge or not. Something else I have to let slide.

"You know what this is about, right?"

"Nah. You do?"

"I think I do," John answers with a nod. "He's gonna make Frankie boss. I know it."

"Where'd you hear that?" Sal asks with a deep furrow in his brow. "You don't know that."

"I didn't hear it from anybody, it's just a hunch," John says, shrugging.

"Hey, you don't know that, so don't go around saying shit like it's fact, especially when it's about a decision from Leo." Big Sal looks pissed, and I can tell he and I are on the same page about John. He's an annoying little asshole who won't last long if he doesn't keep his mouth shut.

"Hey, I'm just talking. I didn't mean no disrespect," John backpedals, still doing that stupid shrug.

The door opens again, and in walks Frankie Leonetti. He's wearing a gray suit with black, shiny shoes. His jaw is strong and his face has a long scar running down the left side, from his temple down to his cheek. It's from a prison fight with a *mulignan* who sliced him with a shank a couple of years back, and it gives Frankie the look of a stone cold killer, which is ironic, because Frankie's been a stone cold killer since the day I met him, so it's fitting. I've known Frankie longer than anyone else in The Family, and I have more respect for him than anyone. He was like a brother to my dad, and he's like an uncle to me now. I fucking love the guy.

Not only is he a killer, Frankie earns a ton of money. This guy came up with a scheme to tax highways. That's right, highways. He started taxing local trucking and shipping companies to use the roads within the city, then he infiltrated the unions just like in the old days. That's Frankie, he's old school, but he'll use a new gun to shoot you in the face without thinking twice about it.

The room goes quiet when he walks in, just out of respect I guess. Frankie ignores the other two and walks straight over to me. We embrace without saying a word—Frankie isn't much for words since he got out last year, after his fourth stint in prison. If anything ever happens to Leo, we all expect Frankie to be the next boss, and he has my full support. He's the oldest capo, at fifty-two, and I trust him more than I trust my own crew.

When Frankie sits down at the table, the rest of us follow suit. That's it, there's four capos in the Giordano family— Frankie, Big Sal, John, and me—and now that all of us are here, we know the next guys to arrive will be the higher-ups, so we wait patiently. I light a Cuban cigar and shoot smoke up towards the ceiling, and Big Sal does the same. The smell of the cigars reminds me of my father and makes me feel right at home in this room. I know I'm meant to be here. I'm Donnie Collazo's son in every way.

After only a couple of minutes, the door opens again, and Jimmy Gravatto steps in, followed by the man himself, Leo Capizzi.

Jimmy's the underboss and right hand man of Leo. Usually, when Leo has something he wants passed down to the rest of us, he gives it to Jimmy to give to us, and we pass it down to our respective soldiers. That's how This Thing of Ours usually works, but today's different.

Jimmy struggles to get his fat body into the chair, and his double chin always gives me the urge to laugh, but I know better. He's been the underboss for a long time, and he's been in and out of prison longer than I've known him. He's ruthless, and he'd gladly give his life to protect Leo, just like an underboss is supposed to. Jimmy is the very definition of loyalty, and if I'm ever blessed to see the top spot, I want an underboss just like him by my side.

Leo Capizzi is the only true boss I've ever known. He was boss when my father was around, and over the years he's been trying his best to avoid prison, which has forced him to do a little running to avoid prosecution. He's appointed a couple of acting bosses over the years, but Leo has always come back to his throne. I look up to him because my father looked up to him. He sits at the head of the table and is sure to make eye contact with everybody in the room, nodding his head in approval. He reminds me a lot of Vito Corleone, with those puffy cheeks and raspy voice. I'd do anything this man asked me to do, so I wait on the edge of my seat for him to speak.

"It's not often I send for you," Leo begins. I perk up in anticipation. "The fact that we're all here should let you know how serious this matter is. What I'm about to tell you is a big deal to this family, so I want your undivided attention. I want you all to look around the room and tell me what's wrong with this picture. Do you notice anything different?"

We all look around, first at each other, then back to Leo and Jimmy. When I see the two of them, I realize what's wrong. We're missing someone.

"Where's Danny?" I ask.

I don't know how I didn't realize it before. I must've been too focused on the fact that Leo was walking into the room to realize that his consigliere, Danny Ramano, is missing in action. I should've noticed that from the get-go, because Leo doesn't go anywhere without Danny. It's Danny's job to be by Leo's side as his advisor. So, now I'm *really* curious about what the fuck is going on.

"Good question, Dominic," Leo replies. "What I came to tell you all is that our good friend, Danny Ramano, has flipped."

The four of us gasp like school girls.

"Danny has turned state's witness, and he has given

information about Jimmy and me. According to my guy inside St. Louis PD, Danny has provided enough information to put us both away for a long time, and it doesn't look like there's anything we can do about it. He's locked up and under witness protection, as is a part of his deal, and the FBI is using his information to press a judge for arrest warrants for Jimmy and me as we speak."

"That rat fuck!" Sal explodes, slamming his large hand on the table.

Leo puts his hand up and shakes his head.

"There's no need to get upset. When you've been in this game as long as I have, something like this is bound to happen. We all know the Feds best weapon is a rat, and all it takes is one. Now that they have their rat, all we can do is prepare. So, I'm not here to discuss revenge. We've had enough bloodshed over the years, and I don't want this indictment to be the end of Our Thing here in St. Louis. It's gonna be on all of you now, to make sure this family keeps going. So, there's something I need to tell you, and it's even more important than the fact that Danny is a rat. When Jimmy and I are sent away, I will not be running The Family from prison. There will be an acting boss initially, like always, but then a new, permanent boss will be selected. The Commission has already given approval, and they're gonna advise on the decision, but I have final say. It's what's best for the family in the long run.

"I also don't want Danny's family touched. None of them. As much as I'd like to send a message to everyone about being a rat bastard, what's done is done, and the new boss of this family will move things forward, not backwards. Danny's family will not be harmed. Is there any confusion about anything I just said?"

The four of us stare at Leo, completely stunned. This is a bombshell being dropped in the middle of the glass table and exploding all around us, and none of us know how to react to the devastation.

"This will be the last time all of us meet like this," Leo continues. "I need all four of you to be on top of your game, because the next boss will be one of you, and I expect the rest of you to show him the same respect and loyalty you've shown me all these years. Do I make myself clear?"

We all nod slowly, still stunned, and we stay that way until Leo and Jimmy get up and walk out of the room.

The air is thin for a few minutes. There's just so much I can't believe. Danny's a fucking rat, but we can't do anything about it, and Leo's appointing a new boss. That's a lot of big information for one meeting.

"This is bullshit," John chirps. He's suddenly filled with an annoying energy, as he stands and starts pacing like he has to piss. "Why don't the four of us get to vote for the new boss?"

"Hey! That's not what Leo wants to do, so you can drop your shit, John. This is a big decision for The Family, and Leo and The Commission are thinking long-term, so they're gonna weigh all the options," Sal snaps.

"Look, I understand The Commission wants to advise, but they're all the way in New-fucking-York; so why are they advising on our business? It doesn't seem right to me. You guys don't have a problem with this?"

"Shut the fuck up, John," Frankie hisses, but John's on a roll.

"Oh, of course *you* don't have a problem with it, Frankie! We all know you're gonna be the next boss anyway. I'm just sayin' it's messed up is all."

Suddenly, Frankie jumps up and points a finger at John.

"I said shut the fuck up! You've been a captain for less than a month, and if you want to keep that title, you better learn to keep your fucking mouth shut. We don't know who it's gonna be, so shut your mouth and wait for the word to come from Leo or Jimmy.

"Now, all of you heard the old man, he's about to get locked away, and we all know Leo doesn't have many years left anyway. So, we'll be supportive, but we also need to be thinking about how this family is about to change. It's on us now. So, go back to your crews and do what you can to prepare them. That's all we can do right now."

We all agree with a nod, and hug Frankie as he makes his exit. Big Sal is the next to go, but he only hugs me, choosing only to eyeball John as he walks out. Everyone needs time to think, and we have to tell our crews about Leo and Jimmy. It's a lot to take in, and none of us are happy about the fact that we're losing a boss and an underboss because the consigliere is a rat. It doesn't matter if we expect Frankie to be the next boss, this is the kind of thing we hope to avoid in Our Thing. There isn't much time to dwell on it, though. It's going to happen no matter what, so I have to get back to my crew and pass the message down.

"Those guys need to learn to relax, huh Dominic?" he says to me, but I ignore him as I put out my cigar and turn to walk out. "Maybe you all need to just loosen up a bit. We're about to get a new boss. No need to be so tense, Boy Wonder."

Before my hand can touch the door knob, I stop. Ice shoots from my heart and runs through my veins as I turn around. John's dumb fucking face stares back at me, grinning playfully. He's a made guy, so I'm not supposed to hit him. I try to remember that as I walk to him and stop only a couple of feet away.

"You don't know me very well, and I'd hate for you to get the wrong impression, so it's important that I'm honest with you. You talk a lot, you know that?" I ask. John frowns, but I continue before he can answer. "And the things you say are gonna get you in trouble. I know you're older than me, so you think you can say little playful shit and break my balls, but I think there's something you should know. If you ever call me that again, I'm gonna rip your fucking tongue out of your mouth and use it to make you lick your own asshole."

I don't ask if he understands, because I can tell from the frozen, terrified look on his face that he knows I'm not kidding.

I don't smile, I don't wink, I don't fucking play. I just turn around and walk out the door.

You better remember it forever. I'm Dominic Collazo.

SEVENTEEN

Dominic

"ALRIGHT, WE ALL HERE? WHERE'S Skinny?"

"He's in the bathroom. Skinny, hurry the fuck up! Dominic's here and we got business to discuss!" Tommy screams, even though the bathroom is only a few feet away.

We're in the conference room of River City Casino & Hotel. "Skinny" Joe Cuzamano flushes the toilet and comes stumbling out of the bathroom as he struggles to get his zipper up. He's the newest and youngest of all of us at twenty-four, so he's always under a lot of pressure. The guy's six-foot two but only weighs a buck sixty, so he's got long and lanky limbs that look stretched out and creepy. He's been with me for three years though, and he's always been a stand-up guy. He's not quite ready to be made yet, but he's a good associate who has no problem setting up a score. He also doesn't mind killing anybody. Skinny Joe's a little quick on the trigger because he's short tempered, so if we don't watch him, he can cause some unwanted attention, but he's a good guy, nonetheless. He's just still learning the business side of Our Thing. The blemishes on his face aren't from acne, they're from fights he's gotten himself into from blowing a gasket when he shouldn't have. He's taken a few too many punches and kicks to the face, but it usually takes two or three guys to get Skinny Joe down. Stringy arms or not, Joe Cuzamano can fist fight with the best of them.

Skinny Joe takes a seat at the end of the table next to

Charlie Mannello. Charlie's the same age as me, and he's not made either, but he's getting there. He's done a ton of robbing on the streets and he's starting to do some decent earning of his own via illegal gambling and loan sharking, so the capos are taking notice. I put in a good word for my guys every chance I get, because This Thing of Ours needs to keep growing, and we need guys like Charlie and Skinny Joe to keep The Family going in the right direction. Charlie's less of a killer and more of a money-maker. He's a thinker. It's not often I need to think of ways to earn fast cash because my three casinos do plenty of that, but when the occasion arises, Charlie's my guy. You need a diamond sold or some evidence to be "misplaced," you talk to Charlie. You want to get information about a guy, you call Charlie. You want to find someone, put Charlie on it. He'll clip a guy if he has to, but he's more the type to find the guy that needs to be killed and watch you do it. He's the smart one of the crew, and he looks the part with thick glasses resting on a thin nose.

Once Joe takes his seat, I take mine. To my right is Tommy "Two Nines" Caprio. Tommy's the oldest of the crew, at twenty-seven, and he's a made guy. Tommy's a captain's dream. When things get hot and need to be handled "aggressively", Tommy's the one who's going to handle it. He got his name from the obvious fact that wherever Tommy goes, he's got two nine millimeter pistols stashed somewhere on him. Sometimes they're in a double holster under each armpit, sometimes they're tucked under his belt, sometimes they're tucked in his socks. It doesn't matter where they are, just know that they're always there, and he's ready and willing to use them. One nod from me and Tommy will put three bullets in your chin just to prove a point. Tommy used to work for Big Sal, but when I got upped to captain, Big Sal gave him up to me as a show of respect, so Tommy belongs to me now. I trust all my guys, but I don't trust anybody more than I trust Tommy Two Nines. He takes no shit, he makes good money from loan sharking and extortion, and he's as loyal as they come.

"Hey, when Dominic shows up, you hold your fucking piss until he says what he has to say," Tommy scolds Skinny Joe just as he's getting comfortable. Joe tightens up with nervousness. "I don't care if he talks so long you end up pissing your pants. You wait for Dominic to finish saying his business, you don't leave."

"I'm sorry, Tommy," Joe says. "I didn't know he came in."

"Did I ask what you fucking knew?" Tommy snaps. The room goes quiet as Tommy stares at Joe like he's ready to slit his throat. Joe doesn't move, and he looks like he isn't even breathing. Suddenly, Tommy smiles. "Ah I'm just breaking your balls! Relax, kid. I'm just kidding."

Everybody in the room busts out laughing.

"That's not funny, Tommy. Why you gotta mess with me like that?" Joe asks as he laughs. I can see the relief on his face, though. Tommy's five-ten and over two hundred twenty pounds. Not only is he crazy enough to kill you, he actually looks the part, with a mean scowl that seems to never fade away. He's either smiling or scowling, there's no in between. This guy never lifted a weight in his life, but you wouldn't know it from how stocky he is. It doesn't matter how short a temper Skinny Joe has either, because Tommy's a made guy and Skinny isn't, so Joe can't lay a finger on him.

"Alright, alright, listen up," I interrupt with a wave of my hand. "We just had a meeting with all the captains, and I've got some news. So, turns out Danny Ramano decided to flip on Leo and Jimmy. Leo got the word that the cops are getting warrants sometime in the near future, so things are gonna be changing in The Family. Leo says there will be an acting boss temporarily, but then he'll choose a new permanent boss with the advice of The Commission. We all expect it to be Frankie, but Leo didn't say anything about who it'd be. So, we'll just wait and see I guess. Nothing has changed for the moment, but it will. That's what came out of the meeting."

The three of them look just as stunned as the capos did when we first heard.

"I always knew Danny was a sneaky little bitch," Tommy snips. "I don't know how he became consigliere anyway. Fucking rat."

"I swear, a rat has always been the downfall of Our Thing," Charlie chips in. "Fucking rats. There's no way to get rid of 'em. Even when things are going good and everybody's happy, there's always a rat lurking in the shadows ready to ruin it to save his own ass. So, when are we making an example out of this cock sucker?"

"Leo doesn't want that," I answer to the annoyance of everyone. "I know it's fucked up, but Leo doesn't want his family touched. What's done is done. So, we're not gonna dwell on it. We're gonna move forward with business as usual until we hear something from Leo or Jimmy. That's it. Understand?" They nod along together, and we move on to the next topic. "Alright, so where are we with Lumiere Place, Tommy?"

"We're in the same place we were before. The fucking guy isn't budging, Dominic. I mean, he's a fucking multi-millionaire for Christ's sake. He could go buy another casino, but he's making life difficult."

"Ugh, fucking Russians," I complain. "This hotel is right off of Highway 44, and if we own it, it'll go a long way towards partnering up with Frankie, who has already taxed the trucks on that road anyway. We can stash merchandise and money right in the building without even having to travel a mile off the highway. The Lumiere Place Casino & Hotel would be a goldmine, and it'd give us control over everything coming through St. Louis. So, I don't give a fuck what that little Russian prick wants, I want that hotel. You tell him to name his price."

"I know, Dominic, but the guy says he's not selling. I mean, there's a way we can get him out, but it might get messy, and you know how Leo is about attracting heat nowadays," Tommy explains.

I know he's right. Leo's been picky about hits the past few years because the Feds are always on our asses, so we have to tread very lightly with this kind of thing. That's why I love having Tommy around. He knows what to say to keep me from flying off the hinges without thinking things through. He's like my own personal consigliere.

"No," I say quietly, thinking out loud. "I don't want to take it there just yet. We've got enough trouble with the Feds and St. Louis PD coming after Leo and Jimmy. Just let me think for a second."

I have to weigh my options here. I know I could send Tommy in there with his two nines to put an end to this Russian asshole in a snap, but then I'd have to worry about the body and the questions coming from the guy's family and friends, which would lead to questions from the cops. I also don't want to let it go. If Frankie actually becomes the boss, it'd be a big deal to be able to help him out through that hotel, not to mention how much money the place makes legitimately. It's good for The Family, and it's good for me personally. I can't let it go.

"Alright, this is what we're gonna do," I start, the imaginary light bulb above my head shining bright. I light another Cuban and inhale deeply. "Tommy, I want you to arrange a sit down with this *coglione*. Somewhere public, so he feels safe. Charlie, I want you do some digging for me. Before this sit down, I want to know absolutely everything there is to know about Abram Baskov."

EIGHTEEN

Dominic

I ALWAYS NOTICED LUMIERE PLACE Casino & Hotel, but I didn't appreciate it until now. We approach on Highway 44 so I can see the route we'd be using to bring in merchandise, and you can see the Lumiere from the road. It's at least twenty stories, with big blue windows that reflect the St. Louis Arch, which can be seen as you stand in front of the entrance to the hotel. It's a beautiful place, and the look of it makes me want to own it even more. I always loved River City, maybe because my father owned it before I did, but there's something about Lumiere Place. Something about the location, and the colors, and the proximity to the Arch. It's just beautiful, and as Tommy and I make our way through the revolving glass door, the inside affects me the same way the outside does. It's mostly white with brown accents, and there's a huge picture of the Arch behind the check-in counter. I love it.

"This is a nice fucking place," Tommy says as we step up to the counter and wait for a clerk to address us.

"Yeah, it is," I agree. "Never seen the inside before. Now that I have, I want it more than ever."

"Between this place and River City, you'd be next level, Dominic. I don't know how you were able to get into all this casino stuff, but it's impressive. You'll be set for life if you can couple this up with River City."

"That's the plan, right?" I reply. "This isn't just about my life. It's about the lives of everybody in my crew. Our kids and their futures, too. We close the deal on this place, and we're talking about *our families* being set for life, not just me. We gotta make this happen, Tommy. We can be untouchable."

"Sounds like you're trying to become the boss," Tommy says with a big smile, but I wave him off.

"Fuhgeddaboutit. Frankie's gonna be the boss, but maybe we can lock us in for the future, and if I get it, you're coming with me."

"Don't get my hopes up, Dominic," Tommy says with a chuckle.

I've never openly talked about what it'd be like to be the boss of The Family, but it's a position everyone wants. When you're the boss, everybody in the family has to kick up to you. *Everybody*. So, for me, if I can get Abram Baskov to stop being a fucking asshole and let me buy him out of the Lumiere, I'd be owner of two hotels, and partner on two more. On top of that, I'd be getting money from everyone in The Family until I die. Tommy's right, I'd be set, and anybody else I wanted would be set too. I could also have anybody who gets in my way clipped with a snap of my fingers, and no one would ever find the body, and it'd never come back to me, because when you're the boss, you're never around when a hit takes place. At least that's how it should be. Leo and Jimmy had a bad habit of breaking that rule, which is why they're in the position they're in now, but I know better than to be thinking about that. Frankie has the position locked in, but I won't need to be the boss if I can make this deal happen.

"Mr. Baskov is ready for you," a voice says from behind me. Tommy and I turn around to find a young, clean-shaven black kid in a dark brown suit staring at us. He's got a bald head and a nametag that says his name is Anthony. "He's in the lobby to your left."

"Kinda sneaky, ain't you?" Tommy says to the guy, who just smiles as we walk towards the lobby.

Tommy and I approach the lobby together, where there's a few people seated in cream and red plush chairs. Some of them are on their phones, others are clicking away on laptops, but they all look like occupied business people—all except for two.

Standing in front of a table in the exact center of the lobby are two men—one large guy, and one average size guy with black hair that's styled like he should still be in the eighties. The big guy is tall and heavier set with a bald head that's covered in tattoos, and a black suit that's struggling to hold his big body inside of it. The average guy is trying to hide the fact that he's covered in tattoos too, but they're still visible as they peek out from under the collar of his black suit when he moves, as if they're trying to escape. His hands are covered in symbols I can't recognize from a distance, but I know they're traditional Russian mafia tats.

I don't know who the big one is, but the average one is Abram Baskov. His father, Ivan Baskov, was the head of the Russian mafia in Chicago a few years back. But that didn't end too well, which is why Abram has resettled here in St. Louis.

I can tell from the look of this guy that he's not someone I'm going to have to worry about. He's young, only twenty-four, with a five o'clock shadow to try to make himself look older. It doesn't help though, because even with the hair on his face, the youth is in his eyes. He's never hurt anyone before and he sleeps well at night. He's not haunted by the faces of the men he's killed. He's not in the lifestyle, he just wants people to think he is because of who his relatives are . . . were.

"Nice to finally meet you, Mr. Collazo," Abram says as we greet them. He doesn't extend his hand, so neither do I.

"The pleasure's mine," I reply.

"Please. Sit."

The four of us sit down and order champagne, and a full two minutes goes by before either of us says anything. It's a test to see who'll break the silence first, and there's no chance it'll be me. We'll sit in this bitch all night before I speak first.

Finally, Abram relents and speaks up.

"Alright, let's not waste each other's time, Mr. Collazo. I know why you're here," he says before pausing to sip his champagne. He's confident. "And your visit is quite unnecessary, because there's no way I'm selling my casino."

I exhale to steady myself.

"That's not the way I hoped this conversation would start, Mr. Baskov," I begin, making sure to never break eye contact. "I know you have your pride, but you're a very rich young man. You could buy another casino without me buying you out of this one, so there's no need for us to start off on the wrong foot."

"I don't care what foot we start on. All that matters to me is that you know I'm not selling, and now that I've said that to your face and you've heard it straight from my mouth, there's no need for us to continue this conversation." Just like that, Abram and his goon stand up like they're leaving.

But they're not.

I clear my throat.

"You don't know me very well, and I'd hate for you to get the wrong impression, so it's important that I'm honest with you," I begin, crossing one leg over the other. "I'm not impressed by your tattoos, or your little bodyguard in the suit that's two sizes too small to try to make himself look bigger. I'm also not impressed with your money, especially since the only reason you have any is because you got a nice, fat inheritance and life insurance when your lunatic uncle, Ilia Baskov, murdered your pussy of a father so he could partner up with his enemy, Kelvin Carter, and become boss of the family. Which was completely pointless, because your uncle ended up getting killed in a shootout with Chicago PD anyway. I know you, Abram. You didn't earn any of this shit, you didn't work for it. It was handed to you, and I'm not fucking impressed. So, you can spare me the little rich kid attitude, and sit the fuck down before I make a scene in front of all your guests."

Abram looks stunned, but he looks downright flabbergasted when he glances at Tommy and sees he has his hand in his jacket pocket holding one of his two nine millimeters.

Abram hesitates for a second, before finally exhaling.

"*Sest', Aleks,*" he says to his bodyguard in Russian. They both sit, and Abram takes another sip of his champagne. "You have my full attention, Mr. Collazo."

"Good." I nod to Tommy and he tucks his pistol back into its harness. "Now, here's the deal I'm offering. I'll buy you out of your ownership of Lumiere Place for five million dollars, which is overpriced for the inconvenience of having to sell quickly and without preparation. See, I'm nice. Your staff and everything else stays in place for now. The only thing that goes is you. You sign it over to me, you take the money and pile it in with the rest of your inheritance so you can buy another hotel, preferably *outside* of St. Louis, because if you think you can escape your family's fucked up past in Chicago by settling down here, you're crazier than that suit looks on 'ole Alex here."

Abram looks pissed. He sticks his pointy nose up in the air and breathes in like the oxygen gives him confidence, and he needs all he can get. He sips the champagne again before finally sitting back and crossing his legs, mirroring me.

"Interesting offer, but allow me to counteroffer," he says with a thin Russian accent. "I know you Italians are a prideful bunch as well, with your La Cosa Nostra bullshit, and your *Omerta* code of silence that no one in the history of the Italian mafia has ever kept. You're not the only one who's capable of doing research, Dominic Collazo. I know your family is having trouble once again, with Leo Capizzi soon to be arrested and spending the rest of his pathetic life behind bars. Acquiring my casino would go a long way to making you the youngest boss your family has ever had. But I also know you already own River City, so you too could buy another casino if you wanted. You Italians think you can just step on whoever you want to get whatever you want, and you're mistaken.

"You come to my casino, you insult my family, you insult my *father*, and you think I would sell to you? You're out of your mind. I will, however, do you a favor out of the kindness of my heart. I'll help you. See, *I'm nice*. I'll help you look like a big shot in front of your family by allowing you to become my partner, but you'll split everything with me fifty-fifty. Anything you and your family bring in through Lumiere gets cut in half and belongs to me. That's the deal, and it's the only deal."

"What is it with you Russians always trying to become partners? Let me make this clear for you, you fucking cock sucker. This ain't Chicago, and I ain't Kelvin Carter. I'm not looking for a fucking partner to split shit down the middle, and you should know better because that's the same kind of idiotic thinking that got your father killed. Partnerships between families is bad for business, because there's no trust. I'd tell you to ask your father, but we see where that got him. That ain't how the Giordano family does business. That ain't how I do business. You got a lot of balls to insult what we do in Our Thing, when your entire fucking family got wiped out just a few hours away from here. You should probably learn to keep your fucking mouth shut about things you don't really know about."

The tension is thicker than ever and I can feel it heavy on my skin. It hangs over us like a thick fog making the air hard to take in. My blood's rushing through my veins and I'm more alert than ever. Beads of sweat are starting to form on Abram's head and I can see his jaw tight with anger. I didn't expect this to get so hot so fast, but I don't fucking care. I'm ready. I tap Tommy on the leg under the table and he responds by pulling out the other nine millimeter he had stashed in his waistband.

He aims it at Abram under the table, and judging from Alex's stiff posture and the nervous look on his face, he's doing the same thing, with his pistol aimed straight at me.

Abram and I glare at each other, waiting for the other person to make a move. I wish for it. I want him to try something, so I can watch Tommy blow his fucking face off right here in the lobby. But he doesn't. He exhales and I see his muscles relax.

"You don't agree to fifty-fifty?" he says with a shrug. "Then you can take your five million dollars and shove it up your Italian ass. I'm not selling. So, make your move." Abram picks up his glass of champagne and knocks the rest of it back before finally slamming it back on the table and folding his arms in defiance.

"You sure this is what you wanna do, Abram?" I ask, giving him one last chance. "Because if I walk out of here right now, you know what that means."

Abram doesn't budge.

"I'm sure if you're sure, Dominic," he says, his face cold and emotionless. "You see, your problem is that you think I'm afraid, but I assure you I'm not."

"And your problem is that you think your fear, or lack thereof, makes a bit of difference," I say as I tap Tommy again. He stuffs the gun back in his waistband so none of the patrons in the lobby see it, and both of us stand together. "Whether you're afraid or not has no effect on me now, and it won't have any effect later."

That's it. There's no need to make any threats or to try to end the conversation like a badass. There's nothing left to say, so Tommy and I turn around and walk towards the exit, leaving Abram and Alex at the table staring daggers into our backs. I don't look back, because as far as I'm concerned, Abram Baskov is already dead.

"Well, that was fun," Tommy quips as we exit the lobby

and head to the main exit. I turn to him and smile, because we both know what's going to happen next. We just have to figure out how we're going to do it. It's when I'm smiling at Tommy that I notice something behind him.

As we walk past the counter towards the revolving door, I see a woman setting her luggage at her feet as she speaks to the clerk at the counter. She has long brown hair that flows beautifully to the middle of her back, and her ass is pushing her jeans to the absolute limit. Something about the way she's standing grabs my attention and doesn't let go.

I stop walking and stare at her as the clerk checks her in and hands her the key to her room. When she grabs the key and turns around to pick up her luggage, my heart drops into the bottom of my feet.

I recognize her pale skin, her brown eyes, her pouty lips.

"Holy shit," I say louder than I mean to, but I can't help it. It's her.

"Alannah?"

NINETEEN

Alannah

OHMYGODOHMYGODOHMYGOD.

It's him.

He's here.

He's right here in front of me.

I just landed an hour ago. I haven't even had a chance to check into my hotel room completely, and Dominic is already here. It's really him. Oh. My. God.

He's staring at me, and I'm staring back. He's blinking, but I don't think I am. I don't think I'm breathing either, because the sheer beauty of this man is making it hard for my lungs to function properly.

He's bigger than I remember, which should be a given since it's been ten years, but my brain isn't firing on all cylinders right now, so I'm surprised by it when I shouldn't be. He's about six-feet tall now, and at least two hundred-five pounds with thick arms and the same pink, pouty lips I've always loved. He's gorgeous and intimidating, and I can't stop staring. It's Dominic. A bigger, sexier Dominic, wearing a suit that's not quite black and not quite gray, but it definitely looks good on him.

"Alannah?" he says to me, his voice low, and sultry, and sexy, and *holy shit*.

"Oh my god," I manage to utter. "Dominic. Is that you?" I know it's him, but I don't know what else to say.

"Yeah. Yeah, it is. I can't believe this. What are you doing here?" He looks confused and adorable with that furrow in his brow that always turned me on and scared me all at the same time. His voice still carries the subtle Italian accent but has dropped an octave.

"I'm here," I answer. I realize that sounds confusing so I try to clarify, but even that's difficult right now. "I mean, I just landed. I'm here. I'm back. Umm, I just moved back here. To St. Louis."

Dominic raises his eyebrows.

"You moved back to St. Louis? For good?"

"Yeah. My flight just landed about an hour ago. I'm just now checking into my hotel room until my place is ready. Umm, what are you . . . I mean, it's really nice to see you. I was wondering if you were still here."

He smiles before he answers, and I'm pretty sure my heart skips a few beats, then resuscitates itself.

"Of course I'm still here. I'd never leave St. Louis. I don't understand. You're here. You're back," he states like he's confused by his own words. Then he suddenly snaps back into reality and looks at the man standing behind him, and I realize there actually is a man standing back there that I didn't even see before, because I was too focused on Dominic.

This guy isn't someone I recognize from school. He's a little shorter than Dominic, but I can tell he's buff even in his suit. He's got really short hair and a scowl etched on his face like it's permanent. The two of them together look like businessmen—the kind of businessmen that would hang you off the roof of a balcony if you owed them money.

Dominic whispers to the guy who I'm already convinced is a hitman, and while the two of them talk, I realize I'm standing here in a pair of jeans and a white Homegrown Alaska t-shirt that I soaked with my sweat on the plane. I'm a hot mess, and Dominic is over there dripping with sexy gorgeousness. Shit. I try to run my fingers through my hair like a brush but before

I get two strokes in, Dominic turns and walks over to me. The other guy exits the building without saying a word.

"You're staying in this hotel?" Dominic says, his expression harder now.

"Umm, yeah. Why?"

"You can't stay here." Dominic scoots his way behind me and places some cash on the counter. "She's checking out. Now," he says to the clerk, who looks puzzled.

"I'm not sure I understand," the young clerk replies.

"You don't have to understand. Just check her out of the room."

"What are you doing?" I interject. "What's going on?"

When Dominic faces me, his expression has softened again and he's smiling.

"Nothing. Why pay to stay here when you can stay in a suite for free?" he replies.

Now it's my turn to look puzzled.

"A suite? Free? Am I supposed to be this confused?"

Dominic smiles again as the clerk finishes checking me out of the room I never stepped foot in.

"I'll explain on the way."

AS WE RIDE IN THE back of the taxi, Dominic sits silently next to me staring ahead like he's driving even though he isn't. There's been no explanation as to where we're going, but I'm not concerned about it anymore. All I can think about is how Dominic is sitting next to me. *Dominic is sitting next to me!* He isn't dead—the victim of some heinous murder with his body chopped up and buried in cement, never to be seen again. The lack of contact over the past decade has made my imagination go to extremes, to say the least.

Now that I know he's not dead, I see him sitting here with his fancy suit and untouchable demeanor. He's grown up to be the man I thought he'd be when we were in school. He's obviously got money, and I can tell he's the kind of man who demands respect.

So, I start to wonder. What's he doing now that he's all grown up? Is he still connected to the mafia like he was ten years ago? Is he a savage killer who likes to cut off the hands of his enemies? Or, is he really a businessman earning a living off of the hotel his father used to own? I don't know, but I want to.

"So, how have you been all these years, Dominic?" I force myself to ask, although my nerves want me to stay quiet.

Dominic peels his eyes off the windshield to look at me, his blue eyes piercing.

"I've been good. I'm a little stunned that you're here, though. I didn't think I was ever gonna see you again."

"I know what you mean."

"So, you're really here for good?"

"Yeah. I got a job at Mercy Hospital so I'm here to stay. I'm glad, too. I've always loved this place, and I never wanted to leave to begin with. I've missed St. Louis."

Dominic doesn't say anything, but he smiles like he's got lots to say in his head. I smile back and we lock eyes again. It's like it's a game to see who'll look away first, and I lose when the cab turns into the parking entrance of River City Casino & Hotel.

I look out the window and marvel at the large structure built to look like a castle in the front. It's bigger than I remember, and you can't tell it's a hotel until you pull around back and see the windows to the rooms. The construction is marvelous and it just breathes fancy, with its pillars made of elegant white brick.

Dominic pays the cab driver with what looks to be a lot more money than the fare, then he steps out. As I reach for my handle so I can get out, I see two valets outside jump to attention and rush over to greet Dominic. I open my door just in time to hear them talking to him.

"Good morning, Mr. Collazo," one says, nodding politely.

"Sorry, Mr. Collazo, I didn't recognize you in the cab," the other says with a bit of pleading in his voice.

Dominic shoos them away with a wave of his hand as he glances down at his phone, before stuffing it back into his pocket and speaking.

"It's fine. Just help her with her bags," he says, and the valets dive into action. When I try to reach for one of my bags, they tell me they've got it, and follow Dominic and me as we walk inside to the counter. Dominic directs his attention to the clerk who stands at attention like an Army soldier when he sees us approaching.

"Make sure she gets the Director's Suite, okay? And charge it to me," Dominic says, and my heart perks up like the clerk.

"Oh my god, Dominic, you don't have to do that. I'll be fine in a normal room. Really," I try to tell him.

"I know you will, but I think you'll like this one better," he says with a smile, then he turns back to the clerk who's already clicking keys on the computer to check me into the suite. "And do me another favor; make sure we have reservations at the VIP Lounge in two hours. *Capisci?*"

"Understood, Mr. Collazo," the nervous clerk replies, then he hands Dominic the keys to my room, who hands them to me.

"So, listen," he says. "I got some business I gotta tend to, but I'm gonna meet you right here in this spot in exactly two hours. Can you be ready by then?"

"Can I be ready for what by then?"

"I thought maybe we could go to dinner. I figure we need to catch up after ten years apart."

My heart explodes, and sends tiny rays of happiness shooting through my body, but I don't let Dominic see my excitement. I let out a sigh like I'm bothered by his pushiness, but I really just want to dance with joy.

"Well, good thing I don't have anything planned, huh?" He doesn't respond, he just flashes his devilishly sexy smile. "Alright then, I'll see you in two hours."

"Okay." With that, Dominic turns on his heel and heads back out the way we came in.

The valets are replaced by bellboys who carry my luggage for me and lead me to my room. I've got two hours to get ready for dinner with Dominic on my first night back in St. Louis. Whether it's two hours or two hundred hours, there isn't enough time in the world to prepare for this.

TWENTY

Dominic

TWO OF THE OTHER THREE captains are already seated at the glass table in The Lodge when I get there. They look confused and pissed when I walk in. Confused because we've all been called on by Frankie Leonetti without an explanation, and pissed because we've been pulled away from whatever we had going on in our lives to come here without explanation.

John looks the most perturbed as he sits with his arms folded across his chest like a pouting child. He eyes me when I walk in like he wants to say something about me arriving last, but he thinks better of it—probably has something to do with how our last conversation ended.

Big Sal is the one who speaks first when I walk in.

"You know what this is about, Dominic?" he asks as he stands up to greet me with a hug.

"No. I just got the message to show up. I was hoping one of you was gonna tell me," I reply.

"Nah, I guess we all got the same message," Sal says as we sit down. The second our butts hit the seats, the door swings open and Frankie struts in.

There's something different about him. There's something about the way he saunters in that makes me do a double take. He has the look of a man who has information that only he knows. The rest of us are out of the loop and he likes it. He sits at the table, which is normal, but it's where he sits that brings the confusion in the room to a peak. He's in the head seat, which is supposed to be reserved for Leo.

I know why we're here now.

"I called on all the captains to let you know that Leo and Jimmy got picked up this morning," Frankie says. His voice is somber, but his face isn't. "Danny Ramano gave a statement and ratted on both of them, and they've been charged with murder, conspiracy to commit murder, money laundering, and racketeering. Looks like the feds are trying to get them both with RICO. We all knew it was coming. Leo and Jimmy prepared us for this, so I guess it shouldn't be too surprising."

It's true we all knew this was coming, but that doesn't make it any easy to accept. I guess somewhere deep down I was hoping Danny would wise up and change his mind, but when the Feds have their hooks in you and you know you can help yourself out by taking a deal, fuhgeddaboutit.

None of the captains say anything. I guess we just let it sink in that Leo Capizzi is, more than likely, gone for good, and so is the underboss, Jimmy Gravatto. The change we all knew was coming is actually here now. Ready or not, here it is.

Frankie straightens out his jacket and does a little stretch with his neck from side to side like he's about to say something huge, but we already know what it is.

"So, until we have an official new boss, I'm the acting boss," Frankie announces like we all expected. He's the senior capo in the family, and we all respect the guy anyway. It all makes sense, and although it sucks to lose a longtime boss like Leo, I think we've all mentally prepared for Frankie to begin his reign. "Now that that's official, you all know how I do business. I don't like being caught off guard by anything, so is there anything going on out there that I need to be made aware of? Is there any beef in the streets that needs to be brought to my attention? If not, I'm gonna assume everything is running smoothly and it's gonna be business as usual for The Family. So?"

Frankie starts making eye contact with each captain one at a time. He starts with John, who's still got his arms folded like a brat as he shakes his head. Then he moves to Big Sal.

"Nah, I got nothing, Frankie," Sal confesses. "A couple of guys not paying their taxes on time, but it's being handled. No worries."

"You do what you gotta do to make sure you get paid," Frankie replies. "I expect everyone's kick-up to be the same as it was with Leo. Nothing changes right now, until this thing becomes permanent. How about you, Dominic. How's the casino business?"

As Frankie looks at me, I think about the meeting I had this morning with Abram Baskov, the defiant twenty-four year old heir to the Chicago Russian mafia fortune. Is this something I need to be passing up to Frankie right now? Is this the kind of thing I can't handle on my own? Would my father pull the boss into his personal business and give him the impression that he can't handle it without help?

Fuck no.

Abram Baskov is a self-righteous little prick whose mouth writes checks his spoiled little ass can't cash. Yeah, he's rich, and he probably has sufficient protection because of that, and yes, his father and uncle were ruthless killers and heroin distributors right next door to our Chicago Outfit. And yes, he even survived a gunshot wound or two to the abdomen a few years back, but those points are irrelevant, because Abram Baskov is *not* a gangster. He's not a street guy. He's merely the son of a dead Russian mob boss, nothing more.

This is something I can handle on my own, and I don't need help from *anybody*. I can tell from Abram's baby-face and slick hair that he'll be easy to get rid of. I just have to push the right buttons and he'll pack up and ship out without much resistance. I'm not worried about him, so Frankie shouldn't either.

"Bellissimo," I reply in Italian with a convincing smile. "We're all good Frankie. Only thing you gotta be concerned about is the headache that comes with being the boss."

"Hey, hey, I'm just the *acting* boss," Frankie says, mirroring my smile.

"Yeah, but you know it's coming. Get over here, man. Congratulations." I stand up and congratulate Frankie with a hug, and the other captains do the same. We exchange some laughter and pat Frankie on the back for getting upped to the top spot, even though it's not official.

I'm genuinely happy for the guy. Frankie's been in Our Thing a long time, and there's no other guy I'd rather see as the boss than someone who was loyal to my father the way Frankie was. That's another reason why I have to secure the Lumiere. The location of that hotel is perfectly off the highway, and I can really put a smile on Frankie's face by giving him the gift of a new place to stash merchandise without having to drive off the main road. We're all in this thing to make money, and the Lumiere helps all of us do that.

Which is why after all the congratulations, and after I leave The Lodge to head back to River City to prep for my date with Alannah, I pull out my cellphone and dial up Tommy Two Nines, who's been waiting for my call.

TWENTY-ONE

Alannah

I'M STILL IN AWE OF everything, even as I stand in the lobby waiting for Dominic. It's not only the room I just changed in, with its king-sized bed, refrigerator, big-screen TV, and massive Jacuzzi and bathtub. It's the fact that I'm here at all. I was in Alaska earlier this morning, and now I'm St. Louis, standing in River City, waiting for Dominic to meet me so we can go to dinner. I mean, how is it possible that this is happening already?

I can't believe I've already seen him, and he's doing so well. He looks better than I imagined he would, too: big, round shoulders, apparent even through the suit he was wearing, and a strong, chiseled face with sexy plump lips. He's morphed from being an awkward kid who everyone called Ugly Dominic, and turned into a sex god who owns a casino. All of it's unbelievable.

But as excited as I am about all of this, I'm anxious to get this dinner started so I can find out about the things I'm most curious about. Like, is he still doing the mafia type stuff he was doing when we were kids? I think I'd be dumb to assume he's not. He was into that when we were in the fifth grade. It's all he knows. But just how deep does the rabbit hole go? Is he a ruthless killer? Does he extort money from people by threatening to kill their mothers? I mean, just how bad is it, and how far is too far for me?

When we were kids, I knew Dominic was into some

sketchy stuff and I still loved him. So, how much is too much now? Is there such a thing as too much? I guess we're about to find out, because he's strutting his way into the lobby like he owns the place . . . because he does.

I have to remind myself to breathe as he approaches with his hands in the pockets of the black slacks he changed into. He's wearing a dark gray button-up with the top button undone, teasing a sneak peak of his muscular chest. Every girl in the lobby is staring, but he's fixated on me. He smiles and chuckles as he stops in front of me.

"Are you okay?" he asks, still grinning. "You look like you just saw a ghost or two."

"Oh, yeah, I'm fine," I reply. I have to snap myself out of it. "I just can't believe I'm here. With you."

"Neither can I. You look phenomenal. What do you say we go sit down so we can catch up?" he says, still admiring the tight black dress I decided to wear.

"Perfect."

Dominic leads me through the lobby and into an elevator. We don't talk as we head up to nearly the top of the building. As soon as the door opens, we're greeted by an amazing view of St. Louis. The windows to the VIP Lounge are as tall as the walls themselves, and it's stunning. Alaska is a beautiful, outdoorsy place, but there's nothing there that gives you a city view like this.

The lounge is mostly dark red, with beautiful gold fixtures and chandeliers. Dominic walks right past the redheaded hostess and leads me to a gold table with red and gold seats. We sit down and are immediately asked for our drink order by the same redheaded hostess we passed. Dominic orders a Sprite and Apple Crown Royal, and I decide to ease into a cranberry vodka. Once the hostess is gone, Dominic eyeballs me with a smirk teasing his lips.

Just breathe, I remind myself.

"Wow," Dominic begins. "I didn't think I was ever gonna see you again, Alannah. It's pretty incredible that you're sitting across from me right now. What made you decide to come back?"

"I told you, I got a job at Mercy Hospital," I answer, trying to play it cool.

"I know, but you could've gotten a job in a hospital in Alaska. You wouldn't have gotten a job here without applying for it. So, what made you decide to come back?"

"Umm," I start playing with the gold silverware on the table because I'm nervous. "Honestly, I came back here because I always wanted to. I never wanted to leave, so when I got my degree, I decided to apply for a job in the place I always wanted to live. It was a longshot, but it worked out."

He smiles like he already knows there's more to it than that.

"That's awesome. So, what have you been up to the past decade? I mean, I figured you would've been married with kids by now."

"Me? No way."

"Not even a long-term boyfriend after all this time?"

"I mean, I've dated, but nothing too serious. What about you? Girls must be flocking to you, Mr. Casino Owner."

Dominic smiles humbly.

"I haven't been interested, and I haven't had the time to really care about anybody else. I've been busy with work."

The mention of "work" sends a sharp tingle down my spine.

"Busy with work. You talking about the casino business, or the other kind of work?" I ask, doing my best to tread lightly but failing. I'm thinking about it too much to just let it go, so I go for it. "Like the kind of *work* you used to do with your dad when we were kids?"

He doesn't look pissed, but he doesn't look happy either.

He shifts in his seat a little and clears his throat like he's uncomfortable, which isn't something he used to do when I knew him all those years ago.

"Getting right down to it, huh?" he says. "You seem genuinely curious, but I'm not sure you actually want to know what you think you want to know."

"I *do* want to know," I reply. "What do you have to hide?"

"I have no need to hide," he snips, frowning a little. "You only hide when you're afraid, and I'm not afraid of anything or anybody, so I don't hide or lie. I just don't know what you actually want to know."

"I learned a lot while I was gone," I answer, just as the hostess delivers our drinks. "A byproduct of growing up, I guess. One of the things I was really interested in was the kind of stuff you used to tell me about. The things you and your father were into were things the police put a lot of effort into getting rid of in this city, so I'm just curious."

"The police can think that they got rid of something if they want to," he says, avoiding the word *mafia*. There aren't many people in the VIP Lounge, but it's better to be careful. "I'd prefer they think that, actually. But the thing my father was a part of will always be around, it just operates differently now. Quieter."

"And you're a part of that now?" I sip my drink to try to prepare myself for the answer.

"I always have been."

My heart picks up pace. I knew it, but now I really *know* it. Dominic is still in the mafia. It's easy to think about the rumors and misconceptions of what people say about the mafia, but I don't really know what that means, in all honesty. I think I want to find out, but maybe now isn't the best time. I think confirmation of Dominic being a member of the St. Louis mob is enough for the first night.

A waiter comes over to the table and takes our order—I

order a steak, Dominic gets the most expensive lobster on the menu—and I use the interlude to change the subject.

"I tried to write you, you know?"

"Oh yeah?"

"Yeah, twice," I tell him. "The letters came back both times. I just figured you moved or something. Which kind of reminds me of something else. So, I have another question."

"Uh-oh. More questions."

"Nothing bad. I was just wondering if you got my letter."

He looks confused.

"I thought you said the letters got sent back."

"Those did get sent back, but this is a different letter," I reply. "I wrote it before we moved to Alaska, and I left it in your mom's mailbox. I guess she decided not to give it to you. Or maybe she never got it. I don't know. Never mind, I guess."

"Hmm. Nah, I don't know nothing about no letter," Dominic says, as he starts devouring his lobster and digging into the baked potato that came with it. As he chews, he leans over so he can reach into his back pocket, then he places a folded piece of paper on the table and looks at me with a grin.

"What's this?" I ask as I reach for it. He doesn't answer, so I unfold the paper and I'm shocked to see that it's my letter to him. The writing is faded, but it's still legible. It's my letter.

"I take it with me everywhere I go. Always have," he says. He smiles at me as tears fill my eyes, then he goes back to his food like it's no big deal.

But it is. To me, it is.

"I can't believe you still have this after all this time. It's been ten years, Dominic. Why do you still have this?" I ask as my voice starts to shake with emotion.

"Because you wrote it," he replies nonchalantly. "My mother gave it to me the day of my father's funeral. It goes where I go."

"This is incredible," I say, doing my best to shake away the tears. I fold up the paper and hand it back to him, and he pushes it into his back pocket, its home for the past ten years.

We finish our dinner—which Dominic pays for without hesitation—and make our way to the elevator. The doors close behind us and I'm filled with all kinds of emotions. On one hand, Dominic admitted he's still in the mob, and on the other hand, he still carries my letter around with him every single day, and he's been doing it for a decade straight. If that isn't love, then what the hell do you call it? But he said it all so casually that I'm not sure how he even feels about me. The fact that he's still carrying my letter around has to mean something, though. Right? I mean, he wouldn't do that if he didn't care. Would he?

The elevator opens and I die inside, because I don't want the night to end. We've stopped on the floor of my suite, and Dominic walks me to my door.

"I'm sure you're probably tired after all the traveling and whatnot," he says. "Sorry I didn't let you rest before asking you out to dinner, but I'm really glad you came."

"It was my pleasure. Thanks for asking. I'll definitely sleep well tonight. I had a good time, though. It was good catching up."

"Yeah, it was. But we still have more catching up to do. Ten years' worth. So, I have to see you again. And then again after that. And probably again after that, too."

We both laugh, and my insides fill up with teeny-tiny butterflies.

"Well, I have to report to the hospital tomorrow now that I'm here," I reply.

"Okay, that's cool. Just call me whenever you're free." Before he leaves, he gives me a River City business card that has his number on it, then he grabs my hand and brings it to his mouth, kissing it softly as he looks me in the eyes.

I melt.

Then he turns on his heel and walks away.

I watch him until he turns the corner and is out of sight. I'm overcome with feelings of happiness, anxiety, joy, and fear. It's a whole buffet of feelings that bring tears to my eyes without me being able to fully understand why.

Once inside my amazing suite, I sit on my bed for fifteen minutes before I'm able to move. I have to take my time breathing all of this in. It's like I'm right back in the ninth grade. Nothing has changed, even though everything has There's so much I don't know, but the things I do know are enough for now.

He's even more perfect now than he was before I left, and this was the perfect beginning to my new life in St. Louis. I have a feeling there's more nights like this just around the corner, and I couldn't be more thrilled.

He's still perfect.

He's still Dominic.

TWENTY-TWO

HE QUADRUPLE-CHECKS BOTH NINE MILLIMETERS to make sure everything's good to go. The knife is there, too. The last thing Tommy needs is to get inside and find out he doesn't have all the necessary tools to do the job.

Everything's good to go, so he slowly and quietly turns the knob. There's an alarm system, but Charlie disabled that about sixty seconds ago, so Tommy doesn't have to worry about cops showing up just because he opened the door.

It's dark inside. Luckily, Tommy's been waiting outside the house in the dark for the past hour so his eyes are adjusted. He can see the end table sitting in front of him, waiting to tell on him if he hits it. There's piles of clothes sprawled out on the floor that Tommy has to avoid just in case there's something loud under them. He can also see the glass coffee carafe on the wooden table in the middle of the messy living room, and in the brown leather recliner next to the table is Alex Romanov. Abram Baskov's right hand man.

The fat fuck is lying there wearing a white tank top and basketball shorts, as if he's ever played basketball or exercised in his entire fat life. Even in the dark Tommy can see the hair on his shoulders arching towards his back, covered in sweat and filth. Who would ever let this guy be their number two? Fucking Russians.

There's no kids in the house, because nobody would be desperate enough to fuck this pig and risk getting pregnant, and of course there's no wife. Alex lives alone and always has. He's had a rough life, growing up in foster care and all, but it doesn't make Tommy feel bad. He doesn't give a fuck about what kind of life Alex may have had leading up to this point, because it doesn't change anything.

Dominic called and pushed the button on Alex a few hours ago, so it is what it is. Tommy doesn't question any of it, because Dominic is nothing if not calculated and smart. He doesn't make a move without thinking about the next three. So, when Dominic told him he had the green light on Alex, Tommy knew the point behind it. Abram Baskov fucked up when he tried to get cute at the sit down. He didn't realize that Dominic Collazo is a guy who always gets what he wants. You can fight and resist all you want, but eventually Dominic will outsmart you. He's been involved in La Cosa Nostra his whole life, and sometimes people just have to learn the hard way. Which leads Tommy back to the glass carafe on the table.

Tommy thought to hit Alex in the head with the butt of his gun, but he didn't want to risk damaging his weapon on this sloppy fucker's skull. Tommy loves his two nines too much to take such a risk. So, he inches his way over to the table and grabs the carafe. Alex's snores are loud and disgusting, and he never knows what hit him as the carafe connects with his face and glass goes flying everywhere.

Alex clutches his face in pain, and yells in terror, so Tommy punches him in the mouth to shut him up, then throws his fat body down to the floor. There's blood gushing from one of the many wounds on Alex's face, but Tommy's not sure which one as he leans forward so Alex can see him. Alex is covering his face with his hands because of the glass that is surely lodged in his skin, so Tommy has to get his attention.

"Hey," he says. Alex tries to look at him through his fingers, but there's too much blood. "Hey!" Tommy snaps. Alex pulls his hands away from his face and they finally make eye contact.

Alex recognizes him, and his body goes numb with paralyzing fear. He knows what's about to happen, and he knows there's nothing he can do about it.

Tommy can see the fear in his eyes and it makes him smile. Russian mafia background or not, you don't fuck with the Giordano family. You don't fuck with Dominic Collazo.

Tommy reaches into his jacket and removes one of his trusty nine millimeters from its shoulder holster. He makes Alex watch him as he slowly chambers a round, screws the silencer onto the barrel, and aims the pistol at his chest.

"No hard feelings, Alex," Tommy says. "It ain't your fault Abram's an idiot."

"Fuck you!" Alex screams at the top of his lungs. He's determined to go out like a soldier.

Tommy is almost impressed.

"Good night."

Tommy pulls the trigger three times and the nine kicks back, but the silencer does its job and suppresses the noise. Alex's body jolts from the impact of the three rounds to the chest, then it's forever still.

He's gone, but the job isn't finished yet. Dominic wants the message to Abram to be loud and clear. So, Tommy removes the knife from his jacket pocket and kneels down next to Alex's lifeless body. He'll have to get rid of this fat fucker ASAP, but not before cutting off every finger on Alex's hand—the same hand he used to point that gun at Dominic underneath the table.

It's gruesome, but Tommy's wearing gloves and doesn't mind a little blood. It comes with the job. As long as the message is received, Tommy's happy. So, he'll be sure to deliver the message—all five parts of it—to Abram Baskov's mailbox first thing in the morning.

TWENTY-THREE

Dominic

IT'D BEEN A FEW DAYS since I had dinner with Alannah at River City. She had work stuff to tend to, and I had business that needed my attention, so when she finally called this morning, I nearly jumped out of bed to answer the phone. She told me she'd be free later in the day after she got off her shift, and asked if I wanted to hang out again. I said "fuhgeddabou-tit," which confused her until I explained what I meant, then I made a call to my staff at Isle of Capri and reserved my favorite outdoor table for a candle lit dinner. Now, as I stand in the lobby of River City waiting for her to come down, my belly is doing summersaults. With all the things I do in my life that should make me nervous, it's the thought of being with Alannah Sullivan that does me in.

I feel like I'm living in a fucking alternate universe. I don't even know how all of this came to be. One minute, I'm doing business as usual, the next minute, Alannah is back in St. Louis and here to stay. She's actually here! It's been ten years, and the only woman I've ever loved has come back into my life. I don't know what I've done to deserve such a thing, but I'm thankful. With Alannah being here now, I have everything a man could want. All the power and respect my dad commanded now belongs to me, and once I wrap up my acquisition of Lumiere Place, I'm going to be good to go. I'll be able to sit back and relax while my businesses make money for me, and I'll have Alannah to relax with. Just one more deal to go.

Speaking of Lumiere Place, it's been quiet on that front ever since I sent Tommy to pay Alex Romanov a little visit. Tommy made ole' Alex disappear, but not before delivering a little package to Abram on my behalf. It's no surprise Abram's been quiet. It usually takes guys a couple of days to get their affairs in order before they move on from a business, especially one as lucrative as the Lumiere. So, while Abram fights over the mental hurdles of accepting the inevitable, I wait patiently, and I watch in awe as Alannah struts her way towards me wearing the sexiest navy blue dress I've ever seen.

Her brown hair flows and sways gracefully behind her as she walks, and I see other guys in the lobby checking her out. I have half a mind to put one of these boys in a chokehold, but I resist the urge. I'd hate for Alannah to think less of me.

"After all this time, you're even more stunning than before you left," I manage to say as she approaches. Her smile is wide and sincere, and I have to shake off the fact that it makes me more nervous. I did a good job of playing it cool at dinner last time, and I've got to keep it up.

"Thank you, Dominic," she replies. "You look very handsome. That's a gorgeous suit. I don't think I've ever seen a gray one with red pinstripes before."

"Well, I know a guy, and he hooks me up with whatever colors I want," I answer, making sure not to go into too much detail about some of the places we extort. What can I say? A captain has to earn.

"So, where are we going?" she asks.

"I've got a place in mind. Shall we?"

I lead her to the car, and she marvels at the metal flake paint on my BMW that shifts from black to dark purple, depending on the angle you look at it from. As we drive, I can't stop my eyes from wandering over to her legs as they stick out of the dress, teasing me, forcing me to reminisce about homecoming night. Fuck how uncomfortable it was in that car, being with her was amazing. Images of that night flash across my vision like a slideshow on fast forward, and I really have to focus just to get us to Isle of Capri without crashing.

Once we're inside and seated, I see Alannah checking out the décor of the fancy outdoor setup. Well, it's kind of outdoors—there are five tables in a glass enclosure that gives you a nice view of the busy street. Yellow and white lights hang from the ceiling, and there are roses and lilies in decorative glass vases on each table. This little section is made for the high rollers who reserve it, and people have to call months in advance to book it. Tonight, I made sure the place was empty just for us.

"So, how has work been so far?" I ask to start up the conversation.

"It's been okay. Paperwork and training. New girl stuff. How was your day?"

"My day was fine. I was excited to get to hang out with you again. I'm still trying to convince myself I'm not dreaming about you being here."

"I know, it's hard to believe for me, too," she says, sipping her white wine. "So, how's your mom been doing? I was so shocked that you still had my letter that I forgot to ask about her last time."

"I haven't talked to her in a while," I admit, although I hate that it's true. "We haven't been as close as we used to be since dad died. I don't think she likes that I got into the same business as him. She always wanted me to avoid it, but once dad died . . . that just wasn't something I could do."

"I see. That's too bad. Did they ever find the guy that . . . you know."

I don't know how to answer the question. Even mentioning Sammy Cestone, the man who killed my father, still makes my blood boil even though I know he's *gone*. So, I end up going with the default answer.

"Nah, they didn't."

But I did.

After my father's murder, I think I went crazy for a little while. I couldn't stand to see him like that—slumped over in his seat with bullet holes in his face, and it took everything in me to get over it. I didn't really get there until the day Sammy Cestone *went to Australia*.

I waited a year before I let myself act on the revenge I was aching for. I was a blood-thirsty sixteen year old looking to make a name for myself—a name better than Boy Wonder.

So, I stepped in my father's place at River City just as a plan was put in place to add a new parking area across the street. The day before the parking lot was to be poured, I met Sammy Cestone at his house after he dropped off his son at school. I'd been watching him do the same routine for two weeks straight, and I knew when I walked into his run down little apartment, he'd be all alone. I shot him in the face with one of my dad's guns. Three shots, just like what he did to my father. Then I buried his body in the spot where the concrete for the parking lot was poured the next day. So, Sammy *went to Australia*, meaning he is literally *down under*. I take pride in the fact that I get to drive by his permanent grave on my way to River City, where I stay in the penthouse suite on the top floor. They never found Sammy, and they never will.

"So, what about you, Alannah?" I start again, making sure to quickly move on from the topic of Sammy Cestone. "Be honest; what made you decide to come back here after all this time? Alaska too cold for you?"

"Yeah, it was, actually," she says behind an adorable giggle. "It's cold as hell there, but like I told you before, I never wanted to leave St. Louis."

"There's more to it than that. You were gone for ten years, you went to college and got a degree, you already had a nursing gig, and you said you were dating even though it was nothing serious. So, why uproot your life to come back to St. Louis? I really wanna know."

She hesitates to think. I don't know what the answer is, but I know what I'm hoping for, and maybe that's a bit crazy. Maybe it's naïve of me to think she came back here for me after a decade. Then again, I was still thinking about her after ten years, so it's not impossible. I wait impatiently, sipping my wine so I don't look so anxious.

"Okay," she says after a big, deep exhale. "I came back because I never wanted to leave . . . and because I needed to know what happened to you. There was a lot of stuff on the news about the FBI and St. Louis PD cracking down in the city, and I saw a lot of names popping up about people being either murdered or thrown in jail for long stretches. But I never heard anything about you. I didn't know if you were alive or dead, and I kept thinking about it. I left when I was fifteen, and the feelings I had for you at that time have never been matched by anything I felt for anybody in Alaska. Anchorage is a nice place, but I felt like something in my life was unfinished. So, when the opportunity to get a nursing job presented itself, I took a shot, and I got it. So, here I am."

I'm a made guy—someone to be feared and respected. I'm not supposed to feel whatever emotions I feel right now, but they're here. Everything she just said is exactly what I was hoping for. All the women I've hooked up with over the years have been one night stands and meaningless situations I never cared about. I never gave them anything real because of who I am and what I do, but also because everything I had to give, I gave to Alannah when I was fifteen.

"Wow, that's deep," I say, doing my best to stay cool.

"Maybe it is," she continues with a serious expression on her flawless face. "But I'm not going to lie to you, Dominic, I learned about the Giordano family and how it works. There was a lot out there on the news, and I learned a lot about the kind of stuff you do."

"Well, I've always been honest with you about the things my father and I used to do," I chime in, whispering, just in case there's ears in the room. You never know.

"I know, and it never bothered me when we were kids because you were always nice to me. You always made me feel special, even when you were scaring the shit out of the other kids. But now that we're grown and I know what your *family* does to make money, it scares me, Dominic."

"Hey, you don't ever have to be afraid with me, Alannah."

"How can I not be? You're a part of what the cops call the mafia. That's scary shit, and I know you own casinos and they make legit money, but is that all there is to it? I mean, what else do you do?"

"Ninety percent of the money I make is legit from the casinos I own, the other ten percent is small time stuff that I started when I was younger. It's just business."

"Business," she repeats as a statement. "Do you hurt people?" she whispers as she leans in so I can hear.

"Do *I* hurt people? No," I answer. It's true, *I don't* hurt people.

Tommy does.

When I tell him to.

"Have you ever killed anyone?"

I feel my face immediately heat up like I'm hovering over a stove. I've never felt the need to lie about anything I do—except to the cops—but if something I say pushes Alannah away, I'll be devastated. I wrestle with how to answer, but Alannah saves me from having to make a decision.

"Don't answer that," she interrupts. "I'm not even sure I want to know. Look, I just want to know if there's anything I need to be worried about. I don't want to be arrested for aiding and abetting, or harboring a fugitive, or some shit like that. I don't want any drama."

I start to laugh.

"Geez, I'm not a fugitive, Alannah, relax. There's no warrants out for my arrest, and I'm not under investigation for anything illegal. You've known me since I was eleven years old, and you know I've always been honest with you. I'm telling you, you don't have anything to be worried about. I promise."

She looks at me like she wants to believe me, but it's hard. That's understandable, I guess, especially if everything you think you know was told to you by the news and police reports. I try to look her in the eye so she knows I'm not lying, but when I do, something behind her catches my attention.

On the street behind Alannah, I see a black SUV parked next to the curb. It wouldn't normally be a big deal, except you can't curbside park in this area, and the vehicle has its headlights on.

How long has that been sitting there?

As questions start to swirl in my head, the SUV turns on its high beams, shining blinding light right into my face. I can't see much, but I notice the obvious silhouette of a person speed-walking up to the window behind Alannah, and I know what it looks like when a pistol is being pulled out and aimed.

I jump to my feet and grab Alannah by the shoulders just as the first shots ring out. The room is quickly filled with loud popping sounds and glass exploding all around us. I drag Alannah to the floor and climb on top of her to shield her body as the shots continue and bullets whiz over our heads. I can hear screaming coming from inside the restaurant and dishes being knocked over as people duck for cover, and the bullets slice through the drywall. Alannah screams underneath me, and my heart is pounding nearly loud enough to drown it all out.

Then, just as suddenly as it started, the shooting stops, and I hear the sound of tires screeching as the SUV peels out and speeds away.

TWENTY-FOUR

Alannah

THERE'S RED AND BLUE LIGHTS bouncing off the walls, and ambulance sirens sing a dreadful melody into the night sky. Three people were hit with stray bullets. One of them died. Stray bullets that were meant for Dominic.

I sit on the hood of his BMW, watching him as he talks to the police with disinclination written all over his face. I know he won't tell them anything, but I also know he knows who did this. There's no way a man like Dominic doesn't know who his enemies are, but a man like him doesn't tell the police anything. He settles it on his own, which scares me nearly as much as the bullets speeding over my head did.

I can't explain what it felt like to be sitting across from him in a restaurant in one of his casinos, admiring his gorgeous face and alpha attitude, then to have it all snatched away in the blink of an eye as I'm thrown to the floor.

At first, I didn't even know what was going on, but I didn't have time to question it for long because there's no confusing the sound of gunfire and shattering glass. I wanted to scream, but the air was knocked from my lungs as Dominic jumped on top of me. I know he was trying to protect me, and a part of me is thankful for that, but there's another part that doesn't give a shit. I could've been killed tonight simply because I was sitting in this restaurant with him. The question now is, well, now what?

After he's finished talking to the police, I watch as he

saunters over to me. Glass and dirt are on the shoulders of his fancy suit that I'm sure cost a fortune, and he locks eyes with me. There's a level of pain in his gaze that wasn't there before. He looks miserable as he stares at me, and I can see it in him—he's worried about me, about what I'm going to say, about what I think. He's nervous, and he should be.

"Are you okay?" he asks as he stands in front of me, that sad look still holding his face hostage.

"What do you think, Dominic?" I counter. "Our dinner was interrupted by gunfire. That's not something that happens to me every day, so I'm sure you can guess if I'm okay or not."

His shoulders slump like my attitude has confirmed his fears.

"I don't really know what to say," he begins again. "I'm sorry all this happened. You just got here, and . . . I'm just so sorry, Alannah. I mean that. I'm sorry."

"What is it that you're sorry for, exactly? Are you sorry that I almost got shot just by being with you tonight? Are you sorry about the man who actually was killed by one of the bullets meant for you? I mean, seriously. What are you so sorry for?"

"All of it. I didn't know this shit was gonna happen, and I didn't expect it, so there was no way to prepare for it. I'm sorry you were put in danger, and I'm sorry innocent people got hurt. I'm sorry for all of it."

"If the people who were shot tonight were innocent, then what does that make you?"

With every word I speak and every word I hear, I feel myself getting more and more upset. I can still hear the sound of the gunshots, I can still smell the gunpowder, I can still hear the screams and the sound of my own pounding heartbeat, and I'm still afraid.

Dominic's eyes shift downward as he finds more comfort in looking at the street than he does looking at me.

"I don't know what you want me to say," he replies, his

voice somber.

"I told you I didn't want any drama in my life. Look around Dominic, this is pretty much the epitome of drama."

"I don't know what you want me to say," he repeats, this time less somber. Angrier.

"Tell me what the fuck is going on!" I snap. "You know who did this, don't you? I don't expect you to tell the police because I know you, but I expect you to at least tell me. I think I deserve to know why I almost died tonight."

Dominic looks like he's teetering on the edge, but he holds his frustration back and sits on the hood of the car next to me. He puts his hands in his pockets and takes a deep breath. I see his shoulders relax like he's ready to spill his guts.

"I don't know for sure who pulled the trigger tonight, but I have a pretty good idea who sent the guy to pull the trigger," he starts, still looking at the street. He has my full attention. "I'm in the middle of a bit of a business deal with a guy who owns a hotel; the same hotel you were about to check into when you first got here."

"Lumiere Place?"

"Yeah. When I saw you that day, I was just leaving from a business meeting with the owner of that hotel. The meeting didn't go well. I wanna buy it, but the guy doesn't wanna sell, which is a problem for me and my associates. So, I sent a guy to visit one of his friends a few days back, which probably didn't sit too well with him. I thought he'd fold up and sell the Lumiere to me, but it looks like I might have pissed him off enough to try to put a hit out on me. And I'm certain about it because I don't have beef with anybody else, not for a long time now. So, I'm sure it's the guy from Lumiere."

I take a moment to soak in all the information. It's a lot, and it doesn't make me feel any better. I shouldn't be surprised about it either. He's in the mafia; of course he has this kind of shit going on, and there's probably more to it than what he's telling me, too. Of course. What did I expect? What the fuck was I thinking believing I could come back here and live some fairy tale life with a mob figure without it being dangerous? Only an idiot would think that, and I'd been even dumber to believe that what happened tonight is going to be the end of it all.

"So, what's next, Dominic?" I ask, although I'm afraid of the answer. "Now that this guy has tried to have you killed, what are you gonna do about it?"

"I don't know," he whispers.

"Don't lie to me. I'm not dumb, okay? I told you I learned all about this, so I know you're not gonna just sit back and let this slide. So, are you gonna kill him?"

Dominic's head snaps up as he looks around to see how close the cops and paramedics are.

"Would you keep your fucking voice down, please?" he snips, still whispering. "I don't know what I'm gonna do. Right now, all I'm thinking about is you. You're what I'm concerned about right now, that's all. I want to make sure you're okay, then I'll take time to think about what I need to do"

"Well, you don't have to waste your time thinking about me. I survived the attempt on your life, now I just wanna go."

"Alannah."

"Please, just take me back to my room, Dominic!" I yell as my emotions get the best of me.

Dominic's head snaps up again, but this time it's for good reason. A cop has heard me and is staring us down. He squints as he eyes us, then he turns and walks our way.

My heart is back on fast forward as the young policeman approaches us with suspicion on his hairless face. Dominic doesn't say a word as the cop never takes his eyes off us, stopping only a few feet away with his hand resting on his holster.

"Is everything alright over here?" he asks, glaring at Dominic before looking to me. "Are you okay, ma'am?"

Dominic puts his head down and awaits my answer. I suddenly feel powerful, like I have his life in my hands at this very moment. I could tell this officer everything right now and Dominic could do nothing to stop me. I could settle his beef for him by telling and sending the cops over to Lumiere Place to question the owner. I could help their investigation and probably do a lot to protect Dominic from whatever else is going to come from all of this.

But if I did that, I'd lose Dominic forever. He'd never be okay with me cooperating with the police. He'd never look at me the same, and no matter how angry I am with him, it'd be a lie to say I didn't care about that. I do care about that. I do care about him.

"Everything's fine, Officer," I snip just as I get up and walk around to the passenger door.

"Are you sure, Miss?" the cop double-checks, still eyeing Dominic.

"Yes, I'm sure. If there was a problem, I would've told you when you interviewed me earlier, but like I told you then, I don't know anything. It's been a long night, and I want to go home. So, Dominic, please take me home." I dismiss the officer with a wave of my hand, then get in the car and close the door, making sure not to make eye contact with the cop again.

Dominic doesn't waste a second. He ignores the cop's glare and gets in the car, starting it up immediately and driving away from the scene.

The ride back to River City is silent. I know he has questions and is probably in his head just as I am right now, but neither of us speak. He parks the car in the garage and we walk to the elevator together. When we reach my floor, I get out without saying a word, but he stops me.

"Alannah, please don't go like this, alright? I know you're pissed, and you have every right to be, but you just came back to me." He suddenly stops talking and looks down at the floor before clearing his throat and looking up again. "I mean, you just got back. You just got back, and I don't want it to end like this."

I don't want it to end like this either, but maybe it has to. Maybe it doesn't matter what we want anymore. Maybe the idea of being with Dominic is better than the reality, because in reality, gangsters are dangerous people who hurt and get hurt. The bad boy persona is undoubtedly appealing and attractive as much as it is terrifying and dangerous. Maybe I was too blind to see that before. Maybe I was wrong all along.

"Good night, Dominic," I reply. Then I turn on my heel and walk away. I hear the elevator close behind me as I open the door to my suite, step over the threshold, and slam it shut with every muscle in my body.

I spend the next few hours crying into my pillow, until sleep finally shows up to comfort me.

TWENTY-FIVE
Dominic

"DID I, OR DID I not, specifically ask you if there was shit going on that I needed to know about? If my fucking memory serves me correctly, I asked all of you if there was beef in the streets that I needed to know about, and every one of you said to me that everything was good to go. You even said *Bellisimo*, or some corny shit like that. But today I learn that one of my captains has a contract on his head, put on by some wannabe Russian mafia cock sucker. So, you better start explaining what the fuck you've got going on, and why the fuck you didn't speak up when I asked about it."

Frankie is genuinely pissed off. I guess I earned it by not telling him about Abram, but then again, I didn't expect Abram to try to blow my fucking head off. I thought he'd roll-over. I was wrong, almost dead wrong.

"I'm sorry, Frankie," I begin as he sits down behind the desk in his home office. He fastens the string on his robe and glares at me as I try to explain. "I was trying to wrap up this deal to buy the Lumiere casino from this Russian prick, and he didn't wanna cooperate, so I sent Two Nines to send him a message a few days back. I guess Abram decided to get his fucking manicured hands dirty and retaliate. It's my fault, but I'm gonna take care of it, Frankie."

I go to sit down in the brown leather chair next to me, but Frankie isn't having it.

"Don't fucking sit down," he snips in a low, angry whisper.

His wife and two kids are asleep upstairs, so he's trying to keep it down, but he's struggling behind his anger. "I can't believe you're bringing this shit to my house in the middle of the fucking night. I expect better out of you, Dominic, you know that. You've been a part of Our Thing a long time, and you know how we do business, so I'm really fucking disappointed in how you went about this. What if that fucker would've got you? Have you thought about that? We wouldn't have known shit, then how would we have hit back? This is unacceptable."

I think to tell him I was trying to acquire Lumiere Place so we could go into business together, but it wouldn't do me any good right now. He's too pissed, so I keep it to myself and let him chastise me.

"Alright, now that everything's finally on the table," he continues, rubbing the length of the scar on his face. "Let's talk about how we fix this. This guy put a hit out on you and tried to carry it out in fucking public. He had the balls to try to have you clipped in a restaurant in your own casino. You know how that makes us look?"

"I know, Frankie, we can't let this shit slide, and I don't plan to. Not to mention he almost got Alannah."

Frankie's forehead immediately grows tons of wrinkles.

"He almost got who?" he inquires.

"I was out with Alannah when they tried to make the hit. If I didn't drag her to the floor with me, they would've hit her."

"Alannah? Who the fuck is Alannah?"

"Alannah's a girl I grew up with. We were at dinner."

"The same Alannah you were always yapping to your dad about when you were a kid? The one who moved to Alaska or some shit?"

"Yeah."

"She's back now?"

"Yeah. She just got back a few days ago."

"Ah, now I get it," Frankie says, leaning back in his chair

and shaking his head with disappointment. "You've never been one to be caught with your pants down, and now that your little girlfriend is back, you lose focus and almost get your fucking head blown off."

Now it's me who's frowning.

"Wait, that ain't how it is, Frankie," I reassure him. "This didn't have nothing to do with Alannah. I just didn't expect Abram to put a fucking contract on my head. It's not about Alannah being back."

"Well, it better fucking not be, Dominic," he snaps. "You're my best earner, and I don't wanna see something happen to you because you're too busy thinking about some high school crush. You're a made guy and the son of my best friend, God bless his soul, and I expect you to be boss of this family after my old ass is gone. So, you need to keep your fucking head on straight, and do what you've always done. Keep your mind on your money, and set this little thing with the Russian right. And you know what I mean when I say that, don't you?"

"Of course I do.

"Good. This is a big mess you've made, now it's on you to clean it up, because it's not just about you now. This Russian tried to clip a made guy—when New York finds out about this, they're gonna expect *immediate* consequences. So, you need to clean this up quickly, and brutally. An example needs to be made. You understand?"

I nod, thinking about how those bullets were only inches away from me.

Inches away from Alannah.

"I got it, Frankie," I reply as I turn to leave. "I'll let you know when it's done."

"WHAT THE FUCK? WHY ARE we just now hearing about this?" Charlie snaps as he takes his seat at the table in the conference room of River City. "You should've called us when it happened, and we would've hit back that same night. We don't fucking lay down for shit like this."

"I know we don't, Charlie," I try to explain. Charlie's fired up though. They all are. "We're not laying down. I just needed a minute to think, and I had to tell Frankie."

"How'd that go?" Skinny Joe asks, with a grin that says he already knows.

"Just like you'd expect. He was pissed," I admit. "Made sure to remind me how this makes us look as a family, which means he doesn't want to look bad, and he doesn't want New York to think he's not handling business as acting boss. So, we've gotta fix this, quick."

"You're goddamn right we gotta fix it quick," Joe snaps, his skin turning red as his temper flares. "You're a fucking made guy, Dominic, and my captain. Nobody takes a fucking shot at you without getting clipped. No-fucking-body. So, now that Frankie knows everything, we find these cock suckers and we hit back. Hard. We make it public and out in the open so everybody in the streets knows you don't come after one of our guys."

As much as I'd like to tell Joe to calm down, I find myself being motivated by his energy. He's right, the last thing any street guy would do is take a shot at a made man. It's street code, and everybody knows it, and when that code is broken, so is your fucking neck.

"Alright, so here's what we're gonna do," I begin, once Joe sits back down. "Charlie, I want you track down this SUV for me. It was dark when it all happened, but I know it was black, and it had a big body, like a Denali or something like that."

"Okay, Dominic," Charlie says, pushing his glasses back up on his nose. "I'll see what I can do."

"What about Abram? He authorized the hit," Tommy chimes in.

"I wanna wait on Abram," I reply.

"What? Why would you wanna wait?" Tommy says, frowning.

"Because I wanna find the shooter first," I answer. "I want the shooter first, and I want an example made of him so big that Abram can't ignore it. I want him to know we're coming for him so he has fucking nightmares about it until the day those nightmares come true. So, find the shooter, and when you do, sit on him. Don't make a move until you call me. I wanna be there."

"Wait, you sure that's a good idea, Dominic? You don't want your hands getting dirty with something like this," Charlie advises.

"No, it *is* a good idea," I snip. "That motherfucker had the balls to come to my casino and take a shot at me, and he almost hit Alannah. He's gonna pay, and I'm gonna be there to watch it happen."

"Who's Alannah?" Skinny Joe inquires.

"Alannah's a girl I was with when they tried to make the hit. Fucker almost shot her."

The three of them look at each other like I just said something offensive.

"What the fuck are you looking like that for?" I ask, scrunching my forehead.

"Nothing, nothing," Tommy answers for the group. "Just not used to you being out with no girls. You've always been focused on business. More of a one night stand kind of guy, not a dinner date guy."

"Well, I was out with her, so I guess you got me pegged all wrong," I reply, and I don't want to talk about Alannah with anybody, so I stand up and change the subject. "Anyway, look, I want the shooter found, like, yesterday. This motherfucker is gonna pay for the shit he tried to pull, and I don't wanna wait. So, I need all of you on this until it's done. Call me as soon as you find him."

I grab my coat and start heading for the door.

"Okay, and where are you gonna be while we're hunting this fucker down?" Tommy asks, gesturing with his hands.

"I told you, he almost got Alannah. I gotta go make sure she's okay."

There's that look again. The three of them have the same expression like they're triplets. They look at each other like they know they're all thinking the same thing, but it's Tommy who speaks for all of them.

"Look, Dominic, I don't know who this Alannah girl is, or why you seem so concerned about her, but maybe it's not a good idea for you to be out and about while there's a contract on your head. Why don't you let Joe go with you?"

Skinny Joe immediately stands up in preparation to come along.

"No," I say quickly. "I don't need a fucking bodyguard, and don't worry about Alannah. Just find the fucking shooter, Tommy. That's it."

"Okay, Dominic, you got it," Tommy replies, but I can still see the confusion on his face as I turn around and walk out.

I can understand the confusion amongst the guys. It's not like me to keep things secret, especially in regards to women. Tommy's right, before Alannah came back, I wasn't interested in anything serious with women. They got one night of my attention and my dick, and then that was it. The possibility of something more was never an option because I never wanted to risk the distraction that emotions cause, and I never wanted some girl finding out more than she needed to know and going and running her mouth to anybody. One night was all anyone ever got. But Alannah isn't just anyone.

Alannah is *the* one. She's the one and only and she always has been. So, it doesn't matter if Tommy and the guys don't understand right now, and it doesn't matter if Frankie doesn't get it either. Every capo in The Family is married, and so are Leo and Jimmy, and almost all of them have a *gumar* on the side, so they got no room to judge me for anything.

I wouldn't give a fuck if they judged me anyway, because when it comes to Alannah, something's different. With her, all of the rules change.

TWENTY-SIX

Alannah

THE BOXES ON THE FLOOR are driving me crazy, but it's worth it to have my own place. It took the landlord a couple of days to get my apartment ready, which is why I had to stay in River City, but I was able to start moving in this morning, and although it sucks having to unpack, it feels good to have a place to call my own.

It's only been a day since I almost died at Isle of Capri with Dominic, and the memory is still a fresh wound that hurts when I think about it. I dreamt about it the night it happened and developed a new level of understanding for people who go to war and experience PTSD. My situation only lasted a few seconds and I'm a total wreck, so I can only imagine if it had lasted days, weeks, or months.

It wasn't long ago, but I've spent every second since then thinking about it. Thinking about Dominic. I haven't heard from him since that night, but I'm glad because I don't know what I'd say or do at this point. I feel like my dreams of what it'd be like to come back to him came crashing down around me like the exploding glass window. I had one thing in mind, and I initially thought that thing was going to come true. However, reality has a way of slapping you in the face, and that's exactly what happened.

Dominic Collazo, the beautiful Italian I fell in love with when I was just a teenager, is still gorgeous, and the emperor of sex appeal. He's even a bigger bad boy now than he was before, but there's a price that comes with it that I simply didn't take into consideration.

A teenager who's a bad boy is almost never as bad as he seems. He probably smokes, or doesn't take shit from anyone, including adults he should fear and respect, or he dresses like he doesn't really give a damn about anything. It's usually something on the surface, but deep down, he's just a kid trying to find himself.

An adult bad boy is much more dangerous. An adult bad boy is the one who's into the illegal things that can bring you the most trouble. An adult bad boy knows who he is, knows he's bad, and doesn't care a bit. It's real when they're bad *men*. That's Dominic.

As a kid, Dominic was everything I wanted, and he's still physically everything, but he scares me now in a way he couldn't before. Maybe it was because I didn't know about everything, and I was a bit naïve when it came to his father and the Italian ancestry. Well, I know about it all now—I know how the police view the mafia and I know the history of it, and after the shooting the other night, I can't help but look at Dominic differently. At least, that's how I think I feel before I hear a knock on my front door.

It's nine o'clock in the evening and I'm unpacking in a new apartment, so I don't know why anybody would be at my door right now, unless it's the landlord checking up on me. So, I pause for a minute, holding a plate in the kitchen and assuming my visitor will realize they have the wrong house and go away. But there's another knock. I put the plate in the golden oak cabinet and slowly make my way over to the door. I look out the peep hole and I'm shocked to see him.

It's him.

It's Dominic.

"Hi," he says as I open the door. He smiles at me, but I don't smile back, and I can see it makes him a little uneasy.

"How are you?"

"I'm okay," I answer, before getting to what I really want to know. "How do you know where I live?"

He smirks as if to say *"You didn't really think you could hide from me, did you?"*

"I had one of my guys look into it."

"But I *just moved in* . . . this morning."

"I know. I looked for you at River City and they told me you checked out, so I had my guy, Charlie, look into it for me. Charlie has ways of finding things out like that."

"Umm, that's a total invasion of privacy, but okay."

"I know it is, and I'm sorry about that. I just really needed to talk to you. Can I please come in?"

I want to hesitate, but there's something in me that wants to let him in. He looks amazing in his white button-up and light gray pants. It's pretty casual but he makes casual look sexy as hell. I move aside and he brushes past me.

"Excuse the mess," I tell him as I lock the door and turn to face him.

His face is serious as he steps around the scattered boxes. He's been thinking about a lot, I can tell, and that expression of worry is still lingering. I try to not to get caught up in the look on his face and just focus on how I almost got shot the last time I was with him. I do my best *I'm pissed off* impression, and stand there waiting for him to speak. It takes a minute for him to realize I'm waiting, then he gets to it.

"Okay," he begins nervously, gesturing with his hands. "Umm, I don't really know how to say everything I wanna say, but I know I need to say it. I know that shit was bad the other night, and I didn't expect all of that to happen, and I swear that's not the kind of thing that goes on in my life on a regular basis. Before that night, everything was smooth. I'm a casino owner and a business man, but I don't want to lie to you, or lead you to believe something other than the truth. It's been ten years, and there's things you don't know about me, and I'd hate for you to get the wrong impression, so it's important that I'm honest with you."

He takes a deep breath and steadies himself, like his words are heavier than his body is ready for. I feel nerves in my stomach, but I let him continue without interrupting.

"The stuff you said you heard on the news is mostly true. I *am* a made member of the Giordano family, otherwise known as the St. Louis mafia, or the St. Louis crime family. My father was a made member as well, and he started prepping me to be a part of it when I was about eight years old. I've seen and done a lot since then, and a lot of that stuff has been bad. I've done things you probably don't ever want to hear about, things I won't tell you for your own safety. This thing is all I know, and I've managed to make it mostly legit, and I've avoided most of the stereotypical mafia bullshit they say on TV. Things went south before you got here, but there's something you gotta know, Alannah. I've been waiting for you since the day you left.

"I tried to put on this tough guy act when I first saw you, and I tried to avoid how seeing you made me feel. I didn't want you to think I was soft, but none of that matters anymore. The truth is, I haven't been able to be serious with anyone because nobody could ever compare to you. The things I've felt for you since the day we met in 2001 could never be replaced by something new. Why do you think I've been carrying your letter around for the past ten years? It's always been you, Alannah. Since I was eleven years old, it's always been about you, even when we were in junior high and I was too chicken shit to tell you. My heart left when you did, and now that you're back, everything I felt has come rushing back with you. It's new, and it's fucking terrifying, especially with the shit that went down at Isle of Capri, but this feeling will never be matched.

"I just need you to know that I would die protecting you. I

would literally lay down my life to make sure you're safe, and you're the only fucking person in the world I'd do that for. I promise I'll take care of you, nobody will ever lay a finger on you, and nobody will ever feel about you the way I feel about you.

"You are it for me, for the rest of my fucking life, I know it. You're it. So, I'm begging you to give me a chance to clean up this thing that went crazy the other night. I'm asking you to forget the other stuff, and focus on us. Focus on what we felt for each other ten years ago, and how those feelings were strong enough to bring you back here, all the way from fucking Alaska. You're it for me, Alannah, and I'm hoping you'll give me a chance to prove that I can be it for you, because now that you're back, I don't think I can handle being without you again."

I should be running for my life. I should kick him out and hide under the covers until he goes away for good. I shouldn't care what he says or how sweet it sounds, or how good he looks. I should get far, far away from Dominic and everything dangerous that comes with him. I just don't want to.

I tell myself I don't care, but the tears in my eyes tell me otherwise.

I tell myself I don't want him, but my body tells me different.

I tell myself he's dangerous, but my heart doesn't care.

I tell myself I can go back to Alaska and get over him, but I know that's a lie.

I breathe hard, like I just finished running a mile, and I can feel the tears stinging my eyes as I stare at his terrifying beauty. I think to say something, but when I start, the words catch in my throat and I feel overcome with emotion. All I can do is shake my head and try to fight off the combination of joy and fear I feel. Looking at him makes it worse, and I have to pry my eyes off of him so I can look at the floor until I recover from what feels like a blow to the stomach.

"Why?" I stammer, still staring at the floor. "Why can't I say no, when I know I should? Why can't I turn off these feelings?"

"Because you've loved me since you were eleven years old, and it doesn't matter what we do now. Nothing will ever turn this off."

As I look down, I'm taken aback by the sudden sound of his footsteps on the hardwood floor. Dominic races over to me and firmly puts his hands on my cheeks. He lifts my head up and forces me to lock eyes with him, then he presses his lips against mine like it's the first and last time he'll ever be able to do it.

My body melts into a pool of hot wax at his feet as I let go and give in. His tongue caresses mine and moves like it's been waiting to be reunited with me. Dominic's breathing picks up and it's now just as heavy as mine as we kiss with more passion than there has ever been in my life. I couldn't pull away from him if I tried, and I wouldn't dare try.

His hands start to explore my body as they slide down my neck and make their way to my hips. He pulls my pelvis to his and I don't even know how to react. Instincts take over and my hands mirror his. I pull him into me, and it's in that moment that I know I'm lost forever. I want him like I know I'll die without him, and once that thought enters my mind, it burrows deep and there's no getting it out. There's no U-turn allowed, and I'm on a one way street to somewhere frightening and exhilarating.

I can't go back.

I don't want to go back.

My fingers claw at the buttons on his shirt, and his tear at my belt. I drop his shirt at the same time he lets my jeans fall to the floor. The cold air hits my legs, but his hands immediately warm them up again as he rubs my inner thighs like he's reading my mind.

His body is picture perfect: smooth, tight, ripped, vascular muscles, pulsating in his chest and arms as he rubs my body. The look and feel of it all takes my breath away, but it's nothing compared to what I feel when Dominic drops to his knees, pushes my panties to the side and rubs his tongue over my clit.

I nearly scream, and my knees buckle instantly. Dominic has to hold my body upright as he works his tongue over and over again on my clit. My body jumps and writhes like it's mimicking the moves his tongue makes, and the sensation is so strong, I start to wonder if I've ever had someone do this to me before. I have, of course, but Dominic is so good it erases the others. No one and nothing existed before this.

I grip his hair and let it slide between my fingers, and then I have to squeeze and pull it as the orgasm hits me like I never saw it coming. I moan, I yell, I whimper, I fall apart, I melt in his mouth, and he loves every second of it.

Once I'm able to stand on my own, Dominic slowly rises. He locks eyes with me for a second, then he bends at the knees and wraps his arms around my waist. His biceps tighten around my hips and his forearms grip my ass as he lifts me up off the floor, and starts to carry me down the hall. I look down at him and wrap my arms around his thick neck.

"Where's your bedroom?" he asks, his voice low and hot.

"Third door on the left," I answer.

Dominic carries me down the hall and into the bedroom, and I pat myself on the back for telling the movers to make sure the bed was setup before they left. There's no sheets or covers on it, but we won't be needing those.

Dominic lays me down on the bare mattress, then he stands up so I can see him. The lights are out, but I can still see his rock hard stomach with the six-pack that looks drawn on. I watch him as he unfastens his pants and drops them to the floor. My heart explodes into a million caffeinated butterflies as he pushes his boxer briefs down and they fall to his ankles.

Every inch of him is beautiful.

Every.

Single.

Inch.

I stare at him. I stare at *it*, and I feel warmth emanating from between my legs like our bodies are communicating. I watch him pull a condom from his pants and slide it on, and every move he makes is laced with sexiness, and I can barely take it. We can't wait any longer.

He pulls my panties off and doesn't waste a second before sliding inside me. The width of his shaft stretches me in all the best ways, and I gasp at the feeling, sucking in as much air as I can to steady myself.

He starts slow, grinding from side to side before thrusting slow and deep. My fingers grip his muscled back as he takes his time, making sure I feel every inch of him. He pushes himself in as deep as our bodies will allow us to go, then he pulls himself out to the point of teasing me with the tip, before sliding all the way back in.

Every.

Single.

Inch.

"I need you, Alannah," he whispers in my ear as his hand runs over the top of my head. When he reaches the back, I feel him grip my hair. "I need you to feel how much I need you."

Dominic's hips start to pick up speed as he pulls my hair, using it as leverage. My fingers tighten on his back differently now, and my nails dig into his skin. He thrusts into me hard and strong, like the time for the appetizer of lovemaking is over, and we've moved on to the main course of fucking a woman the way she wants to be fucked.

The headboard bangs against the wall with every upward thrust and I have to wrap my legs around him so I can hold on. I've never felt anything like this before, and the sound that comes from my mouth surprises me as I scream like I hope my new neighbors will hear. He pulls my hair so my chin is pointing at the ceiling, and the sound of our pelvises crashing together echoes through the apartment.

This is nothing like ninth grade. This isn't homecoming night in the passenger seat of his dad's car. No, this is what dreams are made of. This is what every woman hopes she can marry so she can experience it on a regular basis for the rest of her life. This is everything I never knew I wanted. This is the best I have ever fucking had, and my second orgasm triples the intensity and sensation of the first one. It washes over me like a tidal wave and I scream so loud I know my throat will hurt the rest of the week, but it's a pain I'll gladly carry around with me as a memory of how incredible Dominic is.

As I come down, Dominic's body tightens up. His muscles reach a new level of rock hard, and his breathing becomes labored and staccato as he plunges himself deep into me until he comes just as hard as I did. He moans the sexiest moan known to man and tightens his grip on my hair. It hurts, but I couldn't care less—another pain I'll gladly accept.

Then, it's over. Dominic collapses onto the mattress next to me, breathing heavily on his back as he stares up at the ceiling. My body still trembles from my own orgasm, and I'm sure I won't walk right for a while, so I don't move. I lay there next to him, speechless, and buried inside a bubble that protects me from the truth.

I know I'll never be the same again. I had an opportunity to get away from all of it, but it's gone now. The door is closed, never to be reopened, and I don't know how I feel about being locked inside.

I should care. I should be terrified and screaming for help. I should be thinking of any way I can to escape and find my way back to safety, but I'm embracing it all instead. I'm bathing in the fear and soaking up the excitement, and I feel higher than ever.

I know I shouldn't feel this way, but I do, because when it comes to Dominic, everything's different. With him, all of the rules change.

TWENTY-SEVEN

Dominic

THE SUN RISES AND TAPS on the window until I wake up. She's still next to me when I open my eyes, just as beautiful now as she was last night. The sun touches her cheek and makes her skin glow. She's like an angel lying there, so I try not to disturb her as I get up. She covered us with a light blanket before we both passed out from exhaustion, so I make an effort to keep her covered up.

"Good morning," she whispers as I lean over her, but she keeps her eyes closed.

"Good morning," I answer. Luckily, she can't see my corny smile.

How can I not smile? Am I not supposed to because I've been a street guy my whole life? This is Alannah Sullivan, the girl I fell in love with when I pulled a bully off her back in the fifth grade. I was eleven then, so it's almost like loving her is just as much a part of me as This Thing of Ours. So, I'm not ashamed when I smile at her even though she can't see me. Yeah, it's weird to me, and it's corny, but it's Alannah.

"Go back to sleep," I whisper to her.

"Can't. Gotta go to work."

"Oh, okay then. Well, then you should get up and quit being lazy," I joke. She smiles, still keeping her eyes closed, and I'm shocked by how adorable I think it is.

She finally opens her eyes and locks them on me. We stare at each other for a minute, both of us smiling, thinking things we're not sure we should say yet. Her eyes and lips draw me in, so leaning in to kiss her feels like an involuntary action. Her lips are ridiculously soft, and memories of last night jump out of the bushes in my mind and jolt me awake. This woman makes me think things I shouldn't be thinking. Amazingly good things.

We manage to stop kissing, and Alannah gets up to get ready for work. I grab my clothes off the hardwood floor and start to put myself back together again while she puts on scrubs and throws her beautiful brown hair into a bun.

"You should let me take you to work," I tell her. "Then I can come get you when you get off, and we can go to dinner or something."

She smiles into the mirror as she applies her makeup.

"I'd like that, but if we're going to go to dinner, I'll have to come back here so I can change first. Can't do dinner in these scrubs," she says as she points at the rubber ducky print on her pants.

"So, you're saying you *don't* wanna go out to eat wearing those sexy pajamas?"

"Well, they *are* sexy," she replies behind a soft giggle. "But I'd rather not."

We laugh together, and it feels like it's junior high all over again. It's like we haven't skipped a day, let alone ten years. Something that was dormant inside me feels alive now, and I've missed the feeling of . . . us. I enjoying being around her again, so I'm a little bothered when my phone chimes from a text message.

Charlie: We found him . . .

Alannah comes out of the bathroom just as I stuff the phone back into my pocket without replying.

"Ready?" I ask, as she grabs her purse.

"Ready."

While we drive to Mercy Hospital, I put my hand on her leg, and she wraps her fingers around it. I'm watching the road, but I feel it every time she gently rubs my skin, and I rub hers back. I want to soak up every second of this car ride, because twenty-four hours ago, I didn't think we'd ever be together like this again.

"So, what's work gonna be like today?" I inquire. Not because I'm trying to make small-talk, but because I really want to know.

"Well, I've done all my paperwork stuff—new girl stuff, as I call it. So, I might be seeing patients today and working the nurse's station. I'm actually kind of nervous about it."

"Why? You did this in Alaska, right?"

"Yeah," she answers, looking out the window at the big city buildings. "But this is my first time seeing patients here, and working with these nurses is a whole new challenge in itself. Not to mention the new doctors—learning how they like things done, and which ones of them are assholes. It's a whole new adventure."

"You're gonna do great," I reassure her. "All you have to do is be yourself, and you can't go wrong."

I feel her eyes on me.

"Thank you," she says.

I take my eyes off the road for a second just to look over and see her smile. It shakes me to my core, and I love it.

When we get to Mercy, I'm pissed that we got here so fast. I drive under the overhang, put the car in park, and I clinch her hand so she can't get out.

"I don't want you to go," I kid.

"I know, but I have to," she says, beaming. "I'll see you in a few hours, okay?"

I sigh as I let her leave.

"Okay."

She leans over and kisses me softly on the lips, then she

gets out and walks into the hospital without looking back.

When the sliding glass doors close behind her, my phone chimes again. I pull it from my pocket and read the message from Charlie.

Charlie: We followed him to a house. 1212 Douglas Ave . . .

This time, I send a reply message.

Me: Go inside and say hello. I'm on my way.

IT'S A DECENT-LOOKING HOUSE FROM the outside. Medium-sized with red bricks and a short little driveway with lots of cracks in it. It's not the driveway or the house I hone in on—it's the black Lincoln Denali parked out front. The second I pull up to the curb I know it's the same vehicle from Isle of Capri. This is the house of the motherfucker who tried to shoot me in my own casino. This is the guy who sent bullets buzzing over my head, only inches away from Alannah.

I park across the street from where Tommy's Maroon Durango is sitting, and I quickly make my way inside. I don't waste time looking around like you see in the movies, because all that does is guarantee that you look suspicious to everyone who might be watching, plus give them multiple angles to see your face. I keep my head down and speed-walk up the sidewalk. Skinny Joe opens the door for me so I don't have to knock, and the second I enter the old house, I see my crew standing around a black guy who's tied to a chair with thick rope in the middle of the living room.

The house looks like it can't possibly belong to just this one guy, because it's neat and tidy inside. There's no clothes or porno magazines on the floor. There's bookshelves covered with books and crystal ornaments. When I see it all, I start to wonder if we're going to have company soon. We might have to make this quick, so I turn my attention to Charlie, who's standing over the black guy, wearing blue coveralls and holding a tiny wooden baseball bat that's already got blood on it.

"Okay," I say, glancing at the bald kid with the blood dripping from his mouth onto the stomach of his black t-shirt. "So, tell me Charlie, who the fuck is this guy?"

"This here is Anthony Bennet. He works at Lumiere Place," Charlie says, pointing the bat at the kid's face. "I asked around about the car you described, and a few of our people said they recognized it. So, I went to the places they said they saw it. It was too fucking easy to find this guy dropping off his grandma at bible study this morning. We spotted him and followed him back here. Anthony was just telling us about his employer, Abram Baskov. Ain't that right, Anthony?"

The kid puts his head down like he's ashamed. Blood drips from his mouth, and I can see his face is already swelling up. The guys didn't waste any time putting Charlie's bat to use.

I step in front of the kid and size him up. He's skinny, maybe a buck fifty-five, maybe five-foot-nine or somewhere close to it. He doesn't have any hair on his head, and he looks like he can't be any older than twenty-two. I bend over until my face is directly in front of his. He doesn't look up at me, and it makes me madder.

"A couple of nights ago, you had all the balls in the world," I say softly in his ear. "You parked your fucking ride outside the restaurant of my casino, and you confidently shot at me while I was having dinner. You had a lot of fucking balls then. So, why don't you lift your fucking head like a man? Look at me, you motherfucker!" I scream, and the kid jolts in his seat.

Slowly but surely, he raises his head and makes eye contact.

"There he is," I say with a smile. "So, Anthony Bennet, do you know who I am?"

He nods his head.

"And what do you know about me, Anthony?"

"Nothing," he whimpers.

"Nothing? I'm confused. If you don't know anything about me, why'd you try to kill me?"

"He told me to, but he didn't tell me nothing about you."

"Who the fuck is *he*?"

He hesitates like he doesn't want to be a rat, but we all know he's going to tell.

"Abram," he says, then he lets his head slide down until his chin is in his chest.

"What exactly did Abram tell you, Anthony?"

"He told me he had something he wanted me to do. Said he'd pay me five grand. So, I told him I was down, and he showed me a picture of what you look like. Then he said he knew you had reservations at some casino where it'd be easy to get you. So, I went there at the time he said to go, and I did what he told me to do."

"Oh, no you fucking didn't, asshole," Skinny Joe barks from his seat on the plastic-covered couch. "You tried, but you fucking missed. You're a shitty shooter, Anthony. Not a good trait for a penniless, freelance hitman who lives with his grandmother."

The four of us who *aren't* about to die chuckle together, but I don't let it last long. This business needs tending to.

"Okay, Anthony, I don't wanna drag this out, so I'm gonna get right down to it," I say as I take a seat next to Skinny Joe and light up a Cuban. "You don't know me, and I'd hate for you to get the wrong impression, so it's important that I'm honest with you. You're gonna die here in a few minutes, Anthony. However, before you die, I have one more question. Have you spoken to Abram since your failed attempt on my life?"

Anthony tries to answer, but the words get choked up in his throat as tears start streaming from his eyes. He's scared, which is understandable. He probably should've thought about that before he fired those bullets at me and Alannah.

"Look, I know it's hard to accept impending death," I say, trying to help the guy out. "But if you don't answer my question, I'm gonna make sure my friend over there with the bat prolongs the dying process as much as possible, then I'm gonna make sure your grandmother finds your dead body with your fucking face smashed in the middle of her living room. So, do yourself and your grandmother a favor, and answer the fucking question."

Anthony takes a deep breath and blows the air out.

"I spoke to him on the phone," he says, his words coming out in a trembling heap.

"I see. What'd you tell him?"

"I called him right after I did it, and I told him it was done. I told him I got you, and he said he'd meet me with the money in a day or two, once things quieted down."

"Has he paid you yet?"

"No."

"Why'd you tell him you got me?"

"I thought I did. I didn't have time to stick around and make sure, though. So, I assumed I did."

"See, now that's fucked up," Skinny Joe starts up again. "Abram hires this *mulignan* to do a hit, then doesn't even get around to paying the fucking guy before he gets wacked. So, you literally did that shit for nothing, man. That's gotta fucking suck."

Joe, Tommy, and Charlie all laugh as another tear slides down Anthony's face. He's absolutely terrified and I can see he regrets ever falling for Abram's shit. Abram should've told him who he was dealing with, but he let the kid get fucked instead. I almost feel bad for the guy. Almost.

"Alright," I say as I stand up. "Well, Anthony, I'll let you in on a little secret. I was planning on making our little meeting last a lot longer, and for it to be much more painful for you. But I'm in a good mood today. I'm still wearing the same clothes I had on last night, and seeing as how I'm not a bum on the streets, you know that means I had a good night. So, since I'm in such a good mood, I'm gonna let you off the hook."

Anthony's head snaps up.

"So, you're not gonna kill me?"

"No, I'm not gonna kill you, Anthony," I reply, as I think of Alannah's face and reach for the door. I latch on to that good feeling that she gives me, then I look at Anthony. "*I'm* not gonna kill you, but my friend, Charlie, is." I look at Charlie. "Make it quick and get rid of the body. Clean up in here so his grandmother doesn't know. She can think he ran off or something. After you dump him, find Abram, who apparently thinks I'm dead. That means his guard will be down, which is fucking perfect. I want this thing done and over with."

Charlie nods and I turn to leave, but Anthony speaks up again.

"Come on, man," he yells. "Cut me some fucking slack. I was just looking to make some money. I wasn't trying to get involved in this life. Cut me some slack, please!"

I stop at the door and turn my head to look at Anthony, who's trying his best to give me sad puppy eyes.

"Cut you some slack?" I snip. "Did you know you killed a guy that night? Some poor, innocent bastard took one of your stray bullets to the back of the head while he was eating his fucking mozzarella sticks with his wife. She's a fucking widow now, probably crying over her dead husband as we speak. Can you go cut her some slack? Did you plan on cutting me some slack that night?"

Anthony puts his head down as he starts crying again.

"I thought not," I say, then I nod the go-ahead to Charlie. "Call me when you find Abram."

I stick my cigar in my mouth and walk out of the house,

making sure the door closes behind me. I take the narrow sidewalk back to my car, and before I get halfway, I hear the silencer-suppressed gunshot that ends Anthony's life.

Good riddance.

TWENTY-EIGHT

ABRAM BASKOV'S HEART POUNDS IN his chest as he watches Dominic Collazo climb out of his BMW and walk up to the house. He can't fucking believe it—Anthony lied to him. He said he was sure he got Dominic when he fired all those shots through the window. It was over. It was done, and it was all bullshit.

The plan was to stop by Anthony's house after he dropped his grandmother off at church, so he could give him the five grand he promised, but as Abram drove up the road, he saw someone he recognized. It was the big guy from the sit down at Lumiere Place. He knew it was the same guy Dominic had with him, no mistake about it, and he knew if he was going into Anthony's house, there was no chance Anthony was ever going to see the light of day again. Abram figured the guy and his two friends were there to get revenge for the hit on Dominic, which is exactly why Abram hired Anthony—a young black kid who Abram doesn't associate himself with. They weren't supposed to make the connection to Abram, and for all he knows, maybe they didn't. But once he saw Dominic show up, he almost started to panic.

Now, it's been ten minutes since Dominic walked inside, and the door is opening again. Out strolls Dominic like he doesn't have a care in the world. Abram can't stand seeing him walk around like everything's fine, knowing he just did something terrible to poor Anthony, who never saw any of this shit coming. Dominic gets in his car, but the other three guys are still inside, probably cleaning up the mess. Abram knows he has to do something. He has to get rid of this Collazo fucker, or he'll never have peace. These fucking mob families always think they can just take what they want from people. Well, fuck that. It won't happen this time, not to Abram.

He needs a plan, but Dominic is already driving away from the house, so he doesn't have time to sit there when he already knows Anthony's dead. So, he puts his truck in gear and follows the Italian.

He knows he has to keep his distance. He can't afford to be seen, at least not until he's ready to make his move—whatever that's going to be. As he drives on the highway, he thinks. Dominic is a major player in the Giordano family, not someone to be taken lightly, so he knows it'll be a bad idea to take the guy on straight up. Unlike the crooks his father ran into, the Giordanos are connected to the Original Five Families in New York. This isn't some made up shit, this is the real deal. So, whatever move he makes has to be perfect, or he's sure to be tortured to death in retaliation.

Dominic drives into the underground parking area of River City, where Abram knows he'll be staying, at least for a while. He knows better than to get too close, so Abram parks in the staff parking lot across the street from the underground entrance. He'll wait there until he figures out his next move, or until he sees an opportunity to strike. He doesn't give a fuck how long it takes either, because this thing has to end. Abram refuses to end up like his father and the rest of his family did back in Chicago.

Hours pass before Abram finally sees Dominic leaving River City again. As he prepares to get back on the road to follow him, he still doesn't know what the hell he's supposed to do to get rid of this bastard. He just knows he has to, because there's a chance Dominic and his crew beat the information out of Anthony. If they got Anthony to tell them who hired him, Abram knows he won't last long. These motherfuckers have no problem killing someone in broad daylight. He can't take any chances. He has to make this happen.

Then, the stars align.

Abram follows Dominic to Mercy Hospital, where he watches with a smile as a woman wearing hospital scrubs exits and climbs into the BMW. Dominic quickly drives away and Abram stays on his tail.

He doesn't know who the beautiful brunette is, and it makes no difference. All that matters is that she's someone Dominic cares about in some way. It could be a sister, or a cousin, or a girlfriend. Abram hopes it's the last one. Love brings out the most emotion and garners the best results, so as the BMW turns into a residential area, Abram feels his heart start to speed up.

This woman was gorgeous, and he can feel it in his stomach that this was not a family member. Abram believes the woman is Dominic's girlfriend, and when the car pulls into a driveway and parks, Abram's suspicions are confirmed when the two lovebirds get out and kiss each other like they haven't seen each other in years. Abram watches them from four houses down as they caress one another, leaning against the BMW for support as they engage in a proud public display of affection.

Not too many cousins kiss like that.

It takes a while, but they manage to pull themselves apart, and the two of them playfully walk inside and shut the door behind them, totally unaware that they just gave Abram Baskov everything he was hoping for. He stomps on the gas and drives away, burning rubber as he speeds down the road. He knows they can hear the screech of his tires and the roar of his engine, and it makes him chuckle, because they don't know it's him. They don't know what their carelessness has done.

They don't know Abram finally has a plan.

TWENTY-NINE

Alannah

"IF YOU PUT THAT DRESS on, we might not make it to dinner."

I giggle as I zip up my favorite black dress and Dominic stands in the doorway grinning. He took the time to go home and change while I was at work, and he's a tall glass of water to a woman dying of thirst as he stands with his hands in the pockets, wearing a navy blue suit with sky blue pinstripes. He dresses like he has a tailor living in his closet at River City, so I had to break out my favorite dress just to keep up.

"Hey, I thought the same thing when you picked me up wearing that suit," I respond. "So, you started it."

"Oh, I see. You're one of those people?"

"What? What people?"

"A one-upper."

"I am not," I snip, as we laugh together. "There's just going to be a lot of girls checking you out, so I have to step my game up so they know you're with me."

"Okay, I get it now. Trying to protect what's yours?"

I fight back a smile and glare at him, because it sounds so good to hear him say he's mine. He's right, but I won't tell him that.

"So, I think I'm ready. You?" I ask, changing the subject.

"Am I ready? Fuhgeddaboutit."

The bright city lights of St. Louis shine into the car and help to keep a continuous smile on my face. The speed at which all of this has happened is crazy, and it's a bit surreal to be driving on the highway in St. Louis with Dominic in the driver's seat. It's all so much different than the cold of Alaska, where it's either bright most of the day or dark most of the day, depending on the time of year. I'm here with him, instead of there with my parents and my friends of the past decade. It's a drastic change, yet I don't feel out of place or afraid like I expected. I guess that's because being with Dominic makes me feel so comfortable, plus I lived in this city a while, so it's not completely foreign to me. Nonetheless, it's a trip being here with all of this going on, but my excitement-to-worried ratio is two-to-one. I feel like there's a great adventure ahead of me, but I'm going through it with Dominic, and it's all okay. I'm okay.

We decided on Red Lobster this time, and we made sure to *not* make reservations. The last thing I could handle is another Isle of Capri situation. So, we park and walk into the restaurant hand in hand like a real couple ready for the long haul of commitment.

To be honest, at this point in time, I don't really know what I'm doing. Dominic and I are together, but there's a lot of other stuff that's going on under the surface. I haven't forgotten that he's in the mafia, or that he has a checkered past that probably includes hurting people in the name of "family business." I also haven't forgotten that he has ongoing drama with the guy from Lumiere Place—the one he thinks sent the guy to shoot him. I know things aren't picture perfect with him, so if you're wondering how I'm holding his hand as we walk, I don't have an answer that even I understand. The only thing I do understand is that I want to be with him, and how I feel about the other stuff is the same as I felt about it when we were kids. Dominic treats me the way every woman wants to be treated by the guy she's with, so that's what I'm trying to focus on. I know I have to figure out if I can accept the other stuff, but right now I'm just enjoying being with him. I'm enjoying reliving the part of my life I've always cherished most, and it feels too good to just throw it out. I don't know how to explain it in a way other people would understand, so I'm not looking for an explanation. Instead, I'm hanging on to what I realized when he showed up to my house yesterday; Dominic is the love of my life, and there's nothing more powerful than knowing that's true.

Once we're inside, we're taken to our seats immediately. It's hard not to think about the last time we had dinner, but we both do a good job of acting like it's not in the back of our minds.

Our waiter, a tall guy with a super-thick mustache, takes our orders and we're left alone. I sip my wine and take a second to soak Dominic in. He has grown up to be so incredibly hot that I'm still surprised by it. Who would've known that the lips everyone used to make fun of him for would end up being his best feature. It took a little time, but he grew into everything with absolute perfection.

"What's up?" he says when he sees me staring at him.

"How'd you get so hot?" I ask with a giggle.

"Look who's talking," he replies, and we share another laugh.

"No, really, Dominic. You're twenty-five years old, you make a ton of money, and you're gorgeous. So, I really want to know how you got to this point without at least a long-term girlfriend. Any other guy who has what you have would be taking advantage as often as possible."

He lets out a sigh and sinks into his chair, making himself comfortable.

"Well, growing up, my concern was never about getting girls," he begins. "When I was a kid, everybody made fun of me, especially girls. I'm sure you remember that. So, as a result, I guess I decided I wouldn't give anybody that kind of attention. At least until I met you. You're the first girl I ever had a crush on, and that kinda stuck after you left. Not to mention, I've had some crazy experiences with women in the past, let me tell you."

"Ooh, please do. I love stories about crazy women!"

"Oh yeah? Well, I've got a few. I knew this one girl who told me she was pregnant with my baby three days after we met."

I burst out laughing. I even manage to draw the attention of the table next to us.

"Are you serious? How'd she try to explain that one?"

"She didn't," he continues after a sip of his champagne. "She found out I owned casinos and the next thing I knew, she showed up with a positive pregnancy test. She brought it with her when we went out on a date. Pulled the stick right out of her pocket at the dinner table and told me how happy she was that *we* were pregnant."

"Oh my god! That's crazy and gross at the same time," I exclaim while laughing like a kid with a sugar high. "So, then what'd you do?"

"I laughed a little, then I got up and left her crazy ass at the table alone."

"Wow. That's a good one right there."

"I had a girl lick my face one time," he continues.

"What the hell?"

"Yep. I made the mistake of going to a nightclub with this one chick. We're on the dancefloor doing our thing—I hate dancing, by the way—and the next thing I know, she leans in and licks my fucking cheek like it has tartar sauce on it or something. It was our first and last date."

I laugh so hard it starts to make my stomach hurt. I imagine this woman pausing her dance routine so she can stand on her tippy-toes to lick Dominic's face, and it just splits my side. The neighboring table looks at me again, but I couldn't care less.

"Don't laugh too hard," Dominic says, still chuckling himself. "I'm sure you've had some crazy stuff happen to you, too. We're both twenty-five and unmarried, remember?"

"Oh, I know," I reply as the waiter brings my steak and delivers Dominic's giant seafood platter. "I didn't have the best luck with guys when I was in Alaska, which is why it was so easy to leave."

"Alright, so let's hear it."

"Okay," I begin. "Well, I don't know how much you'd want to hear about this, but it's pretty weird and funny. I knew this one guy who refused to have sex with me unless I used a vaginal foam."

Dominic nearly spits out the wine he just sipped.

"What the fuck is vaginal foam?"

"It's a foam that has spermicide in it, and he refused to have sex unless he had a condom and I had the foam. He was really worried about having kids."

"Aw, fuck. Well, that's new. Did you do it?"

"I hate to admit it, but I did try it once. It was horrible, and I still feel gross about it. In fact, I think I need a shower right now."

"I can't believe that one," Dominic says between bites of fried shrimp. "Spermicidal vaginal foam. So, so sexy."

"Right? Ooh, I've got another one. Wanna hear it?"

"Of course."

"Okay, so I'm on a first date with this guy from work. We're in a nice, quiet restaurant, and everything's going okay for the first fifteen minutes or so, and then he gets a phone call. He answers, and after about ten seconds of silence, he starts screaming into the phone. When I say screaming, I mean veins popping out of his neck. He keeps yelling, 'Stop calling me! Stop calling me, goddammit.' So, I'm thinking he's talking to an ex or something, and I'm already telling myself I'll never go on another date with this crazy screamer ever again. Well, he's not finished yet. The next thing I know, he goes, 'If you call me again, I'm gonna get a fucking restraining order on you like I did before. Do you understand me? Do you want another restraining order on you? No? Then stop calling me while I'm out on my date. I'll be home when I get home. Stop being in my business and just go to bed, Mom.'"

I laugh as I finish the story, and Dominic nearly falls out of his seat with laughter, too.

"Holy fucking shit! He was talking to his mother?"

"Yep, and that's when I got up and left. And as I'm walking away, I hear him say into the phone, 'Great. I just lost another date because of you.'"

The two of us laugh together like we're kids all over again. That's what it all feels like—like we're right back in junior high and high school, having a great time, being absolute best friends while the rest of the world watches us. It's like that ten year gap never existed, and my heart feels complete in this moment. It could be like this every day. It could be like this for the rest of our lives.

We finish our meals and I order dessert—just a little slice of cheesecake that I share with Dominic. As we finish it up, I reach across the table and place my hand on top of his.

"Thanks for bringing me out tonight," I say. "This was great. I haven't laughed like this in a long time."

"I know, me either," he admits.

We lock eyes, and I think to tell him something that I haven't told him since we were fifteen, but before I can get the words to form, our eye contact is interrupted by his phone ringing. He looks frustrated as he apologizes and answers it at the table.

"It's not my mom, so there won't be any yelling," he kids before listening in to the call.

As soon as he puts the phone to his ear, I know something's

wrong. I don't know who it is or what they're saying, but I know it's bothering Dominic. It's not making him mad, though. From the looks of it, he's scared, which terrifies me much more than his anger would've.

"Are you fucking kidding me?" he says into the phone. "Is he alive?"

I feel a strong chill run down my spine. Here it is—the other side of this beautiful thing we have. The ugly side I was hoping I wouldn't have to see.

"Son of a fucking bitch," Dominic says as his head lowers like a child being scolded. "I'm on my way."

"What's going on?" I ask as soon as he puts the phone on the table.

Dominic runs both of his hands over his face, steadying himself as the information he just received sinks in.

"Dominic, you're scaring me. What's going on?" I ask again.

"One of my guys got shot," he says. I watch as his eyes begin to water and he fights back the tears. "My three closest friends were walking into a bar, and a truck drove by and started shooting. My friend, Tommy, was hit in the back twice. He's in the hospital. I have to go, I'm sorry."

"You don't have to apologize," I assure him. "Do what you've got to do. Go see your friend. I can take a cab home."

"It's okay, just come with me."

I immediately start to think about what kind of characters might be at the hospital, and instantly know I don't want to be there. I'm definitely not ready to meet anymore gangsters.

"No, it's okay," I say. "This is your thing, and I'd just rather go home."

"Well, at least let me take you," he pleads, but I want to be supportive. I want him to know I understand he has friends that I don't know. Friends he's known a long time, and I can tell from the tears in his eyes that this is serious.

"I'm fine, Dominic," I insist. "Go check on your friend, I'm gonna take a cab home. Just let me know what's going on as soon as you can, okay?"

He's reluctant, but he nods his head. He pulls a wad of cash out of his pocket and places some on the table to pay for dinner, and then hands some to me.

"This is for the cab," he says as he stands up. "I'm so sorry about this. I'm gonna call you as soon as I know he's okay, then I'm gonna meet you at your house when I'm free. Is that okay?"

I force a smile.

"That's perfect. Okay, now go."

He leans over and kisses me softly on the lips, then he hurries out of the restaurant.

I wait for the waiter to acknowledge the money for the check and the tip, then I get up and make my way outside. I flag down a cab within a minute, and as I ride home, I feel frustratingly anxious. I hate this part of it—the wondering if he's going to be okay or not. I hate trying to figure out if this is something mafia related, or if there are going to be more consequences for it. That's two shootings in two days, yet Dominic insists this isn't how his life usually is. Is it usually rainbows and butterflies? I highly doubt it.

So, when the cab pulls up to my apartment, I'm filled with anxiety and confusion. All I can do is go inside and wait to hear from him. With my nerves being on high alert like this, and my brain drawing its own scary conclusions, I hope I don't have to wait long. I don't think I can take much else.

THIRTY

Dominic

"WHERE IS HE? I WANNA see him."

I run over to a group of people sitting in the waiting area of Mercy Hospital. My crew is there, as well as all the other capos in The Family, plus Tommy's fiancé, who's being consoled by Skinny Joe. Charlie sees me coming and cuts me off before I can force my way through doors I'm not supposed to go through.

"Hold on, Dominic," Charlie pleads. His eyes are red like he's been crying all night long, and he has blood on his shirt from when he sat with Tommy waiting for the ambulance. "He's in surgery right now. The doc is trying to get the bullets out."

I feel tears rushing to the surface, so I cover my face so no one can see me. Charlie knows it's coming though, so he grabs me and forces me to hug him.

"He's gonna be okay," he tries to reassure me, but he doesn't sound so confident himself.

"Fuck! How the fuck did this happen, Charlie?" I cry into his shoulder. Charlie pulls away and looks me in the eye.

"It all happened so fast, Dominic, I can barely believe it all," he begins, wiping away his tears. "Me, Joe, and Tommy were walking to that little bar across the street from River City. We'd just crossed the road, and this black truck pulls out of the staff parking lot. We don't think nothing of it, of course, until we reach the sidewalk and the truck slows down behind us. It's back there creeping, so I turn around to see what the hell this guy's doing, but the windows are tinted so I can't see him. So, I grab Tommy's attention and tell him to check it out, and as soon as Tommy starts to turn around, the window lowers and a hand comes out blasting away. There's nothing we can do except run for cover, but Tommy gets hit and drops. As soon as Tommy hits the ground, the truck fucking speeds away."

"Goddammit!"

"I don't know, Dominic, the shit looked real fishy to me. It was like the guy in the truck was making sure we were who he was looking for before he started shooting. He was back there watching us as we walked. This wasn't no random shooting, Dominic, I'm telling you. I fucking know it."

My first thought is Abram Baskov. We don't have beef with anybody else, so it had to have been him. He must've recognized Tommy from the sit down and thought he had to get him before Tommy came looking for him to avenge me, because Abram thinks I'm dead, thanks to Anthony. This motherfucker has more balls than I thought. This is what I get for underestimating him.

"Fuck," I think aloud. "I bet it was that Russian cock sucker. I know it."

"Yeah, that's what me and Skinny were thinking. So, when do we go get this motherfucker, Dominic? First he puts a hit out on you, then he gets Tommy. This fucker has to die, now!"

"I know, and we're gonna fucking get him," I tell him, but I pause a second. "But we're gonna wait until we here from Tommy's doctor first."

"Why the fuck would we do that?" Skinny Joe says as he approaches. His thin face is scrunched into an emotional, tear-filled expression. He looks like he's on the verge of a full-on mental collapse. "This bitch shot at you, and then he actually shot Tommy. This is Tommy we're talking about. Fucking *Tommy*! We go and kill this motherfucker right now!"

"Keep your fucking voice down," I snip. "I know we need to go get him, but we're gonna wait a minute, goddammit. We're gonna wait until we hear Tommy's okay. Once we know . . ."

"What the fuck did I tell you?" a voice says from behind me. I turn around to find Frankie glaring at me with his arms folded. He looks miserable, and the scar on his face makes miserable look terrifying. "I told you to handle this fucking Russian, didn't I? I told you to take care of this, and this prick is still on the streets shooting at you and your crew. What the fuck, Dominic?"

I'm not really sure how to respond. There's too many emotions to pick one, and it feels overwhelming, to say the least. I just stare at Frankie, who glares back like he's utterly disappointed in me.

"I told you to fix this. Now, The Commission has to hear about a made guy actually getting gunned down in fucking public," Frankie says, snarling. "We don't let this shit happen to our people, Dominic. Why haven't you fixed it yet?"

"I've been fixing it, Frankie," I snip. My emotions are running high, and respect for the acting boss isn't exactly a top priority right now. "We found and handled the shooter this morning, for your fucking information, and we were working to find Abram, he just found us first. What the fuck was I supposed to do?"

"And where were you when Tommy got shot, huh? You're his captain, so where the fuck were you, Dominic?"

"I was having fucking dinner. What do you want from me?"

"Out with your fucking little girlfriend who nearly got *you* shot last time. Of fucking course."

"What the fuck is your problem with me having dinner with a woman? This is ridiculous," I bark. Everyone in the waiting area is starting to look at us, and I know I'm walking a thin line talking to Frankie this way, but I'm fed up right now.

"You're distracted, Dominic, and it's making it dangerous for everyone," Frankie yells back. "When you're off your fucking game because of some chick, and bullets start flying at our people, that's a problem for everyone. Do you know what I'm saying?"

"You're fucking married, Frankie! I go to dinner with a woman, and it's the end of the world, but you being married is perfectly fine. That's bullshit!"

"You better watch your mouth, Dominic. You're in enough shit with Leo and The Commission, so I wouldn't start burning any bridges right now."

"You're unbelievable."

"Your father would've never let this happen to someone in his crew. If this was your dad's crew, he wouldn't even be here right now. He'd be out tracking this Abram fucker down, but you're standing in here with tears in your eyes. I expected more out of you, Dominic."

"And I expected you to be a better fucking boss, so I guess we're both surprised at how fucked up everything has turned out," I respond.

The whole room goes quiet. Even the people in the waiting area who aren't with us are watching like we're their personal soap opera.

Frankie glares at me with a look I've seen before. He's fuming, and I know what he's thinking. Frankie isn't the guy you want to piss of, but then again, neither am I. I should probably apologize, though, because Frankie's probably only days away from being officially named boss, but I'm emotional. Tommy is my guy, so I'm allowed to be upset too, but I know I'm going to have to fix things with Frankie soon, or I could end up getting clipped over this.

I try to catch my breath and calm down, but it's easier said than done. Frankie looks furious, and I know I have to fix it.

"Look, Tommy just got shot, and I'm all fired up," I begin. "I don't mean no disrespect, Frankie. You know that. You've known me since I was a kid, and you're like an uncle to me."

Frankie cuts me off by turning his back and walking away.

I turn to Joe and Charlie, and the looks on their faces tells me they know what that means. I may have just royally fucked up. They look scared for me.

I think to follow Frankie to plead my case, but before I can, my phone rings. I look at the display, and I'm comforted by Alannah's name. She's probably worried to death about me, and I hadn't had a chance to call her and tell her anything. Right now, I just want to hear her voice.

"Hi, beautiful," I say when I pick up.

Then, everything stops.

"Oh, how fucking sweet, lover boy," a deep voice replies.

A man's voice.

Abram's voice.

How does he have Alannah's phone?

"What's the matter? Surprised to hear from me, you fuck?" he says when I hesitate to speak.

"How do you have her phone?" I manage to say as my heart beats faster by the second, and tears blur my vision.

"How do you think, Dominic? Me and your little girlfriend are hanging out right now, and if you ever want to see little Miss Alannah again, I suggest you get your ass here to her house, right now. And you better be alone, or all that'll be left of her is five little pieces of her hand."

He hangs up, and my heart falls into my feet. I can barely breathe, and my skin feels like it's on fire. Charlie and Joe stare at me, wondering what's wrong, but I can't tell them. I can't risk Alannah's life.

Abram has Alannah.

My body fills up with more fear and rage than I've ever felt, as I break into a full sprint towards the exit.

THIRTY-ONE

Dominic

ONE GUN TUCKED INTO MY pants, another with a silencer in the holster under my jacket, plus a knife in my pants pocket.

I approach the house from the front, because I don't want Abram to think I'm doing anything he needs to be suspicious of. I won't risk him hurting Alannah, so I get out of my car and close the door loudly, like everything's normal. I walk to the front door, and before I can knock, it opens all the way. Abram fucking Baskov greets me with a nine millimeter already pointed at my face.

He's wearing black sweatpants and a white tank top. His ugly fucking face is just as bearded and soft as it was the last time I saw him. He doesn't have the look of a street guy, yet here he is pointing a gun at me, with the love of my life tied to a fucking chair in her own living room.

I see Alannah's teary eyes and it makes my blood boil. I have half a mind to lunge at this fucker, but I have to keep myself under control. She doesn't seem hurt physically, which makes it a little easier for me to keep it together, but just seeing the rope wrapped around her and weaving through the legs and arms of the chair is enough to make my knees shake with anger. She has duct tape over her mouth and her eyes are locked on me like she's trying to communicate telepathically. I wish I could read her mind, but I'm stuck on the outside, trying to figure out what she needs me to do to save her.

"Nice of you to show up, Dominic," Abram says as he steps

back into the house but leaves the door open for me. "Get in here and close the door behind you."

I don't say anything, I just walk in and shut the door. Glaring at him, I stand there waiting for him to say whatever dumb shit he's going to say, hoping a plan on how to end this as fast as possible will pop into my head.

But it turns out, I don't need to read Alannah's mind, because I can see her. Her eyes are still locked on me, but her right hand is slowly shifting from side to side, and the rope isn't tight in that spot. She's already trying to get free, so all I have to do keep Abram's eyes on me. Who needs mindreading when your woman is independent and smart on her own? Just another reason she's irreplaceable—another reason I can't let this motherfucker hurt her.

Abram stands there staring at me for a while, just pointing the gun and twisting his lips. I can see he's pissed and trying to figure out what he wants to do, like he never really had a plan, and now that I'm here, he's trying to come up with what's next.

"Take off your jacket," he demands.

Shit. I was hoping he wouldn't come up with that.

I have to keep Alannah in mind, so I do as he commands. I unbutton my jacket and toss it on the floor in front of him. Now my shoulder holster is fully exposed.

"Take that off and throw it on the floor, too. Then spin around with your hands in the air so I can see what else you've got."

Again, I do as I'm told and toss the harness with the gun still inside. Then I put my hands above my head and do a full turn. He sees the gun and tells me to toss that one too, and I comply. I'm down to only one more weapon, and hoping he doesn't think to make me empty out my pockets since he already found two guns.

"Do you know how much you've screwed me, Dominic?"

he finally says, satisfied that he can't see a weapon. "Do you know how much damaged you've caused? You killed my best guy. Yeah, remember that, you fucking Italian asshole. You had Alex killed just to try to intimidate me, but you can't intimidate me. I have the blood of my father running through my veins. I'm a fucking Baskov, motherfucker. You don't get to take from a Baskov without suffering consequences.

"So, here's what we're gonna do; I'm gonna take from you the same way you took from me. You took Alex, you took Anthony, and now I'm gonna take something of yours. Because that's the way love works, Dominic. When it comes to someone like you, love will always hurt you more than it'll help you. That's the reason you were willing to come here alone—love. You left your friend at the hospital, where I put him, so you could save your love, and now you get to watch your love die."

He turns around and aims the pistol at Alannah, and my insides explode. I clench my teeth and take a step towards him as a tear falls from Alannah's eye. Then I take another step . . . and Abram spins back around, gun pointed in my direction.

BANG

That's what it really sounds like when a gun goes off inside a house. It's a loud pop that makes you jump, and you spend the next second trying to figure out if you got hit or not.

Well, I did.

Abram squeezes the trigger, I start falling to the floor, and Alannah screams behind the tape on her mouth. My body gets spun around and I land on my stomach, face down on the hardwood. I immediately see blood on the floor beneath me, and then comes the sharp pain in my shoulder and shooting down my left arm. I still hear Alannah's muffled screaming as my eyes bulge at the sight of the blood.

"What'd you think this was, a fucking game?" I hear Abram say behind me. "I figured you'd try to pull some shit like that.

Oh, but don't worry, I wasn't even trying to kill you. At least not until I make you watch me pull all the fingers off your little bitch's hands, and then put a bullet right between her eyes. After you watch that, then I'll kill you. Now turn over. Turn over!"

I wince as I have to use my shoulder to push myself off the floor and turn around. He's aiming the gun at Alannah again, and I feel helpless. If I move, he'll shoot me, but not to kill me. If I don't make a move, I'll have to watch him kill Alannah. One of those is worse than the other. I'd rather die trying to save her than watch her be killed right here in front of me. I've got to do something.

I look at Alannah as Abram turns to face her. She doesn't look at him, though, she looks at me. We lock eyes, and I can tell she's trying to communicate still, so I look down at her hand. She's still wiggling it, and the ropes are starting to give way. She keeps her eyes on me, and I know what's next. I raise myself off the floor some more so I can be ready.

All of a sudden, Alannah's right hand breaks free of the rope with one quick jerk. The second she has it free, she reaches up and grabs ahold of Abram's gun, and I jump into action. I hop to my feet and spring towards him. I hit the Russian with a linebacker style tackle that sends all three of us crashing to the floor in a heap, one on top of the other, while the gun goes skidding down the hallway. Abram quickly tries to go get it, but I hold him down and punch him in the face with everything I've got.

The pain of the bullet in my shoulder steals my strength, though, and the impact isn't as strong as I'd hoped. Abram recovers from the blow with ease, and quickly turns the tables with a punch of his own, knocking me off of him. Alannah struggles on the floor next to us as we wrestle, trying to keep the other away from the gun. I swing a right hook and it lands in Abram's ribcage, knocking him back, then I throw a left cross that hurts my shoulder, but it connects with Abram's temple and he collapses. In that moment, I remember I'm not totally unarmed.

I pull the knife from my pocket and jump on top of Abram, who uses both hands to try to keep me from stabbing him. I aim the knife at his throat and push down with everything I've got, but he's got a death grip on my wrist. We struggle for far too long, and my shoulder is getting weaker by the second, but I won't quit until he's dead. I keep pushing, but Abram's attention shifts to my shoulder, and he takes a hand off my wrist and plunges his finger into the bullet hole.

I let out a blood curdling scream as I succumb to the pain and my arm goes limp, releasing the knife. Abram punches me in the chin and tries to scramble to get up, but I gain my balance and grab him from behind. I wrap my arms around his neck and start to squeeze.

I dig my forearm into his throat and squeeze every muscle in my body. It hurts like hell, but I don't let go, even after he tries to dig his fingernails into my skin, I keep squeezing. His legs go kicking in every direction as his air supply is cut off, but I don't stop—not until he stops moving all together.

It only takes a few seconds, and then the kicking stops. Abram's arms go limp and drop to his sides, and in that exact moment, my muscles seem to reach complete failure and I have to let go. I push Abram off to the side, and fall backwards, completely exhausted.

I can hear Alannah struggling still, and trying to talk behind the tape, so I muster up some strength and pick myself up. I grab the knife off the floor and use it to cut the rest of the rope off of her and she pulls the tape off herself.

"Are you okay?" I ask.

She looks me in the eye and as tears start to stream down her cheeks.

"You're asking me if I'm okay, and you're the one who got

shot," she says as she rubs my face.

"I'll be fine as long as you're alright." I help her up off the floor, and we both look down at Abram, whose eyes are closed, but fluttering.

"He's not dead. He just passed out. We have to call the cops," Alannah says. She looks at me, wondering what I'm going to say. I can tell she knows what I'm thinking, and it sure as hell isn't to call the police.

"We can't do that," I say to her. Alannah freezes and stares at me blankly. "Alannah, I need you to listen to me. This motherfucker put a contract on my head that resulted in an innocent man being killed while he was out to dinner. You and I barely made it out of Isle of Capri alive. He also shot my good friend, Tommy Caprio, in the back and put him in the fucking hospital. Tommy's a made guy, too. And now, he's broken into your house, tied you to a chair, and shot me in the fucking shoulder. There's not a fucking chance in hell I'm gonna let this cock sucker walk outta here. It's fucking over for him."

Alannah keeps staring at me, and I know she's thinking about the difference between right and wrong right now, but I need her to understand the depths of this situation. I need it more than she realizes.

I hear her breathing starting to pick up as I walk over to where I dropped my jacket and my guns, and I pull the nine millimeter with the silencer out of the holster. I chamber a round and walk over to Abram. His chest rises and falls as he breathes, and his eyes are still fluttering with life, fighting their way back to consciousness as I stand over him. He doesn't even realize I hold his life in my hands right now. After all he's done, it's me who holds his life in my hands in the form of a nine millimeter pistol.

"Dominic, wait," Alannah says, almost screaming it. She's breathing hard, like she's about to hyperventilate. "I don't know how I feel about this."

"How do you not? He forced his way into your house and tied you up, Alannah. You think if we send him to jail, he's gonna just forget about it all? You think he doesn't have people on the outside who'd be willing to force their way in here too? It wasn't Abram who shot at us at Isle of Capri. It was some kid named Anthony who worked for him. He did it for five thousand dollars. That's all it took was him offering some poor kid five thousand dollars, and the next thing you know, there's bullets flying over our heads as we wait for our food. If we let him go, it'll never be over. We'll never be safe, and we can never go anywhere without looking over our shoulder. Not ever. So how do you feel about *that*?"

I can see the realization dawn on her. Her face tightens and her shoulders slump, because she knows it's true. We can't let him live.

Abram's eyes start to flutter more, and I know he's on the verge of waking up. We don't have much time left. Something has to be done, but I'm trying to be patient for Alannah.

"Alannah, I know this is hard for you," I continue. "But I gotta end this, and I gotta do it now."

"I know," she replies as a tear rolls down her cheek. "You're right. We'll never be safe if he lives, and after all he's done . . . he deserves it. I can't believe I just said that, but I know it's true. He was going to kill me. He was going to kill both of us . . . he deserves it."

Alannah looks me in the eye, her face blank and stiff, and she wipes a tear away. She glances down at Abram just as his eyes start to flicker open.

"Okay," she mutters, almost in a whisper, then she turns on her heel and walks away. I watch her make her way down the hall and turn into her bedroom, where she slowly closes the door behind her.

Abram comes to just as her door latches, and I aim the weapon at his torso. I let his eyes focus on me and the gun before I do anything. I want him to know what's about to happen. I want him to see it coming. So, I wait until it's as clear as day.

When he sees me, he looks afraid at first, but he pushes it away and tries to toughen up.

"You're not gonna do it," he says. "If you were gonna do it, you would've done it already, motherfucker. You need one of your goons to do it for you."

I let him finish, then I smile.

"You don't know me very well, and I'd hate for you to get the wrong impression, so it's important that I'm honest with you," I say, as I grin and tighten my grip on the pistol. "The truth is, Abram, you died the day we met. Now, we're just making it official."

I squeeze the trigger and smile at the sight of blood spurting out of his stomach. He tries to scream, but the pain is too much, so all he can do is inhale and try to clutch his belly. When he reaches for the wound, I pull the trigger again, sending another bullet through his hand. This time he does scream, and I don't want him to make Alannah too uncomfortable with all that noise, so I pull the trigger again. Another bullet tears into his body and finds a home in his lung, stealing his breath away. The pistol kicks one last time as I fire another round into Abram Baskov's forehead. Blood splatters across the hardwood and starts to pool underneath his body, just as his lungs release their last bit of air and life.

He's gone.

After another minute, I hear the bedroom door being opened, and Alannah walks back into the room. She looks down at Abram, but only for a second as she realizes it's actually over. I don't know what to expect from her, but to my surprise, she walks over and wraps her arms around my waist. I drop the gun on the floor and hold her close as she lays her head on my chest.

"Now what do we do?" she asks as she lays on me like she's trying to listen to my heartbeat.

"You don't have to do anything," I answer. "I'm gonna clean this up, and it's gonna be over. I just gotta make a phone call."

"Okay," is all she says as she goes to sit on the couch and I grab my cellphone.

I dial up Skinny Joe and Charlie first, then I call Frankie so I can tell him it's over. He doesn't say too much, but I can tell he's finally satisfied with something I've done. He even volunteers two of his guys from his crew to help Joe and Charlie get rid of Abram's body.

When they show up, I let them in so they can get to work. They bring in plastic and supplies to clean up the mess, while Alannah and I pack a bag for her so she can come stay with me at River City until she's ready to come back to the apartment. It might be a while, though. Seeing a dead man in your living room tends to have long-term effects.

We leave and let the guys take care of the mess, and once we're at River City, Alannah and I take an hour-long shower together after she works her nursing magic on my gunshot wound. The bullet went through and through, so she cleaned up the wound and bandaged me up real nice. We don't say much after that, and I can see she's trying to wash the image of Abram's lifeless body out of her memory. I understand it may take a while, and I'll be here to support her if she needs me. The same way she wanted to be there for me when my father died. I'll be whatever she needs me to be.

Once we're clean, we lay in my bed and hold each other. I don't need her to say anything. The fact that she accepted what had to be done says enough for me. It takes a special kind of woman to accept a man like me, and to accept the things I have to do in my "line of work". Alannah is no ordinary woman. She's special, and she's mine.

I never needed another reason to love and trust Alannah, but she gave me a million more reasons tonight. The bond we share is unbreakable now.

We're in this.

Together.

THIRTY-TWO

Dominic

ALANNAH NEVER MENTIONS ABRAM. SHE never asks what the guys did with his body, or how they did such a great job cleaning up the mess in her living room. She never asks me how I feel about it, and I never ask her. It's over, and everything goes back to normal. At this point, she probably doesn't even believe there's such a thing as normal for me, and that's fine, because the most important thing is that she has accepted it. So, as I drive her to Mercy Hospital after two days of privacy and separation from the rest of the world, I find comfort in her comfort. She's able to believe she can relax and let her guard down now. We have a real shot at happiness now that the drama is over. At least, that's how she sees it.

I know better.

There's always drama in Our Thing. I haven't gone back to the hospital to see Tommy yet, because I didn't want to risk seeing Frankie and starting up a whole new dramatic scene for the people in the waiting area. I do know, however, that Tommy made it out of surgery just fine. The docs at Mercy did a great job removing the bullets from his back, and he woke up from surgery yesterday. He'll be in the hospital for a few more days, so I plan to go see him since I'm taking Alannah to Mercy anyway. I don't know if Frankie is going to be there or not, but Tommy's my guy, and I've got to go see him. So, I'm just hoping everything stays as cool as Alannah believes it is.

"You nervous?" Alannah asks as I park my BMW. She looks

better now, if that's possible. Her face doesn't carry as much stress as it did when the Abram thing was going on. Even with her hair in a bun and the purple scrubs, my Alannah is untouchable. She's perfection.

"Umm, no, not really," I reply, although I'm not sure if I'm telling the truth or not. "I don't have a reason to be nervous, I guess. I'm just glad I can tell him the guy who shot him is gone for good."

"Yeah, that'll be good for him to hear, and it'll be good for you guys to talk. I'm sure he wants to see you."

"Yeah, I'm sure."

As we walk inside, I'm not sure what the hell Tommy might be thinking. The guys in my crew know I killed Abram, and I'm sure they told Tommy, but this shit with Frankie makes things a little murkier. When there's a beef with the boss—or the acting boss, in this case—The Family always chooses the side of the boss. So, if you're on the other side of that, the people you trust most could be the ones to put a bullet in the back of your head. That's the life we live in La Cosa Nostra. It doesn't make sense to anybody but us, but it's our way of life. We love each other, and we hope to make money together, but we kill each other.

Alannah and I walk into the hospital together, but I make sure no one sees us holding hands. After what we just went through with Abram, I don't need anybody else seeing us and thinking they can use her as leverage against me. What I love about Alannah is that when I told her public displays of affection might be a bad idea, she didn't snap at me about it. She understood. I guess being tied to a chair because someone saw us together is enough to convince anybody.

I walk Alannah to the nurse's station, and I tell her goodbye and that I'll see her when she gets off. We kissed in the car, so we don't do it here. In fact, we barely look at each other as I walk away. Better safe than sorry.

I walk down the hall with my hands in the pockets of my black suit, looking far ahead at the end of the hall to see if I can see anyone from The Family. Skinny Joe told me what room Tommy was in, so when I get close to it, I'm surprised I don't see anyone around. I told Skinny I was going to be here around this time, so I'm a little confused as to why no one else is here, not even Skinny Joe or Charlie. Tommy's room is completely unguarded, which I guess is because Abram's dead now, so they figure the threat's gone. I guess that makes sense; but why isn't anybody else with Tommy?

I make it to the room and glance inside to see him. He looks normal, honestly. There aren't any tubes sticking out of his mouth, and there's no machine breathing for him, and he's not surrounded by doctors with clipboards and stethoscopes. That's all good, because it means he's doing okay. He's out of the woods and just waiting for time to pass so he can recover, so I feel good when I walk in to find his eyes open and a smile on his face.

"Look what the fucking cat drug in," he says, grinning from ear to ear. "How you doing, Dominic?"

"I'm fine, man, but I ain't worried about me, I'm worried about you," I reply as I lean over to give him a hug, making sure not to handle him too roughly. "How you feeling, *paisan*?"

"Well, aside from the two holes in my fucking back, I'm doing alright. I'm ready to get the fuck outta here, I tell you that much. I heard you caught up to that Abram motherfucker."

I pull a chair from the corner of the room and take a seat next to Tommy's bed with a smile pulling at my lips.

"Fucking right," I reply. "It was crazy how it happened, but it happened. He's gone."

Tommy's face doesn't seem as happy as I expected it to be. I figured the other guys would tell him about Abram's demise, but I expected him to seem more grateful. His face goes blank as he looks at me, then it shifts to something else entirely. He seems pissed, and I'm confused.

"What's the matter, Tommy?" I ask, never the one to wait for an explanation for something like this.

"Why'd you kill him, Dominic?" Tommy asks. He looks me in the eye and doesn't look away.

"What do you mean?"

"You know what I mean. Why'd you kill Abram?"

"I killed him for a lot of reasons, Tommy," I try to explain, as the realization that I'm unsure of the answer dawns on me.

"Where'd you kill him?" Tommy asks, and I know where this is going now.

"At Alannah's house."

"Right, so did you kill him because he shot me, or because he shot at you, or because he threatened your girl?

I want to answer, but I'm not sure of what the truth is, so the words never come out.

"Frankie seems to think the only reason you killed Abram, is because he went over your girl's house and tied her up. He thinks it had nothing to do with avenging me."

"Fuck that," I interrupt. "I don't know what Frankie's deal is with Alannah, man. He never liked that I was spending time with her, even though you have a fiancé, and every capo has a wife, including him. I don't understand why he's so bothered by me seeing her, but it doesn't even matter, Tommy. You and I both know I wanted Abram dead before I started spending time with Alannah."

"Do I know that?" he chimes in. "As far as I can remember, you saw Alannah right after we left the sit down with Abram. It was on the same day."

"Oh come on, Tommy. I sent you to go see Alex before I went on my first date with Alannah. Remember that? You know that's the truth, so don't let whatever Frankie's saying get in your head. You know me, Tommy. I've always been all about The Family, and my relationship with Alannah has never affected that, and it won't. I've known her since I was eleven, and I know I can trust her. So, there's no need for all this drama. No matter how you look at it, Abram's dead, and if we want to make a move to acquire Lumiere Place, we still can. This is a fucking win for us, so that's all I'm focused on, and when you get back on your feet, it's gonna be business as usual with us."

Tommy knows me and I know him, so I can tell from the look on his face that he knows I'm telling the truth. The situation with Abram would've happened whether Alannah was in St. Louis or not. Her presence here only made things harder once Abram saw he could use her against me.

Tommy starts to nod his head, and his face finally starts to go back to the smile he had when I came in earlier.

"You're right about that," he says, still nodding. "You told me to set up the Alex thing before you went out with her. That's true, but I'm telling you Dominic, Frankie wasn't too happy about whatever conversation the two of you had the night I got shot."

"I know, but you had *just got shot*. Tension and emotions were high that night, and shit got a little heated. I tried to apologize to him, but he wasn't trying to hear it. In all honestly, he should be happy. He was on my ass about Abram still being alive, and I killed him that same night, so he should be good."

"Well, he didn't seem too good, according to Joe and Charlie. You might've pissed him off, so maybe it's a good idea for you to go see him and fix it. You know Frankie's got that temper, and the last thing I wanna see is you getting clipped over some dumb shit that worked itself out anyway."

"Yeah, maybe you're right," I admit. "I should probably do it before he thinks I'm plotting against him or some shit, and definitely before they up him to boss officially."

"Oh, speaking of the boss," Tommy says, changing the subject. "Did you hear about Leo?"

"Nah, what about him?"

"He's out on bail."

"Oh yeah? When did this happen?"

"Yesterday, while you were snuggled up with your girl. It probably won't be for long because they're gonna go to trial real soon, but he's out for now. He's not supposed to have any communication with any known criminals, but you know Leo."

"Yes, I do," I say behind a chuckle.

"So, there's a chance the decision about . . ." Tommy starts, but he's cut off by the sound of someone entering the room behind me.

I turn around to see Big Sal Bagano and John Salvatore walking into the room. They both look pissed off in their black suits, and when they come in, they don't say anything to Tommy at all. They just look at me like my presence here offends them.

"Hey there," I say to them both. "Why the long faces, fellas?

Sal and John both glare at me in a way that would kill me if it were possible.

"What the fuck, guys. You ain't got nothing to say?" Tommy asks from his bed.

"We need you to come with us, Dominic," Sal says in response.

"What? Why would I need to go with you? I just got here." I can feel my body starting to heat up by the second as my nerves kick in.

"You've been sent for," Sal explains, and I feel my lungs freeze. I can barely breathe as the words repeat in my head.

I've been sent for.

In Our Thing, being sent for means somebody above you wants to see you, right now. So, you drop whatever it is you're doing, and you take a ride with whoever was sent to come get you. In Our Thing, that ride could very well end up being your last ride. A lot of guys have pissed off the boss, or their captain, and got sent for so they could be killed immediately. All it would take is the okay from The Commission if the guy being killed is a made guy. So, if you piss off the acting boss, and he asks The Commission if it's okay to clip you, and they give the go ahead . . . need I say more?

I turn around to look at Tommy, and I can see the fear in his eyes. He knows I made Frankie mad, and we all know you don't want to make Frankie mad. But is Frankie willing to go this far over a woman he doesn't even really know? Frankie never met Alannah all those years ago, so the only thing he knows about her is that I used to talk about her all the time when I was a kid. So, why would he be willing to clip me just because she's back and we're trying to be together again? It can't be that fucking serious. Right?

"You know you gotta come with us, Dominic," Big Sal persists.

"Wow. After all these years we've known each other," I say to Sal, but he's unmoving. He just looks at me with a "it's just business" look on his face. "Alright, well at least let me go say bye to Alannah."

"We can't do that," John Salvatore speaks up.

"You just gotta come with us, Dominic, and we gotta go now," Sal says.

I look at Tommy one last time before pushing myself out of the chair. I take a deep breath and blow it out, then I walk out of the room.

Big Sal and John walk behind me, making sure I don't try to run as they escort me out of the hospital. We walk across the street where Sal's car is waiting, and they make me sit up front for the ride, with John sitting behind me. None of us speak a word as Sal cruises down the highway towards the heart of the city. I can tell we're headed for The Lodge, but what I don't know is whether I'll live to see the outside of it once they take me in. I don't know if this is my last car ride, or if I'll ever see Alannah again. If this means what I think it means, there's a chance Alannah may never know what happened to me. They may never find my body at all, and she'll be haunted for the rest of her life, wondering why I disappeared.

This is the life we live in Our Thing. Piss off the wrong guy, you get clipped. It's something I've learned to accept, even though it's fucked up. But that's not the worst part of it. The worst part is knowing my life will end before I ever got the chance to live it with her.

THIRTY-THREE

Dominic

"ALRIGHT, LET'S GO."

Big Sal has to remind me that we've arrived and it's time to get out of his car. I sit there in the passenger seat, my breathing heavy and my nerves on high alert, feeling frozen. I can't move. I don't want to move. I'm not ready for whatever is waiting for me behind those doors. John has to open my door for me from the outside, and even then, I'm not still not ready.

Again, they walk behind me like guards escorting a prisoner, and with each step, I ask myself what I'm going to do when we get in there and I see Frankie waiting for me. Am I supposed to just lay down and let him put a bullet in my head? Do I not fight back out of respect of La Cosa Nostra and his title as acting boss? How can I possibly continue respecting This Thing of Ours if Leo and The Commission gave the okay for me to be clipped over my feelings for a woman who hasn't broken any of our rules? The questions are many and the answers are few, and my heart can barely take it all. But when we push through the doors, it's not just Frankie I see.

Inside, The Lodge is filled with every made member of the Giordano family. Every made member of Big Sal's crew is seated on one side of the long glass table, every member of John Salvatore's crew on the other. I even recognize the two made guys from Frankie's crew at the back of the table, and seated in the middle of them, is Frankie Leonetti himself. He has the meanest face out of every man in this room, and when he sees me, he doesn't even acknowledge that I've arrived. He doesn't do or say anything.

John takes a seat with his crew, while Sal leads me to a seat closer to the head of the table. His crew greets me with smiles and open arms as I go to take my seat, and I feel even more questions being born in my head and crying for attention. Why the hell is everyone here? Why didn't Frankie acknowledge me? And if he sent for me, why isn't he saying or doing anything? What. The. Fuck.

I sit down and look around the room at the made members of The Family. Some of these men are absolute killers who wouldn't hesitate to put a knife in your throat if you rubbed them the wrong way, but I've known these guys since I was a kid.

Jim Costello is the top solider of Frankie's crew, and I re- member meeting him when I was just thirteen. He latched on to the Boy Wonder bandwagon after he watched me hold up an ice cream truck at gunpoint, and he always told me I was going to be a big deal in this family.

Then there's Raphael Barissi, the youngest made guy in Big Sal's crew. He was the first guy who was made after me, and we've been good friends a long time. We used to hang out a lot when Alannah left, getting into all kinds of trouble, putting our names on the map at the same time. We used to call him Raphy for short, because nearly everybody in The Family has some sort of nickname. Raphy's only problem was that his fa- ther became a rat back when the FBI was all over The Family's ass, and he got a lot of the old heads sent away for a long time. So, even though Raphy was a good kid and a decent earner, his father's legacy always kind of stuck with him, like a ball and chain attached to his ankle.

These are guys I haven't seen in a while, and it's good to see all of them in the same room again, but it's also rare. Usually, it's only the captains who come together like this, and it's because Leo only deals with the highest members of The Family, and it's our job to pass down the information to our respective crews. That's the way the hierarchy of Our Thing works. We don't get to hang out much, because it's safer for us if we're apart, but I'd go to war for the guys in this room, and regardless of what went on between me and Frankie, I think they'd go to war for me. Which brings me back to my original question; why the hell is everyone here?

"Sal," I lean over and whisper. "What the fuck is going on? Why is everybody here, and why isn't Frankie saying anything to me if he sent for me?"

Sal scrunches his big forehead in confusion.

"It wasn't Frankie who sent for you, Dominic," he says. "It was Leo." As soon as the words leave his mouth, our boss, Leo Capizzi, and our underboss, Jimmy Gravato, walk through the door.

He was pinched only a few days ago, but it looks like Leo's been away for a year or two already. His hair looks grayer, and his eyes look baggier. His confidence is gone, and I understand. Charges like the ones he's facing are enough to stress anybody out, even someone as strong as Leo. He's still my boss, though. He's my father's boss, and my level for respect for him is through the roof. The same can be said about everybody in this room. Everybody loves Leo. He's always done what he thought was best for The Family, and we've thrived because of it. When the Feds and St. Louis PD torched The Family a few years back, it was Leo who survived it and brought us back to life. Our loyalty to him is unbreakable.

Leo comes in and sits down in the head seat, and Jimmy stands behind him with his arms folded. He looks around the room at everyone, taking in all of our faces as the voices die down so we can hear what he has to say. Once again, I'm on the edge of my seat in anticipation, because so far, this isn't going anything like I expected it to. I'm still alive.

"It's good to see you all here," he begins in his low, raspy, Godfather-style voice. "We don't do this often, and I'm saddened by the fact that this will be the last time I see you all together like this. As you know, we're only here because we're out on bail, and it won't last long because the trial is set to start in two weeks. They pushed for the trial to start faster than usual because they wanna see me go down, and they want to be able to put my former consigliere, Danny Ramano, on the stand before something bad happens to him and they lose their case. So, this is going to be the end of my era as boss of this family. However, with the end of one era, comes the beginning of a new one."

There it is. The lightbulb in my head finally clicks on, and I realize why we're here. Leo is about to push for Frankie to be the new boss, and we're all here to show our support and pledge our allegiance to him. The Family is about to change forever.

"So, I won't waste time or beat around the bush with this," Leo continues. "I've spoken to The Commission, and they've given me their two cents on who they think has done enough for The Family and been a steady earner. They told me what they thought, and I informed them of who I thought was respected enough in this family to take control and start a new era. We all agreed, and we're here now to make sure we won't have any internal feuds or plays for power in the future. We've seen too many families in Our Thing destroyed because of that type of greed, so we want the support of all of you. Does everybody understand what I'm saying?"

We nod along, and I'm wondering why we're dragging this out. We all know what's coming next.

Leo clears his throat and continues.

"So, after a lot of thinking and phone calls to New York, I've come to a decision, and I want to put my weight behind who I think should be the new boss of the Giordano family . . . Dominic Collazo."

The air rushes out of the room. My eyes bulge and stop blinking until they start to dry out. My stomach heats up and explodes into a butterfly-filled zoo, and I immediately feel nauseous.

Did he just say Dominic Collazo?

Everyone in the room turns to look at me, and I have no idea what I'm supposed to do now. I know Leo is getting up there in age, but did he forget Frankie's name? Is the old man coming down with Alzheimer's?

I look around the room and to my surprise, no one looks shocked. Big Sal and John nod along like this is a great idea, and even Frankie nods his head like the person who was nominated for an Oscar but didn't win. It's like I'm sitting in an alternate universe where everyone is insane, but totally fine with it.

"So, before anything else is said," Leo continues, driving his point home, "I want you to know how we reached this decision. You all know Dominic has been around Our Thing his whole life. The Family is all he knows, and he's been an earner for this family since he was eleven. His father, Donnie, God bless his soul, taught him everything, and you all know Donnie was one of our best guys. We chose Dominic because he'll be around for the long haul, and he doesn't rely on seniority. He relies only on the fact that he knows what he's doing. I think Dominic's era can last longer than mine did, and even though he's young, I know he's ready to lead this family.

"So, I want to know, right now, who agrees with this decision. I want to see a show of hands in support of Dominic as the new boss of The Family."

I'm scared to look, because I know *someone* has to be against this. But I look around, and one by one, the hands start reaching for the ceiling. It starts with Big Sal, who raises his hand and smiles like a proud father, and it spreads down the table like a virus. Every single one of them raises their hand, and when the line reaches Frankie, he does something I never expected. He smiles at me, and nods his head as he raises his hand. There isn't an ounce of anger or resentment in his eyes. Just like Sal, he looks proud of me. Once Frankie's hand goes up, I know it's official. I don't know if it's because everyone is so loyal to Leo that they'd go along with anything he suggests, or if this is a legit acknowledgement from the entire Family, but it's happening.

I'm the boss of The Family.

"Alright then," Leo says as he looks at me and smiles from ear to ear. He stands up, and everyone in the room stands with him. "It's settled. Dominic, do you accept this responsibility?"

My smile in uncontrollable.

"Yes, Leo, I do accept it."

"Do you pledge to think of The Family before anything else?"

My heart could explode.

"Yes, I do."

"It's your responsibility to keep this family on the path to prosperity," Leo advises as he puts his hands on my shoulders. "Don't let your age hold you back. Think big, and go with your gut in all things. We didn't come to this decision lightly. We trust you, and we can't wait to see how you carry the torch."

My father would be so proud.

"Thank you, Leo. Thank you, Jimmy." I hug both of them, and it has never felt this good to be me. I have everything I've ever wanted now.

"Now, as for the rest of you," Leo says, addressing the rest of The Family. "Today is a new day. From now on, I am no longer the boss of this family, but I expect all of you to pledge your loyalty to your new boss. Let us all agree, any mutiny or disobedience will be punishable by death, as supported by The Commission and every made member of this family. *Salute*."

Every member in the room repeats, *Salute*, and it becomes official.

I stand behind the head seat at the table as each member approaches, one by one, and gives me a hug and pat on the back. I hug them all, and I can feel the love and respect emanating off of them. When Frankie approaches, it's no different.

"I'm proud of you, kid," he says in my ear. "I really mean that. I'm sorry I gave you so much shit about the Russian. You did what you had to do, and you earned this. Your old man would be so fucking proud of you, too. The youngest boss in our history. Fucking Boy Wonder," he says with a smile as he hugs me again.

The old nickname usually strikes a nerve and sends me on a tear, but the look in his eye when he says it makes it alright. He never mentions the beef we had in the hospital, and it looks like I was worried for nothing. We embrace and pat each other on the back, and in that moment, I know it's real. He's genuinely happy for me, and I'm thankful I have him around, because he's the closest thing I have to my dad. So, I let go of the bullshit.

I have the whole family in my corner, and the woman of my dreams by my side. All the craziness I've been through all seems worth it now. I'll never forget the day my dad was killed in the seat right next to me, but I know if he could see me now, his smile would be even wider than mine. I think even my mother would be proud of this moment. So, I pull out a Cuban cigar and light it up with a huge smile on my face.

It usually doesn't happen for guys like me. It's rare for anybody to actually get all the things in life they really want, but it has happened for me. I have everything now, and nothing can stand in my way. I'm on top of the world. I'm the fucking kingpin.

You better remember it forever. I'm Dominic Collazo.

THIRTY-FOUR

Alannah

"WHAT TOOK YOU SO LONG? I was starting to worry," I snip as Dominic steps over the threshold with a smile on his gorgeous face.

I haven't seen him since yesterday when he dropped me off at work, and I had to get a ride home from a coworker because he was too busy to get me. After all we just went through, I worry easily. I hate to be the clingy girlfriend, but I was just tied to a chair a few days ago, so I need to be in the loop all the time.

Dominic doesn't answer my question. Instead, he keeps on smiling like the Cheshire cat and comes to give me a kiss before taking off his jacket and hanging it on the coat rack by the front door. The apartment is mostly furnished now, so it feels a little more like home. All I have to do now is forget all about the night I was tied up and Dominic was shot in the shoulder, and I'll be good to go.

"Are you going to answer me, or what?" I say as he keeps on smiling. He sits down on the couch across from me and leans back, but that smile doesn't leave his face. "What are you grinning at? What's the matter with you?"

"I've got something to tell you," he says. He spreads his arms over the back of the couch, making himself good and comfortable.

"Okay. Should I be worried?" I inquire.

He smiles more, even as he starts to answer.

"No. No, you don't ever have to worry again, Alannah," he says.

"Alright," I say, dragging out the word. "Are you okay? Your face is weird."

We both laugh a little, but Dominic's laugh is different, I just can't tell why.

"I'm fine. I'm better than fine," he continues. "Listen, what if I told you that I could guarantee that the shit that happened with that psychopath, Abram, will never happen again?"

I think about it for a moment, squinting.

"Okay, keep talking."

"What if I told you that it was within my power to make sure that my business is completely legit from here on out? What if I told you that nobody would ever dare mess with us again? What if I could guarantee it?"

I can't stop squinting now.

"Well, that would be awesome, I guess," I say, too confused to say anything with certainty. "Dominic, what's all this about? It'd be nice if you could guarantee that, but let's be honest, the stuff your *family* is involved in kind of breeds violence. It's a part of the mafia history that'll probably never go away."

"Well, what if I can make it go away?"

"How could you possibly make it go away?"

"Because I'm in control now."

I pause, staring at him, hoping my face shows just how vexed I really am.

"Alannah, I'm in control of the entire family now," he says, the smile involuntarily returning. "They made me the boss."

My body freezes in its place. I don't really know what to make of the announcement, so I just sit there, staring off into space, barely blinking. I'm not sure if I'm breathing or not. I'm just sitting here.

"Alannah," Dominic says. "This is a good thing."

"So, what you're trying to tell me is you're a *mob boss* now?"

I inquire. I can't even believe the words that just came out of my mouth.

Mob boss?

Dominic exhales loudly, then he rocks my world. "Yes, I am."

"Umm, what am I supposed to say to that?" I ask, as nervous butterflies come to life in my stomach. "I was worried enough when you told me you were a made member, which Wikipedia says is a big freaking deal, by the way. Now, you're telling me you're the *boss* of the Giordano crime family? Am I not supposed to be fucking terrified, Dominic? Because I am."

"Wait, wait," Dominic pleads as he stands up and approaches me. "That's what I'm trying to tell you, Alannah. You don't have to be afraid for me. I run everything, and if anybody fucks with you, it's fucking with me, and fucking with me means war with the entire family. Nobody wants that. So, you don't have to worry about anything."

"Dominic, this is fucking insane. If there's one thing I learned when I was in Alaska and looking up mafia shit, it's that the boss always gets killed."

"Alannah, this isn't the nineties, okay? Internal beef doesn't happen anymore, and when Leo passed the torch to me yesterday, everybody in The Family pledged their loyalty to me. *Everybody.* In Our Thing, that's a big deal. Loyalty means a lot to us. I'm the boss, and no one's changing that. I made Tommy my underboss, and Frankie's my consigliere. We're a unified front that nobody would ever want to fuck with. You have to trust me, Alannah. I've never lied to you, have I?"

I don't even have to think about the answer, because I know Dominic has always told me the truth.

"No, you haven't," I whisper.

"Exactly. So, I need you to trust me. I know it's scary, and I know you didn't exactly expect this when you decided to come back here, but this is all I know. This Thing of Ours is all I've ever known, and I know how to do this. You don't have to worry about me getting hurt, and you can rest assured that no one will ever hurt you. I'll *never* let that happen. The days of elementary and high school are over. We're grown up now, and we can have anything we want, because I'm the most powerful man in the whole fucking city."

I fight off a smile as Dominic leans in and kisses me on the neck.

"The most powerful man in the city?" I ask. Something about the way it sounds sends an excited chill down my spine. It's that bad boy persona no woman can resist, even when we probably should. There's something undeniable about a man who looks this good and has this much power. It's almost unfair. How's a girl supposed to resist?

Dominic smiles as he kisses my neck again.

"That's right. The most powerful man in the city," he says as I turn and kiss his cheek. "And the fucking richest, too."

He kisses me on the lips and I can feel myself giving in to him. By body temperature is climbing and I feel a new sense of adventure wash over me. This man has a spell on me.

I watch him as he stands and walks over to the front door. He steps outside, and after a minute or two, he comes back and makes sure to lock the door behind him. I notice he's holding a black duffel bag, and that Cheshire smile has returned.

"What's that?" I ask.

"I gotta show you something," he replies as he starts walking down the hall towards the bedroom. "Follow me."

I get up and follow him into my room. Once we're inside, Dominic closes the door as if there's somebody else in the house and he wants privacy. He unzips the bag, and turns it upside down over the bed. Countless stacks of money come pouring out and scatter across my floral-patterned comforter.

It's more money than I've ever seen at one time, and the sight of it takes my breath away. I'm filled with two emotions that are starting to become all too common: excitement and fear. I know eventually one of them will win the battle between the two, and I'm either going to settle into this, or run for my life. Right now, however, the combination of the two mixes into a heightened sense of arousal. It's all so new to me. The money, the power, the love—all of it is addicting, and I feel like I'm becoming strung out. Something in the back of my mind screams for me to quit, but I can't.

Even when I know I should be saying *no*, and running away, I think there's something in me that likes it. All of it: the excitement, the love, the fear. I like it all. I want it all. I don't know what I have inside of me that makes me feel this way, but whatever it is, I like that too.

"What is all this, Dominic?" I ask, doing my best to fight back a smile.

"Every member of The Family has to kick up to the boss every month," he says, looking down at the stacks of cash. "This is their first payment to me."

"So, they're paying you just for being the boss?"

"That's right. Perks of being the boss, babe.

"How much is it?"

"I don't know. I don't even care. This is why I can go legit and keep heat off of me. I'm gonna drop all of my rackets off to other guys in The Family, and everything with my name on it will be legal now. I run the casinos and rake in what The Family kicks up to me every month. There won't be any heat from St. Louis PD or the FBI, because I won't be attached to anything illegal. I'm untouchable."

"This is fucking crazy, Dominic," I say again, because it's all I keep thinking.

"Yeah, it is," he agrees as he wraps his arms around my waist from behind, and nuzzles my neck. "You know what else is crazy? Me . . . about you."

"Aww, look at you being incredibly corny for me. How

sweet."

"I know it's corny, but it's true," he says into my ear. I feel the warmth of his mouth on my skin and I become weak in the knees for him. "I've loved you since I was eleven years old, and nothing comes before you, Alannah. Nothing. And now that I've been put in this position, nothing can stand in our way. You and me are gonna rule this fucking city. Because I'm the kingpin, and you're my queen."

He kisses me on the neck again, and I let my head fall backwards to give him more room to work. He licks my skin and heat spreads throughout my body, warming me up in all the right places.

Dominic pushes me forward and I fall onto the stacks of money as he starts to pull down my pants. I feel hot in a way I've never felt before as I hear him undoing his pants and ripping open a condom wrapper. I bend over and give him access to all of me, as I lay my face on top of the money and breathe it all in. It's like a scene from a gangster movie, as Dominic slides himself inside of me and fucks me on top of the stacks of cash. He thrusts hard and deep, like he's been waiting all day to do it—like his newfound power has given him the hardest, most sensitive erection of his life, and he can't hold back any longer.

I let him do it, because I love it. I love feeling his skin slam against mine, and I love his sweat dripping onto my back as I lay on top of the money. I grab it and squeeze as the orgasm hits me like a freight train, and I smile as Dominic flips me over and continues giving me everything I need, right here on top of more money than I care to count.

I know it's dangerous, I know some would say it's wrong. They may even say I'm stupid for staying with him. People may judge me and tell me how bad of an idea this is. Those people don't understand, and I don't need their approval.

I've known Dominic since I was eleven—that's fourteen

years of my life, and there's no erasing that. Like I said before, when it comes to Dominic, the rules change. So, everyone can save their judgements.

I didn't have a choice when I was fifteen. I had to move to Alaska because I was a minor, and it broke my heart into pieces that were never put back together until I came back. I have a choice whether to stay or go this time. And I choose Dominic.

He's the kingpin, and I'm his queen.

We're in this.

Together.

EPILOGUE

"OUT OF ALL THE PEOPLE in the world, the last person I expected to hear from is you."

"Well, it took me a while to come to this decision, so I guess I surprised myself, too."

"Alright, well, I'm here. In private, like you asked. So, what's this about?"

"It's about Dominic."

"Well, I figured. Why else would you be talking to me?"

"Look, I think we both know that what just happened with The Family isn't the best idea. I think he might be in a little over his head."

"Maybe he is, but what the fuck is the point? He's the boss now, so everybody in The Family has to just suck it up and accept it. There's nothing anybody can do about it now."

"Why not?"

"What do you mean, why not?"

"Why can't anybody do anything about it?"

"Because that's not the way it's supposed to work anymore. This ain't the nineties where John Gotti kills Paul Castellano to take his position as boss. It's 2016, and things are done differently. So, as much as we may not like it, and as much damage as it might cause, we have to deal with it."

"I don't want to just deal with it. Look, I don't want to see Dominic in this position because I don't want to see him hurt."

"What the fuck are you talking about? He's the most powerful, protected man in St. Louis. Nobody would dare lay a finger on him now."

"They would if he starts to ruin things. They would if he starts changing traditions put in place by The Commission. I bet they wouldn't be happy about that, and you know how it would go if he did something that rubbed them the wrong way."

"You say that like you already got some information about his plans as boss. Do you?"

"No, I just have a hunch. Look, I love Dominic, and my loyalty to him is unbreakable. I just don't want him to be the boss of The Family, and I know you can help me come up with a way to change things."

"Wow. I didn't expect this from you. It'd break his heart into a million fucking pieces if he knew you were doing this."

"It's for his own good."

"Alright, you called me because you thought I'd help you with this. But like I said, we don't put a hit out on our own bosses."

"Jesus Christ, is that what you think this is about? I don't want him dead, I just don't want him to be the boss. I'd never try to have him killed. I just said I loved him, didn't I?"

"Okay then, what are you suggesting?"

"I don't know. That's why I called you."

"Well, I don't know either. He's only been the boss for a couple of weeks. If anything suspicious happens now, it'll be bad for everybody. It's too soon."

"Okay, so we wait."

"Yeah. Whatever we come up with will have to wait. If you really want him removed from power, it's gonna take some time. It'll have to be a slow process over a stretch of time. And we'll have to be careful, because like I said, if he finds out we're doing this, it'll destroy him. Especially with you being involved. Who knows what the fuck he might do?"

"Yeah. I know."

"Don't look so sad. If you're patient, you're gonna get exactly what you want. I'll take some time to think on this, and we can meet up again in later. For now, just relax, alright? It's gonna take some time and some patience, but we'll figure something out."

ACKNOWLEDGEMENTS

THERE'S SO MANY REASON WHY this book is special to me. I feel like the road to *Kingpin* was very long, and it had a lot of bumps and potholes to get over and maneuver around for me to make it to my destination. I've been trying to get to this place for a long time, and I kept getting lost along the way. It's so easy to get distracted and sidetracked in this game. It's easy to get pulled away from what you want to do when you're doing something different from what's popular, and I've fallen victim to this . . . well, five times before this. I didn't want to get pulled away from the story I wanted to tell this time, becasue Dominic Collazo is too awesome to be watered-down.

Kingpin is my seventh novel, and those who know me best know my favorite number is seven, so I had to make this one special. I wanted a story that would have a subject that I love, with characters I'd want to read about. So, when I decided that book number seven was going to be one hundred percent WS Greer, three things popped into my head: Dominic, Alannah, and the title. Dominic and Alannah's story had to start in the fifth grade so their love could be indestructible by the time they were in their twenties, and no other title could fit this novel. Even when I found out some news that made me change a character name and almost made me change the title, I decided I wasn't going to give in this time. This was my seventh book, and I absolutely had to write everything exactly the way I wanted to write it. And with just those three things in mind—Dominic, Alannah, and the title—I knew I couldn't go wrong.

I also took the time to think about my fans who've been my fans since the beginning. I thought all the way back to *Frozen*

Secrets, and I realized that fans of *Frozen Secrets* are probably pissed because after I wrote that book, I never went back to that genre. *Kingpin* is my first full-on romantic suspense since *Frozen Secrets*. It took me six books to get back to doing this the way I wanted to when I first started, but now that I'm back on track, I feel more confident and comfortable than ever. I can't go wrong now. Everything is the way it's supposed to be, and I know it's true because *Kingpin* is not only my best book, it's also my favorite of the seven I've published. That's a big deal, because my first book had always been my favorite until now. I finally beat it!

So, on to the acknowledging, huh?

There isn't anyone I'd thank before I'd thank my wife. So, give me a minute while I speak directly to her . . .

Baby, thank you so much for sticking by me through this long process. I'm seven books into this thing now and I know I've nagged and complained, and I've said one thing and done another, but you've had my back. You've supported me and let me work all this shit out, and you've helped to guide me as well. We've been partners in this from day one, and there isn't a hair on my body that would want to do it without you. Thank you for always being there for me when the going got tough, and thank you for putting me back on the right path when I felt like I was getting pulled off of it again. Dominic ends this novel with the same mentality he had when it started because you made sure of it, and I'm very thankful for that. Dominic and I thank you! I love you, baby!

I'd also like to thank my mother for being there during the writing process for this book as well. Your excitement is always telling when you're reading something of mine, and it lets me know I'm doing the right thing with these characters. Thank you for your support.

A huge thank you to my brother and his family, and to my father for his support as well. Thank you to all my family in E. St. Louis who've been in my corner, showing me love and support since I started writing. I love and miss you all!

I'd also like to thank my closest friends who I told about this book when I first started writing it. I made a point to tell guys about this book, because I wanted to see if I could write something that would draw men in, and when I saw your faces light up, I knew I had it. Every time one of you said, "That sounds like something I'd read," knowing good and damn-well you're not a reader, it motivated me to keep going. This book is exactly what I wanted it to be, and I have all of you to thank for helping to bring it to fruition.

Lastly, to the fans of *Frozen Secrets* . . .

I'm sorry I switched gears on you for a while. Admittedly, I got pulled into the popular thing, and I jumped on bandwagons when I knew I hated it. I compromised what I wanted to write for what I thought everybody else wanted to read. That's always a bad idea. I'm sorry it took me so long to figure it out, and I'm sorry I left you hanging, wondering if I'd ever write the genre that made you like me in the first place. Well, I got it all figured out, and I'm back now!

Kingpin is only the beginning. I feel like it's my debut novel all over again, and I'm excited as hell to build my empire off of this. I'm back, and I'm here to stay!

Book Mode!

MORE FROM WS GREER

THANK YOU FOR PURCHASING KINGPIN (An Italian Mafia Romance). Please consider leaving an honest review wherever you purchased your copy. It'd be very much appreciated!

Check out these other titles from WS Greer

Frozen Secrets (A Detective Granger Novel)
Claiming Carter (The Carter Trilogy #1)
Becoming Carter (The Carter Trilogy #2)
Destroying Carter (The Carter Trilogy #3)
Defending Her
Worth Saving

Want more from WS? Follow him everywhere!

www.facebook.com/AuthorWSGreer
www.facebook.com/authorws.greer.5
www.wsgreer.wordpress.com/
www.goodreads.com/author/show/7044361.W_S_Greer
www.twitter.com/AuthorWSGreer

ABOUT THE AUTHOR

WS GREER IS A BESTSELLING romantic suspense author, and an active duty military member with the US Air Force. He's been serving his country since 2004, and has been an author since his debut novel, *Frozen Secrets*, was released in 2013.

WS was born to military parents in San Antonio, Texas, and bounced around as a child, from Okinawa, Japan, to Florida, to New Mexico, where he met his high school sweetheart, who'd become his wife in 2003. Together, the two of them have two wonderful children, and are currently living overseas on the tiny island of Guam.

WS has tackled different genres throughout his writing career. From romantic suspense with his debut novel, to erotic suspense with his bestselling *Carter Trilogy* and *Defending Her*, to contemporary romance with *Worth Saving*.

WS has learned a lot about writing over the years, and his goal is to build a loyal and thriving fan base in the romantic suspense genre from here on out. His stories are deeply rooted in suspense, but WS loves the added drama of intense, emotional characters. Emotion, suspense, and drama is what WS does best.

WS loves connecting with his fans and readers, and does so whenever he gets the chance, and he would love to hear from you. You can find him on his personal blog, Facebook, Twitter, and Instagram.

Stay tuned, there's more suspenseful stories coming from WS Greer!

TURN THE PAGE FOR A SNEAK PEAK INTO CLAIMING CARTER, BY WS GREER, FEATURING ABRAM BASKOV FROM KINGPIN!

CLAIMING CARTER

"OKAY, SERIOUSLY, THIS IS THE worst movie I have ever seen. Why the hell are we still here?"

"It's not that bad, Abram," Vlad said, as he laughed at the picture on the screen in the dark theater.

Abram shook his head in disgust. "Not that bad? It's a tornado made of sharks, Vlad. This is a waste of money, man. Let's fucking go. I could have spent my money on McDonald's or something."

"Alright, alright. We can go," Vlad replied as he rose from his seat and started towards the path leading to the exit, ducking down to keep from blocking the view of the patrons who'd chosen to stay and endure the film. Abram stood and followed Vlad out, but he decided not to duck down. He figured if he blocked the screen, he'd be doing the other movie goers a favor.

Once outside the theater, Vlad and Abram began walking towards the parking lot.

"Dude, I have no idea where I parked the car. This place is surprisingly packed for a Thursday night. You'd figure people would be at home trying to get some rest for work tomorrow," Vlad said.

"Maybe they have the day off, unlike us. We're the ones who should be in bed. I have to open tomorrow," Abram replied. "My mom will be pissed if I don't wake up on time. And *I'll* be pissed if I don't wake up on time just because I wanted to come see the most horrible movie ever with your crazy ass."

"Oh calm down, it wasn't that bad. You're just sleepy and cranky from working in that madhouse you and your mother call a restaurant, or meat shop, or whatever the hell it is. Ten-thirty was the best I could do to accommodate you and your busy ass work schedule."

"Well I appreciate the effort, bro. It was a total failure, but at least you tried. I'm off again on Saturday, so maybe we can hang again. We can bring some chicks over here or something. What's up with you and the Chinese chick you were telling me about?" Abram said as he closed the door to Vlad's 1987 Ford Mustang. The door squeaked and rattled loudly as it slammed shut.

"Whoah, careful with my classic piece of shit, okay," Vlad joked as he started the engine and pressed lightly on the gas pedal. "Anyway, yeah, me and Min are still kind of feeling each other out. But you mark my words, bro, any day now I'll be telling you the story of how she begged me to have sex with her right there in the backseat. You just wait and see."

Abram let out a resounding laugh, smacking his knee. "Okay, so you are still feeling each other out. That's the same thing you said about Mellissa Clark a few months back. If I recall correctly, she never got around to begging you to fuck her in your back seat, did she?" Abram mocked with a chuckle.

"That's not funny, man. We were this close to making a sex tape together and selling it to TMZ," Vlad responded as he began laughing at himself. Vlad continued to giggle as he made a right onto Huntington Road. He was too busy laughing to notice the black Cadillac that had just began following them as they exited the movie theater parking lot.

"Whatever, bro. Anyway, enough about me and my highly active sex life. What's up with you and Sarah?" Vlad inquired.

"We're doing good. She's pretty busy with her job and stuff during the day, plus I'm working my ass off at the restaurant, but then she is still doing work stuff at night, too. Papers, and shit like that, which she has to have ready by the morning when she goes back to work. So, she's busy a lot. Busier than

I am. But she is a great girl, and I hope that it works out. She hasn't exactly asked me to have sex in the back of a car yet, but other than that, it's all good."

What?" Vlad exclaimed. "You haven't fucked this chick yet? What the hell is wrong with you? How long have you guys been dating?"

"First of all, nothing is wrong with me, and we've been seeing each other for about six months or so. She's a good girl, bro. She believes in building a relationship with a foundation of friendship first. That's her thing. I kind of like it, actually."

"You are so full of shit!" Vlad said excitedly. "There is no way you like that shit. Since when do you like good girls who don't want to fuck all the time?"

"Since I met her, I guess. What can I say, bro, the chick is just cool," Abram said calmly. "Slow down, asshole. You're about to run the stoplight."

Vlad had to press hard on the brakes to keep from sliding into the intersection, and the Mustang came to a screeching halt in the middle of the crosswalk.

"See there? Too busy thinking about fucking Min in your backseat to stop the car," Abram joked.

Just then, the black Cadillac that had been following the young men pulled up next to the passenger side of the Mustang. Vlad and Abram didn't notice the black man that exited the backseat of the driver's side of the vehicle until Abram's door was being yanked open.

"What the fuck!" Abram screamed as he turned and noticed the man, wearing a black suit with white pinstripes and a red tie, pointing a large gun at his stomach.

"Eye for an eye," the man uttered as he pulled the trigger. The two shots from the nine-millimeter pistol rang loudly inside the vehicle as the bullets struck Abram in the chest and stomach. Some of Abram's blood splattered onto Vlad's face and clothes as the gunman walked back to the vehicle, climbed into the back seat, and the car meandered away as if the getaway driver were out for a Sunday drive."

"Oh my fucking God! What the fuck! Abram, you're fucking bleeding, man! Talk to me. Are you okay?" Vlad screamed in a terrifying panic.

Abram clutched his stomach as blood poured out of his wounds in a steady pool.

"I'm not okay. I'm hit, bro. Oh my God! Somebody fucking shot me!" Abram bellowed.

"Oh my God! We have to get you a fucking hospital," Vlad said as he opened his door and ran to Abram's side of the car and closed the door. He then ran back to the driver's side, quickly climbed in and stomped on the gas pedal before he even had his door closed.

"The hospital is only two blocks away. You're going to be okay, Abram. Just hold on, bro. Who the fuck was that? I don't get it. Who the fuck would do that? He didn't even try to rob us. What the fuck?" Vlad rambled as he shifted the Mustang into fifth gear and sped down the road, blowing past every red light he passed on the empty street.

Vlad reached into his pocket and pulled out his cell phone. "Abram, I need your mom's number so I can tell her what the fuck just happened and to meet us at the hospital. What's her number?"

Abram shook his head slowly from left to right.

"What, Abram? Don't you fucking die on me, man. Come on, bro. Just hold on! We're almost there," Vlad screamed.

"No, don't call my mom," Abram mumbled as he began to slip into unconsciousness.

"What are you talking about?" Vlad asked. "We have to call your mom!"

Abram continued to shake his head slowly as his eyes began to close involuntarily. "No," he said. "Call my dad. We have to call my dad."

CPSIA information can be obtained
at www.ICGtesting.com
Printed in the USA
LVOW01s2130220516
489484LV00012B/70/P